A Ghost of a Chance

A *Ghost Trilogy* story

A Ghost of a Chance

By Minnette Meador

Resplendence Publishing, LLC
http://www.resplendencepublishing.com

Resplendence Publishing, LLC
2665 N Atlantic Avenue, #349
Daytona Beach, FL 32118

A Ghost of a Chance
Edited by Wendy Williams and Brenda Whiteside
Cover art by Les Byerley, www.les3photo8.com

Print format ISBN: 978-1-60735-389-8

Print Release: April 2012

*To Matt, my constant inspiration
To The Portland Police Bureau and
especially Officer Robert Pickett
To all those who believe that ghosts are real,
that humans are greater than the sum of
their parts,
and that laughter and love will always
conquer evil*

Chapter One

Living with Strangers

Keenan was used to living with hundreds of people. He no longer felt crowded, talked to himself, or went to therapists. Not that he liked it, mind you; given half a chance, he would have buried them all.

So stepping into a full elevator was a relief. They didn't follow him, as a rule. Ironically, they detested crowds.

Keenan nestled into the throng like a warm winter coat, fiddling with the change in his pocket while he watched the glowing "1" above his head. The group smelled of new coffee, sweet perfume, and peppery deodorant. The only sound was the door swooshing closed. The metal box lifted with a jolt and rushed him to the twenty-third floor. The crush of humanity was somehow comforting.

When he stepped out, Keenan paused at the immense reception desk to check for messages. The huge plate glass windows behind the desk framed a glimpse of the Portland skyline and Mt. Hood looming gray and white against a cloudy blue autumn sky. The tilt of the earth must have been just right; the mountain filled the sky to the east, making the city look small and insignificant… like him.

The site didn't make him feel any better. They would be waiting for him in his cubicle.

To postpone the confrontation, he decided to take his time getting there.

Standing at the coffee machine, he yawned and muttered a stifled *morning* to two half-awake fellow graphic designers stumbling past him. He tapped in a heaping teaspoon of creamer to make the coffee a nice tan, gave it a brisk stir, blew the steam away, and took his first sip.

Oh, yeah. Perfect.

When he turned around, an electric blast traveled down his back, paralyzing his legs.

There she was.

Isabella.

The name flowed through his neurons like fine brandy.

It took Keenan a microsecond to drink in the full extent of her dazzling loveliness. Since she was busy talking with one of the secretaries, he took his time appreciating every inch.

Flowing chestnut hair, fawn-like eyes, and lips that begged for a long hot hiss. He loved the way the black dress accentuated the enticing inward curve of Isabella's back and the soft mounds of her ass. It took everything he had to keep from crossing the twenty feet between them and running his hands over those gorgeous contours. Keenan liked the way the dress isolated and displayed each of her delicious breasts. The dark line of cleavage peeking out at the top blended well with Isabella's dusky Mediterranean skin.

Heat rose in Keenan's cheeks. It had been a long time since a woman could arouse him with a glance. He liked that about her. Despite his pleading, his cock stiffened painfully on its own and crept up the inside of his pants. He had to shake his leg to get it to behave. It had been doing that a lot lately.

He remembered their first meeting two weeks ago. Isabella had appeared as if by magic at his cubicle, peeking around the gray fabric wall and voicing a hardy, *Hi, I'm Isabella, the new head of HR. I brought you your insurance package and...*

Keenan didn't hear what she said after that, finding himself distracted enough to go deaf. He would have made his move then, if his posse hadn't intervened...again.

Isabella looked up at him now and smiled, the delicate lines around her eyes crinkling and perfect white teeth bright against her dark skin. The slightest gleam of playfulness danced around that mouth. It caused his heart to drum an African rhythm against the inside of his ribs, and his mouth smiled back insipidly. His brain ceased to function. Only last night Keenan imagined those lips kissing him, trailing down his chest, wrapping around the head of his…

He had to shake his leg a second time.

Since we've gone this far in my imagination, I guess I should ask her out. Yeah…it was the least he could do.

All right let's go, buddy. Get your blood up. Move that leg. Just walk…right…over…to her and…

…and it was no good. That niggling little *problem* that shadowed most of his motivation went into full gear. His nerves crumbled into piles of broken resolve.

Isabella went back to her conversation, and Keenan went back to his coffee, filling the void with another scenario…

"Good morning, Isabella. How's your day going?"

"Oh," she said in a breathless whisper, pressing her hot body into his and opening the first button on his shirt. *"It would be much better if you'd rip my clothes off and take me right here, stud."*

"Oh…ok." He ripped the front of her shirt open, exposing lovely bundles of…

"Sinner!"

The female shriek made him spill scalding coffee all over his hand.

"Fuck!"

Keenan's fantasy went up in smoke and his cock shriveled. He set the cup down so he could grab a few napkins.

"Shut up, Agnes," he sneered under his breath.

"Sinner! You will burn in hell for all your carnal thoughts, Keenan Swanson. Sinner. Spawn of the devil." The disembodied voice behind him shifted to his right, but he didn't bother to look. He knew there wouldn't be anyone there.

"Constance…" His lips barely moved when two office execs flittered by him laughing on their way to a meeting. When they were gone, he jerked his thumb toward where he figured Agnes would be. "Please come get Agnes, will you?"

"Sorry, Kee." Constance's deep southern voice shifted in from the ether and reverberated from one ear to the other. "Come along, dear. Don't bother the poor man. He's trying to work. We promised, remember?"

A shimmering outline appeared at Keenan's elbow, and he had to jerk his arm away fast to avoid the blood freezing touch of those skeletal hands. When Agnes materialized, a shiver vibrated against his skull and arms. Only the top half of her appeared, but the lucent face staring up at him solidified, crowded by stacks of wrinkles and a cold, milky gaze. *Why do they always look so creepy?*

"Sinner!" Agnes shrieked again.

Another pair of hands appeared, wrapped around her shoulders, and pulled her back into nothingness. Agnes's body faded, then her face, and finally those white accusing eyes.

Keenan whirled around and searched the cubicle walls receding like lines of staunch gray soldiers, but Isabella had disappeared. His heart dropped, and he tried to relieve it with a misted sigh. No dice.

He knew he would see her later, so he played another scenario in his head to keep him company (she felt so nice in his arms). Grabbing what was left of his coffee in one hand and shoving the other into his pocket, he headed to his cubicle.

As he rounded the opening, Grumpy sat in Keenan's chair, trying without success to touch the computer.

Grumpy was a new addition to the *family*, a tall black man without legs, and a creased bald head. Keenan figured the ghost used to work for the railroad because of the greasy overalls and engineer's hat, but since he only swore,

Keenan had no way of telling. The specter's hands kept slipping through the keyboard, and Keenan snorted a laugh.

"Sorry, old man, not today. Out of my chair."

The apparition turned his face and got his mouth working. His hands flailed in the air above the keyboard, making the papers on Keenan's desk whirl into a miniature tornado. A stream of muttered profanities filled the air around Keenan's head. He covered his ears until Grumpy dissolved in pieces leaving only his mouth for a couple of seconds to finish the tirade.

When he vanished, Keenan blew out a breath and watched the cold billow of white drift through his cubicle. It dissipated once it warmed. He shook his head.

That cold spot never ceased to amaze him. Of all the hundreds of ghosts and ghoulies surrounding him every day, only a few generated that kind of cold, and he was still trying to figure out why. Even Constance didn't know, though she thought it might have to do with strong emotion: anger, hate, fear, or sadness. It seemed to fit.

Keenan took his seat and turned his computer on to start the day's work. He pulled a pile of clear envelopes towards him and thumbed through them. There had to be at least fifteen graphic design and rendering requests. *Christ!*

Keenan peeked into the first envelop looking for the DVD that should have been tucked inside with the layout. It wasn't there, which meant he had to download the graphics from the server and *fix* the artwork before he could even start.

Why the hell don't people follow instructions?

He slapped it down on his desk and yanked up the second. No DVD. This one he tossed across the desk, knocking over his pencil cup.

What do you know? An independent 'disaster' that doesn't involve the dearly departed. He probably shouldn't take it out on his work, but who gave a crap?

Gathering his pencils, he shoved them back into the cup and decided he had seen enough. The thought of spending his precious weekend redesigning bad graphics and inane copy to sell pharmaceuticals to a gullible public made his hackles stand on end. He slammed his fist against his desk. *Looks like another all nighter.*

"Fuck!"

"Language, mon frère."

Reggie materialized at his elbow, one hand on his hip and smoking a brown English cigarette with the other. Keenan rubbed his face to take the edge off his irritation.

He liked Reggie, in fact, he considered him his best friend. They had met in college where Reggie had terrorized the co-eds by stealing their clothes (while they were still in them), and he had taken an instant shine to Keenan. Reggie told Keenan that he reminded him of younger days long ago.

He was a good-looking man, as ghosts go: tall, thin, muscular, dark. His proper English gentleman façade masked the true scoundrel lurking beneath. A guy Keenan knew the ladies adored when he was alive. Hell, they probably still adored him dead. Who knew? He was always the consummate gentleman and scholar. He had been an anthropologist at the turn of the century and died in Persia during a dig, at least as far as Keenan could gather; if even half of what Reggie told him was true, the ghost's experiences could fill a library of adventure books.

Reggie was what Keenan called a "solid" since he could see all of him and not just bits and pieces. It took him a long time to figure out that the longer a ghost had been dead, the more translucent it became. The solids were preferable to the really old ones, the ones he called "transes" since they were largely transparent. Those guys could make you piss your pants if you weren't ready for them. That caused some embarrassing moments in Keenan's past and earned him the nickname "Pissy" in high school.

God, he hated ghosts.

"Hey, Reg. How'd you do with the twins?"

Reggie floated into a side prone position a few inches above the desk. "Try as I might, I could not get them to feel me. But I had loads of fun attempting it." He rolled his eyes. "Oh, those perfectly symmetrical tits." He took another long draw on the cigarette and Keenan laughed. "You staying home tonight?" Reggie asked.

Keenan drew his brows together and folded his arm. "Yeah, like I'd have a date. Why?"

"No reason. I'm attempting the girls again." Reggie tossed the butt into the ether where it disappeared. "Thought maybe you'd like to join me."

"What? Spy on the twins?" Keenan snorted. "Putting aside the fact that I would probably be arrested for voyeurism, I've got all this work to do. Rain check?"

"As you wish." Reggie got himself upright and adjusted his sleeves. "I'll come over after. Might have something of interest to report. I'm feeling lucky."

Keenan laughed at his friend's persistence. A rustle from the next cubicle told Keenan his neighbor had just come in. Reggie tossed him a sloppy salute and disappeared. Keenan busied himself with the stack of requests.

A living head materialized above the gray divider. "What's so funny?"

Keenan cleared his throat. "Just this email."

"Send it over. I freakin' love a good joke."

"Sure thing, Mike."

Keenan bit his lower lip and gave himself a mental smack to the head for not being more careful. People thought he had just stepped out of a loony bin as it was without adding disembodied conversations to the list. Not that he cared much what Mike thought, he had to remind himself. But the truth was Keenan was lucky *anyone* talked to him. Now he had to come up with something to email Mike.

"Hey, did you hear about Susan in accounting?" Mike asked. "Randy said he went out with her and…"

And so it began: the endless office gossip, the exchange of bad jokes, the politics, the lies. Everything Keenan hated about his job. Whenever he focused on the computer clock, it seemed to be moving backwards.

When lunch finally slogged in, Keenan decided he wasn't going to work through like he normally did. His stomach and his nerves were both growling at him.

Four spirits, two solids and two trances, floated in and out of the cubical entrance playing some kind of tag. The group included a Chinese woman named Sadie who liked to turn herself inside out when she was upset, a clown they called The Bounce whose makeup had run together a long time ago, a little old lady without hands or feet, and Constance, the closest thing Keenan had to a sister...or a mother, if it came to it. His own mother had tucked herself inside a vodka bottle and he hadn't seen her in years.

Constance broke off from the group and touched his hand. It went instantly cold and he yanked it away, wincing at the sting shooting up his arm. When it numbed Keenan gave it a quick shake to get the feeling back.

"Oh, sorry, Kee," Constance said. "I always forget."

He wondered if she really did forget. It was hard to tell with Constance. Her mothering instinct usually got the better of her and she hated not being able to comfort him with a touch. Those cow-like eyes studied him, and her teeth shone like a lighthouse beacon from the elegant dark chocolate face. Since she only came up to his chin, he had to bend his neck to show her a loving smile.

"It's all right, Cee. What's up?"

The solid upper half of her sported, as it always did, a worn blue housecoat. Faded flowers speckled the fabric in pinks and greens, and a long half butcher's apron completed the ensemble. Her salt and pepper hair (heavy on the salt) lined up in curlers that surrounded a plump kind face, making her look like an English barrister. She tilted her chin toward feet that had vanished into the other side a long time ago, and her hands rested firmly over the apron. Unlike the others, Constance had the slightest white aura around her.

"Sorry about Agnes this morning. She can be a handful that one." Constance lifted those lined old eyes and winked at him. "She didn't spoil your chance with that girl, did she?"

Keenan let out a snort. "Cee, how is it you always know."

Her dark eyes solidified when she folded her arms together and drummed her fingers against a substantial black bicep. "Oh, child, how long we been together?

Nineteen years this summer. Remember? I think I know ya better than anyone, Kee."

Constance wrinkled her brow and Keenan braced himself. Every time she did that, he could hear a lecture coming. He settled back to absorb it.

"This one's special," she said. "She's not just for your bed. You gotta be careful, baby... there's something else coming. Something important."

That jovial round face puckered, and her eyes rolled back into her head. When an eerie light spilled from her hands, she lifted them towards him and her voice came from miles away. A sharp scent of something burning twitched at Keenan's nose, the hairs on his arms stood at full alert, and a chill rushed from ass to neck, making his skin crawl.

"Ya got some strange times ahead, boy." The words sounded like they were coming from behind him. "Your life's in danger...ya could fall into darkness, yet light stands at the threshold. Always follow your heart, boy, even when your head tells ya no. Be mindful of strangers... and friends. Watch the night." With a shudder that made her fade out and then back in, the old ghost gave her head a vigorous shake. The curlers clicked like a flock of birds. She squinted one eye up at Keenan, and a broad smile traveled from ear to ear.

"Ooo, that was a good one. It'd make my Creole papa proud, conjurin' like that."

This was the only thing that drove Keenan nuts about Constance. Her father had been some kind of famous Creole voodoo priest from New Orleans. Because of that, Constance thought she was psychic. Problem was she really wasn't. Not a single prediction had come true in the nineteen years he had known her. He would never tell her that, of course. He loved her very much.

"Sure, Cee. I'll be careful."

The other three apparitions slid in and out of the walls of the cubicles, exposing themselves to each other, hysterical with laughter. Keenan reached for his coat and tucked his arms into the sleeves.

"Listen. I'm going to lunch. Can you please keep the posse at bay for a bit? I need some space."

"Sure." She floated over to the group and whispered to them. They gave Keenan a dirty look, mooned him together, and flicked out of view.

Constance smiled and swirled into the fluorescent light above his desk.

Whistling an off-key tune, Keenan headed to the elevator.

When he got there, it was empty. He slipped inside, looking forward to being alone, if only for a few seconds. As the doors closed, a hollered "*hold please*" made him slam his palm against the rubber door jam.

A whiff of Isabella's spicy scent entered before she did. He was certain it was just testosterone muddling his poor male brain, but she seemed to sashay into the elevator just for him. Keenan liked that about her.

"Going down?" he asked with what he hoped was his most charming smile, ignoring the innuendo.

"Yes." The sweet hum of her voice made the muscles at his center jump, adding a log or two to the fire growing inside his pants.

A bright red blush traveled up Isabella's cheeks making her eyes sparkle (with what he convinced himself must be desire). When she reached past him to hit the already lighted "1" button, a flash of cleavage sent his pulse pounding against his ears. Man, she was amazing. The thought of pressing her hot body against the cold elevator walls was almost too much.

"Isabella, isn't it?" Keenan hadn't seen a ring on her finger, around her neck, or a *Love John Forever* tattoo any place noticeable, so he assumed she was available.

"Right. You're Keenan. We met the other day."

"Right."

Usually he didn't have problems talking to girls, but now it was harder than it had ever been. A hundred witty comebacks crowded his brain for attention, but not one of them could make it past the lump in his throat. His growing cock wasn't going to be much help either; all it wanted him to do was blurt out, "*Ya wanna?*"

Bracing himself against possible rejection, and telling his cock to shut the fuck up, Keenan gathered his courage and charged into the fray. "Say listen, if you're not..."

The elevator jarred to a halt and the doors burst open in front of them. At least fifteen people piled into the box, disregarding the "maximum occupancy" sign.

Keenan hit his back hard against the railing and suddenly found his arms full of warm, healthy girl.

The sounds around him came to a crashing halt when he fixated on those gorgeous almond eyes and full red lips. The urge to devour that mouth was irresistible. He felt like he was home. Her balmy scent marinated his brain, clouding out everything else. The velvet skin of her naked arms made his palms tingle.

A sudden terror seized him when he realized his rod stood at full attention, shouting, "Yippee!" Since the crowd had crushed Isabella against him, she must have felt it jumping like an excited dog against her stomach. To Keenan's amazement, she didn't say a word and smiled sweetly up at him. Her expression was almost pleased. It boggled his mind.

"Sorry," he managed after a few precious seconds.

He let go and fully expected her to scrunch as far away from him as possible, a murmured "pervert" escaping her lips. Instead, she slid up next to him and stayed attached to his shoulder, turning her lovely breasts to the doors.

Keenan had a hard time keeping his eyes off them, noting with interest that both nipples were little rocks against the black fabric. He forced himself to focus on the bald spot on the head of the guy in front of him. He hoped to God the man wasn't pushed back; in Keenan's current state, it might be difficult to explain what rested against the man's ass.

"It's all right," Isabella whispered. "You were saying?"

"Oh. Yeah." An irritating rush of fear crept into Keenan's back and he had to fight to keep it out of his voice. "I wonder if you'd like to have dinner with me tonight."

"Tonight?" Isabella's lyrical words were an elixir for his fear. "I'm busy tonight." Was it Keenan's imagination, or did she sound disappointed? "I'm free Sunday... would you like to have breakfast instead?"

"Yeah, that would be great. I could pick you up at..."

"Actually, do you know *The Hotcake House* on Ninth?"

"Sure."

"How 'bout I meet you there at ten on Sunday. All right?"

"Sure." The schoolboy monosyllable stammering irritated the hell out of him, but Keenan couldn't help it.

The elevator bounced to a stop and people poured out, pulling Isabella along with them. Keenan wanted to ask her to lunch next, but they drew her away from him in the rush.

When he finally disentangled himself from the retreating throng and an influx of new riders who almost trapped him, he scanned the lobby, but the girl was gone. Growling at the innocent air, he slammed a fist into his thigh and immediately wished he hadn't. He grabbed a hotdog at the corner vendor and sulked the rest of the day.

Chapter Two

Night Visitor

Keenan's sex life hadn't been exactly what he would have called promiscuous. Not by choice, mind you, but by lack of opportunity. He considered himself a good looking guy, at least that's what the few women in his life had told him, and he always left them laughing, usually as they waved goodbye. Under the (dare he say it?) *debonair* façade, however, lay the true introvert he was; Keenan was shy right down to that little grain of psyche lodged in the middle of his personality.

Fortunately, he loved bold, confident women who took the initiative. Because of that he had managed to pull in talented partners who taught him how to navigate a woman's body without a compass and demonstrated when, where, and how to launch the final sequence. He was almost certain he was not bad in bed.

Even though it had been a couple of years since anyone but him had cranked up the engine, he remembered where everything went. However, the further away he got from that last naked body under him, the more preoccupied he became with the *drive*. The thought of sex had now taken over about eighty percent of the real estate between his ears. Keenan had even tried a prostitute, but, unfortunately, it wasn't until he had his pants down and his hopes up that he realized the girl belonged to the "passed on" parade. Nothing kills arousal faster than a dead person.

With these deliberations doing the mambo behind his eyes, Keenan nodded off in front of his home computer for the fourth time. He rubbed the back of his neck and yawned at the half-finished stack of graphic requests. Knowing he had the rest of the weekend to finish, he pushed himself away from the desk, shut off both the lamp and computer, and headed to his bedroom.

On his way out, he kicked one of the many oil paintings collecting dust next to the door of his office... or was it *studio?*

Keenan picked it up and held the half-painted canvas under the light coming in from the hallway. The eerie red figure that dominated the center was one he had started in college but never finished. It was good, really good; in fact, several of its predecessors had won competitions during his college days. *The next Picasso,* they told him.

He set it on top of the other incomplete paintings also collecting dust. That same old remorse gripped his heart; *one of these days, I've got to finish these.* That probably wouldn't happen anytime soon...if ever.

As he passed through, twenty or so ghosts littered his living room watching the last few minutes of the news. Keenan pulled air into his lungs before picking up the remote.

They were costing him a fortune. The TV, the radio, and even his computer were always on. Lights went off and on constantly. The heat would soar to eighty degrees in the middle of the summer and then plunge to fifty when the winter freeze set in. He couldn't keep any pets; the instant they came into the house they hissed or yelped in terror and ran away. The neighborhood was full of cats that had once belonged to Keenan.

He couldn't keep girlfriends either. The closer they got, the more convinced they were that he was on drugs, a serial killer, or terminally cracked. He hadn't had a girl at his house in years; for some reason they got all heebie-jeebie on him when things started flying around or cold blasts of air unexpectedly lifted their skirts. One girl even had her panties removed, but not by Keenan. He was in the kitchen at the time.

Friends? Forget it. They had a tendency to search for the exit when he told them he saw dead people...and not in the good way. Moviemakers had it all wrong. These weren't people who wanted release; they were freeloaders who wanted nothing more than to torture the living, especially those who could see them. Keenan had lost count of how many pranks he had endured over the years. Somewhere in the thousands, he was sure.

When Keenan clicked off the power to the TV the crowd of specters growled en mass. The box sizzled back on. Keenan held the remote defiantly toward the set and banged the power button again. It hissed off. Three male ghosts, a solid and two trances, pounded on their chests like apes, and the TV came back on.

"Leave the God damned thing off," he bellowed, thumb wrestling the remote one last time. The few spirits visible faded away, but not before four of them flipped him off. A barrage of couch pillows and cushions appeared out of nowhere, knocking him to the ground.

When Keenan shot back to his feet, the ghosts were gone.

Ignoring the mountain of pillows, he tossed the remote onto the naked couch and, with futile exactness, turned off the light, knowing it wasn't going to make the least bit of difference.

When he entered his bedroom there were three young, lucid women with blond curls hovering over a pile of dirty boxer shorts on the floor. The rustle of taffeta and titter of giggles resonated through the room, grinding against Keenan's last nerve of the day. He wondered if he would get any sleep tonight. *Thank God for sleeping pills and earplugs*. He didn't like taking them, but it kept him sane...well, saner anyway. He pulled off his shirt and let his jeans fall around his feet to step out of them.

The tittering reached a new crescendo. "Me thinks he must be well-endowed indeed to have a loin cover so immense. Can you imagine the size of his rod?"

The girls giggled again then screamed like banshees when he shooed them away from his laundry basket by snapping his T-shirt. When they were gone, he tossed it in with the rest of his dirty clothes and kicked his jeans to join them.

Keenan wished he were this popular with his own kind. Every day he drifted farther away from the living and closer to the dead. They occupied each waking hour and even some of his sleeping ones. Over the years, he had grown used to their constant chattering, the multitude of jokes and pranks, the crazy ethereal noises twenty-four hours a day. Silence was as foreign to him as pantyhose.

Even the loss of his privacy was something he missed less each year. But it all came with a price; the effort to bottle up what happened to him all the time made him quiet and withdrawn. Keenan wished there was someone he could talk to about it, someone living.

Doctors were no good; they all thought he was crazy. Three hospital stays, thousands of dollars in therapy, and nightly handfuls of meds hadn't even made a dent. He gave up on conventional treatment long ago and surrendered to the reality... or sur-reality, as he liked to call it. He knew something had to give soon. The thought was a sobering one.

A crowd of six men stood by his closet heatedly debating eighteenth century politics and smoking phantom cigars. As usual, an old residual couple hunched near the window. Residuals were not aware they had passed over, choosing instead to act out some scene in their life repeatedly. These were rare, but Keenan had two living in his house, the other a civil war soldier who pissed on the dining room curtains around nine o'clock every night. The room reeked of it for about an hour then it just disappeared. Keenan avoided that part of the house as a rule. How they ended up there was anybody's guess.

The rest were what paranormal researchers called *sentient*, which meant, as far as he could tell, that they were intelligent and aware of their surroundings. *Intelligent.* For some of them that was a stretch.

Three children played ring-around-the-rosy on top of his bed. The room sounded like the Rose Quarter during a Blazer's game.

"Come on. Give a guy a break."

The ghosts continued without giving him so much as a glimpse.

Keenan flipped his middle finger uselessly and stepped into the bathroom, disregarding the three guys in the bathtub arguing and the naked ebony-skinned woman sitting on the vanity swinging her legs and singing. Their combined voices echoed against the porcelain.

"...*not going to take it anymore, I tell you...*"

"...*hush little baby, don't say a word...*"

"...*shut up, Luke. It's nothing to sneeze at...*"

"...*mama's gonna buy you a mocking bird...*"

"...*I hate this place, man! You tell them they can suck my dick...*"

"...*if that mocking bird don't sing...*"

Rubbing his face with both hands to relieve the constriction in his cheeks, Keenan leaned against the sink, lifted his chin to the mirror, and frowned at the brown eyes staring back at him. The glaring red saturating the white accentuated their color, and dark circles made them look sad. Keenan slapped the faucet handle and splashed cold water against them. An icy headache formed. He reached for the small towel hanging to his right and held it against his face until the chill passed.

The noise stopped.

When he yanked the towel down, the spirits in the bathroom were gone and everything went dead quiet. He gave his reflection a fleeting look, ran a hand through the thick black hair, and turned to go into his bedroom.

It was empty and silent too.

The last time this happened was in Florence when he searched for a corner where he could sell paintings. When he walked onto one of the back cobbled streets, the ghosts had just disappeared. It was the only other time in nearly twenty years he had been completely alone. It was kind of spooky…and this coming from a man who lived the way he did.

Constance, he thought. She must have talked them into cutting him some slack for a change.

Not one to pass up a blessing, Keenan stripped off his boxers and socks, slid into the unmade bed, and popped a pill into his mouth. One of his ghost friends must have "touched" the water bottle; ice cold chased the pill down his throat. He hit the switch on his lamp and burrowed into his pillow. It wasn't long before sleep settled over him, encouraged by the silence.

* * * *

The dream was so real.

Hands slithered over Keenan's body, but they were detached somehow. It was hard to describe. Starting on his scalp, the hot tickling sensation sent tendrils of pleasure down his gut and directly into his cock. It was painfully erect, aching for a good hard squeeze, but he couldn't reach down to touch it.

A weight pressed down on his body, holding him to the bed. Keenan could actually feel his body sinking into the mattress. Something heavy, like invisible clay, pressed against his face. He couldn't move. He wasn't scared at all…just horny as hell.

The *hands* massaging his scalp moved down to his face, pressing his eyes closed with what he could only assume must have been thumbs. They moved down his face and found his lips, parted them, and thrust a slender finger into his mouth. There was no taste, but the soft, warm texture electrified his senses. He sucked on it instinctively. It was deeply sexual and made his cock throb in anticipation. To his utter dismay the finger slipped from his mouth and trailed down his chin.

Keenan opened his eyes. Light from an outside streetlamp illuminated the foot of his bed and half his dresser. When she appeared in a wisp at his feet, he had to struggle to lift his head enough to see her.

Naked heaving breasts came into view; the nipples were long, slate hard, and the areolas black against dark skin. Her waist and hips were slim. Stretched fingers pinched the nipples, making them longer, more rigid. The triangle of her pussy was bald, the slit dark and inviting. Hazy clouds covered her face, making it soft and featureless, but billowing tendrils of black hair twisted out from around it, flowing in a wind Keenan couldn't hear. It moved in a watery dance.

The covers glided slowly down his body. The soft touch of the silk made his cock twinge in agony, and he gritted his teeth to hiss his pleasure. Electric shocks ignited the nerves in his neck, shoulders, and arms. When Keenan was completely exposed, he wasn't cold. His cock sprang into ready position. The hair on his arms and legs snapped with static.

Rising from the floor until her naked body hovered horizontally inches above him, the entity's nipples brushed his chest scattering goose bumps across every pore. The creature reached down and wrapped a hot hand around his erection making it pulse when she squeezed. Her grip was like iron.

Keenan pulled a gasping moan into his lungs. He could only watch as she slid down to put her mouth above his agonized member.

She brushed her tongue several times across the tip then pulled it hard into her mouth. Barbs of lightning convulsed Keenan's body, intensifying his senses. The sucking sound of her mouth against his flesh, the sweet smell of her juices mixing with his own musky scent, the feel of those hot soft lips caressing the sensitive flesh as they slid over the head of his cock, and the strong grip of her warm hand, all fought for his attention.

When he saw his cock disappear inch by inch into her mouth, he was amazed at how big it was. The need to cum, now, quickly, overpowered his better judgment. Something held him back. Keenan had never felt anything like this even during the best sex of his life. The needles of pleasure shooting through his blood carried lust to every inch of his skin. He wanted to scream, but all he could do was open his mouth in ecstasy, gurgling a groan.

The apparition put her hands out to her sides and floated above him. Sliding her mouth in a slow, even progression, she moved down his shaft until it disappeared into her throat. Keenan could feel it give way to his engorged muscle. His hips, suddenly free, moved to her rhythm, and she let him thrust his cock deep into her throat. It was incredible.

The apparition finally moved away from him, sticking out a long tongue that wrapped around his cock twice. If it wasn't so erotic, he probably would have been scared shitless, but the thought didn't even enter his mind; Keenan knew he was too far-gone by then.

Bringing a breast to his mouth, she ran a swollen nipple against his lips until it *pushed* them open. Keenan didn't hesitate. He pulled the long bud into his mouth and sucked it forcefully, biting it from time to time, and running his tongue over the rough skin. The sensation of that warm flesh in his mouth sent shivers down both arms. He ached to touch her, but his arms were lead weights at his sides.

She pulled the nipple from his teeth and settled her knees on either side of his hips. Lifting up on her haunches, she forced his cock to lay flat against his stomach then slid the soft petals of her pussy along it all the way to his balls, saturating them with moisture. Keenan wasn't certain, but he could have sworn her pussy lips were squeezing them. She moved up to the head of his cock and slowly widened them with his shaft. She was soaking wet.

Careful not to take him inside her, she rubbed the soft folds of hot flesh up and down, slowly, back and forth, all the while squeezing her nipples and wrapping that long tongue around them one at a time.

A soft distant moan sounded everywhere at once inside Keenan's bedroom, as if the room itself sighed in pleasure. In a split second, he saw her eyes; they were black opals shining in the dark, but they clouded over immediately.

Finally, the creature slid all the way forward until Keenan's cock stood straight up. She lifted herself onto her knees and allowed the bloated muscle to linger for a few moments against the tiny bud of her ass then the dripping wet creases of her pussy.

Without stopping, she thrust her hips down on his cock burying it deep inside her body.

She was so tight when he slid into her. His muscles pulsed, sending tremors to his hands and feet. The feeling was unbearable, and Keenan thought he would pass out soon if he didn't cum. But he couldn't. The agonizing pleasure forced air out of his lungs and fireflies spiraled in front of his eyes. Keenan had to concentrate to take a breath.

The creature placed her hands on either side of his head and crushed his mouth with hers, softly biting, running her tongue against his teeth, and sucking his lips into her mouth. Moving her hips and rubbing her clit firmly against his pelvic bone, she impaled herself on his cock over and over again until he couldn't stand it anymore.

The climax exploded so intensely he lost all sense of time and place. He could hear screams far away. It took him a moment to realize they were his.

He came a long, long time, somewhere between eternity and no time at all. The woman's pussy gripped his cock like pulsating iron until she sucked every last seed from his body, leaving him dry.

When everything was empty, Keenan passed out.

Chapter Three

Imbibing Spirits

Keenan's eyes fluttered open expecting to be in his bed. Instead, he had his face buried in the porcelain altar, throwing up his guts, listening to Reggie cooing encouragements.

"There you go, old bugger. Get all of it out. That's the lad."

Coughing until he thought his lungs would come up, Keenan tried to figure out what had just happened. All he could focus on was the splattered white inside of his toilet, his splitting head, and a persistent ringing in his ears. The sexual encounter was very fuzzy.

"What the fuck?" His voice was sandpaper against his throat.

He pulled his head out of the toilet and drew as much air into his lungs as they would take. Sitting on his haunches, he held his stomach and rocked, giving Reggie the dirtiest look he could muster. The shining specter smiled down at him, floating nonchalantly by the sink. Everything else was black. A random thought scampered through Keenan's addled brain. *I wish I glowed in the dark.*

"Are you better, my friend?"

"What the fuck?" Keenan repeated more forcefully and lurched to his feet.

"You asked that already."

Keenan stumbled to the sink. Turning on the tap lighted only by Reggie's ghostly glow, he put his head under the water and tried to drown himself in it.

The cold made the ringing and the muddle go away, but his head still pounded like murder. Keenan grabbed the towel from the shower curtain rod and ran it violently over his head and face, hoping the weird sickness would saturate the towel instead of his brain.

He felt dirty, violated, as if someone had pulled his pants down in front of cheerleaders. Yet, there was another part of him that wallowed in fulfillment, satisfied, satiated. It made him want to puke again.

Keenan threw the towel through the specter, stomped into his bedroom, and then stopped with a jolt. Reggie almost ran "into" him.

In the soft light from his window, he could see the bed. The mattress tilted sideways and touched the ground like a beached whale. Everything not otherwise tied down was on the floor. Three pictures looked like someone had pitched them against the wall. Worse, except for the window, there was not a single piece of glass in the room that had not been shattered including the screen to his rabbit-eared TV. The fragmented remnants covered everything.

"I think you need a drink, my friend." Reggie pirouetted across Keenan's path and glided to the door, but Keenan only blinked at him.

"What?"

"A drink. You know…ice, booze, perhaps soda or a wedge of lime."

Keenan shook his head long enough to get the daze out of it then tip-toed through the minefield of glass to pull on his coat and step into his sneakers. He didn't even bother to untie them. Miraculously, the shoes were glass-free and the coat was right side out, though, in his state, it probably didn't matter.

It dawned on Keenan as he followed Reggie out to the living room that the familiar disembodied noise was back. Arguments, low conversations, whispers, and even a little song flitted in and out of the air around him. It was reassuring.

The group of visible ghosts was light: three screamers Keenan couldn't see very clearly, a Hindi named Nihar who was standing on his head amongst fake flowers on the windowsill, and a crowd of loggers dancing on the kitchen table. Three of them were swilling pale mugs of beer. The stringent smell of faded incense and warm beer made Keenan's eyes water.

Keenan searched the room. "Constance?"

Reggie spun around and gave him a ghostly wink. "Sorry, old chap. Not here tonight. Besides…" He floated over to the door and made a grand gesture with his arm. "…for this, you'll need a gentleman's perspective, I think."

"What do you—"

"I'll explain all of it after you've had a drink or two. Off we go."

Keenan's head throbbed enough to make him not care where he was going. He lifted one numb leg after the other. When the front door slammed behind him, it sent a cartoon sound wave that should have caved in his skull. It must have been very cold outside…he could see his breath come out in solid clouds…but he was warm. *Thank God for small favors.*

He stumbled after Reggie who was whistling a happy tune just to torture him.

The haze around Keenan's brain didn't get any better the further down the block Reggie led him. He wondered what time it was; *would the bar be open this late?*

When they rounded the corner, the neon blue and red *Taps* blinked in and out, boring into the headache under Keenan's right eyebrow. The white *OPEN* sign underneath looked misty in the late night fog. The heat that blasted his face when he opened the door smelled of cigarettes and humanity. It was one of his favorite sensations; nothing better in his mind than local color mixed with cold micro-brew. The flashing *Terminator Stout* signs always reminded him of happier days.

Once inside, Patrick eyeballed him briefly without comment and went back to chatting with the drunk at the end of the bar. Patrick had been here when Keenan moved in years before, but Keenan still didn't know if he was the owner or just the bartender. They were on a casual head-bobbing basis.

Keenan didn't feel like lively conversation, so he just pointed to the tap. Patrick nodded once, yanked a glass from the stack behind him, and filled it. Keenan disregarded the twenty or so incorporeal customers that Patrick didn't see. The chatter from the group was smoky, bouncing dully from the dark oak rafters.

It was only then that Keenan realized he was naked under the long coat.

No pants.

No shorts.

No wallet.

He froze and sweat followed the jolt of realization down his armpits.

Can anyone say flasher?

Cramming his hand into his coat pocket without hope, he touched the soft crumpled surface of a bill and several coins. When he pulled the ten out, the sight sent momentary relief through the tight muscles in his neck, followed by a chill that rippled just under his skin. He slid it over the bar and took his beer, hoping to God that the two men staring at him didn't notice his bare legs. Neither said a thing when Patrick passed the change to him and went back to cleaning glasses behind the high bar.

The dead patrons laughed their asses off.

When Keenan settled into a booth at the back of the bar, he downed half the beer in a single gulp and came up breathless.

"Steady, man," Reggie said softly, sitting across from him. "You'll need your wits."

Keenan ran one shaking finger around the rim of the glass and curled his lip. "What just happened to me?"

Reggie lit a mirage cigarette and blew billowing clouds into the ether. "You're not going to like it."

In reply, Keenan snorted irritably and looked around to make sure no one was close enough to hear him talking to himself. He didn't need psychosis on top of public indecency tonight.

"Spill it," he hissed.

Reggie flicked the cigarette into the air where it disappeared. "Have you ever heard of a succubus?"

"Sure." Keenan sat back and tapped on the beer mug absently. "Don't they suck out your life when you're asleep or something?"

"Not exactly." Reggie's smirk deepened and the ghostly light in his eyes intensified. It was obvious he was enjoying this. From time to time, Reggie showed a spark of something that bothered Keenan and even frightened him a little. His eyes were now so bright Keenan sat back a bit and put one foot outside the booth.

"A succubus is a type of female spirit that lives off the sexual energy of men. They visit you in your sleep, stupefy you, and then…well, have their way with you, not to put too fine a point on it." A mischievous grin split his lips and another cigarette appeared between his teeth. "How was it?"

Keenan snarled and took another drink. "Dandy," he replied, looking back at the bar again. "I feel like shit. What did she do to me?"

An eerie laugh escaped Reggie's mouth. It was almost gleeful. "Actually, you are lucky to be conscious at all. I've known men who can't walk for a week afterwards." He gave Keenan a lascivious wink and leaned against the table, pulling his elbows back when they slid into the wood. Heat traveled through the table and into Keenan's hands, warming the icy condensation on the mug. Reggie was the only ghost, as far as he knew, that gave off heat instead of cold. "You must have some endurance, my lucky friend, to go so long with one."

The suds in Keenan's mug laced into dark liquid as he watched. "So, is she a ghost?"

"Not really." Reggie pulled a long draw on his cigarette.

"A demon?"

Reggie tilted his head and regarded Keenan for several ticks of the grungy clock hanging above the booth. The smoke coming out of his nose gathered in a wreath above his head and lingered there for a long time.

"No, not a demon either. She's...very unique. I don't know of many still *practicing*, so to speak. Not in the U.S., anyway. You find them in Germany and parts of Italy, of course, but they don't travel over the pond much. You are quite lucky."

"Lucky?" Keenan hollered. When Patrick and the other man shot looks at him, he lowered his chin and tilted the beer toward his chest. "You call this luck?" he mumbled.

Light shone from the pale face and that spark ignited a second time. "Are you telling me you didn't enjoy it?"

Keenan opened his mouth, but shut it just as quickly. Fact of the matter was he had enjoyed it...very much. He wasn't going to tell his misty friend that, however.

"So, if she's not a ghost and she's not a demon, what exactly is she?"

When Reggie pulled the equivalent of air into his lungs, the cigarette fumes disappeared into his nostrils and came back out as fog. "I'm not an expert, mind you, but I've heard things here and there." He made a show of steepling his fingers and looking intellectual. "The myth tells us the original succubus was Lilith, Adam's first wife..."

"Adam's *first* wife? Adam's wife was Eve." Keenan wanted the words to be adamant, but they came out plaintive instead.

Reggie leveled a condescending leer at him and raised one eyebrow. "Honestly. The ignorance of you modern living could drive one barmy. In a nutshell, God created Lilith when He created Adam. She decided that since she came out of the same clay, she had the same rights as her husband. Apparently someone disagreed since she was turned into a succubus by Lucifer."

"All right, so what exactly is a succubus then?"

Reggie leaned back into the bench and floated his arms over the worn red leather seat back. "As I said, it is a hapless creature that lives off of sexual energy, i.e. the arousal of men. The incubus is the male counterpoint and seduces women...and sometimes men, depending. Think sexual vampire, and you're halfway there. They must roam the world in search of new prey to stay alive. Most hate it; it goes against their natural instincts, but there is nothing they can do about it. The only difference between a succubus and say, a demon, is she is not endemically evil, despite all that two centuries of Christian propaganda have convinced people otherwise. These poor creatures are usually a seraph enslaved by a demon and then forced to become what they are."

"A what?"

"Seraphim angel...part of the choir of angels. Pretty close to the Big Man, from what I've heard."

Keenan blinked at Reggie. "You trying to tell me this...thing is an angel?"

"Well..." Reggie tapped his fingers against the backrest and gazed up at the murky faux Tiffany light above the booth. "Not anymore."

"So what does it want with me?"

Reggie shrugged and rubbed his nose with a long forefinger. "They are drawn to powerful men...psychics."

"That's horseshit, Reggie. I'm no psychic."

Reggie nailed him with a cold gaze and chuckled under his breath. "Let's see...you see dead people. Not only do you see them, but you talk to them as well. As a matter of fact, some of your best friends are dead. Sounds rather psychic to me. But what do I know?"

Keenan licked his lips. "Oh."

"May I continue?"

Keenan nodded miserably. He had never considered himself psychic and the idea left his chest tight. But it made a certain kind of sense; he had to live with the fact that his whole life had been a magic bag of paranormal bullshit. Wasn't a thing he could do about it. Psychic was as good a word as any.

"Anyway, given your history, it's not surprising she would select you. Maybe she wants a child..."

"Angels can have kids?"

Reggie drummed his fingers twice against the greasy oilcloth. "Not in the strictest sense. The succubus seduces a man, collects his seed, and transfers it to an incubus who changes it and delivers it to a human female. Seems to me that would just produce your garden-variety human offspring, but apparently not. The child born to the woman is called a cambion." A shadow of a warm smile touched his cold lips. "Now, *these* little fellows are really something… ugly as sin when born, no breath or heartbeat, but it runs around like the very dickens for the first seven years or so. Then it becomes increasingly difficult to differentiate one from a human. A cambion eventually becomes devilishly cunning with the face of an angel. Persuasive too. Can talk a saint into dropping his drawers on Sunday and a nun to give up her habit."

"So what the hell am I supposed to do?" Keenan's senses turned to melting marshmallows the more Reggie talked.

"Haven't the foggiest."

"Great." A cold breeze snuck in between Keenan's legs, shrinking his already shriveled privates. He smashed his knees together and adjusted his coat. "Why didn't you guys warn me? Where the hell did you all go?"

"Ghosts are not omnipotent, you know. They *are* human," Reggie said, lifting his chin. "There are certain spirits that scare even the dead. Ghosts usually flit away before anyone can say, 'Bob's your uncle.' Not me, of course," he added, clearing his throat. "I wasn't even there at the time. Checking the twins out again, you know."

Anger was beating the hell out of Keenan's better judgment and the earlier warmth was turning into a deep chill. He wasn't sure which feeling was making his knees shake when he leaned across the table.

"So what do we do about it?" he whispered.

Reggie inspected the nails of his right hand. "Dashed if I know. Let her do it again and see how it goes?" he asked hopefully.

"Fuck you."

Reggie smiled and rose to his ethereal feet. "Sorry I can't be more help, old cocker, but I have to hurry off to a previous engagement." A pair of gloves appeared out of the air that Reggie slipped onto his hands in a blink. Tucking a walking stick under his arm, he tipped his head to Keenan. "I know I'm coming across all mouth and no trousers, but I wouldn't worry about it any. It's probably an isolated incident, never happen again. You survived. That should bring you some comfort."

Keenan scowled up at the apparition as he drifted past the table. "What the hell does that mean?"

Reggie stopped and regarded Keenan over his shoulder. "A succubus can kill you, old buck…and usually does after a while. I think you…how do you Americans say it… dodged a bullet?"

Without another word, Reggie disappeared, leaving Keenan to contemplate his mortality.

Chapter Four

The Spirit Is Willing...The Flash Is Weak

One blustering night years before, Keenan found himself lost in the Oltrarno district of Florence, Italy. Flanked by towering cement buildings on both sides and a narrow cobbled road under his feet, try as he might, he could not seem to find his way out of the ancient maze. Finally, being young, bold, and relatively ignorant, he stumbled into a smoky tavern.

He knew at once that this was probably a local hang out. Dark, angry men, some old, some young, glared at him when he came through the door, dripping rainwater onto a stone floor that bowed in the middle where hundreds of years of footsteps had worn it away. Keenan adjusted the portfolio tucked under his cloak when an old woman approached and led him to a table without saying a word.

She set a mug in front of him and filled it with Chianti, grabbed a bowl from a nearby sideboard, wiped it out with her apron, and then filled it from the pot sitting over an open flame. Keenan liked ribollita, a bean stew common to the area, and imagined the place only served one dish per day. The woman held out her hand in the universal gesture of "pay me" and Keenan fished some coins from his pocket to give to her. She counted the coins with a huff, then grabbed a rough loaf of black bread from the same sideboard, plopped it onto the table to accompany the stew, and then scuttled off into some hidden recess of the tavern.

Keenan ate as he watched the patrons going about their own personal business. There were four men decked out in fine clothes sitting at one table. The Italian equivalent of a bachelor party? Keenan assumed so from their merry making and what few words of Italian he could catch. They were very drunk and kept toasting a cheery faced young man sitting at the middle.

Over to his right was a wrinkled fisherman by the smell, sitting alone and concentrating on his dinner. Behind him, in the shadows, sat another man.

Keenan tried to make out his face over his bowl of beans, but the only thing coming across were the glints of the stranger's eyes and the smoke from a cigarette. It may have been Keenan's imagination, but it looked like the stranger was staring at him.

Without warning, a woman plopped into the seat across from Keenan, uninvited. She might have been beautiful once, but several decayed teeth and the leathery hide of an alcoholic smoker made her look as dry as yesterday's ashes. The micro mini skirt and dangling halter-top she wore left nothing to the imagination; it was all she had on. Her bright blue eye shadow was thick and hypnotic.

"*Vuoi un buon tempo?*" The checkered smile shooting from behind large strawberry red lips looked predatory.

Keenan sat back, dropping his spoon into his bowl. His Italian was sketchy. All he could think to say was, "Scusi?"

From out of the shadows, the strange man rose and crossed to them with assured, graceful strides. He was tall, handsome, with a bushy black beard and piercing black eyes. He took the woman's bare shoulders into his hands and squeezed. Her smile turned upside down in an instant and the look of terror was unmistakable in her eyes. She shot Keenan a pleading glance then lowered her face to the rough brown table.

"Questo non si è per voi." The stranger's voice was deep and menacing. The woman bolted from the chair and rushed to the door without looking back. The wind and the rain sucked her into the night.

The man gave Keenan a quick nod and bow. "Enjoy your dinner, signore." He left the building almost as quickly as the woman had, leaving Keenan to scratch his head and wonder what just happened.

That memory crept into his thoughts as he watched the beer in his glass disappear, sitting there at *Taps*. It had always creeped him out. The disconcertion of both nights echoed one another sending a frigid quake up his sides. He was so sick of that feeling.

After finishing his beer, Keenan left *Taps* and pulled his collar up around his ears. The heat from earlier had leaked out of his arms and legs. He was freezing. Walking fast seemed the best solution until the wind meandered up his legs and into his balls. *But, baby, it's cold outside...*

Eventually, the moving muscles started to warm up and by the time he rounded the pathway to his front door, it was bearable. He took the painted cement steps two at a time and then stopped dead in his tracks.

His keys were in his jean's pocket, sitting on top of his laundry, inside the locked house.

He tried the door but it was locked tight.

"Son of a bitch," he said to the tall green door. The sinking feeling mingled with his frozen head and blasted a pang of panic between his ears.

Keenan scurried around the house, rubbing his hands together, trying to figure out what he should do next. The cold was getting worse. He searched the blank wall, forgetting there weren't any entrances on this side. Running more to get his legs warmed up, he sped around the back of the house and then the other side testing every window. No luck.

When he got to his bedroom, he stopped. From outside, the beached mattress looked like a giant teeter-totter, but it wasn't obstructing the window. The beer chose that moment to take over Keenan's reasoning. It apparently figured a little more glass on the floor wasn't going to hurt anything.

Grabbing his right fist in his left hand, Keenan lifted his elbow and slammed it against the window as hard as he could. As was expected, the glass gave way and shattered into the room. As was unexpected, pain bolted up Keenan's arm, set bells and whistles off in his eardrums, and burst out of the top of his head.

He jumped up and down holding the injured arm, sending scattered profanities out into the street. When he saw a light go on in his neighbor's house, he stopped. *Steady, boy.* The beer decided it had done enough. Keenan was instantly sober.

He flexed his arm carefully several times and knew it was still intact. He couldn't see any blood (*small comfort*), but he knew it was going to be black and blue for a while.

It looks so flippin' easy on TV. Pain radiated in a tidal wave through his arm.

The shards of glass in the window beamed back at him like funhouse teeth. He pushed one back and forth until it loosened and then pulled it out, careful not to cut himself. When he got the second and third out, he was feeling a little better, but it didn't last long. A blinding white light threw a gigantic Keenan shadow against the outside of the house.

"Freeze. Put your hands out where I can see them."

"Fuck." The elongated word floated out of Keenan's mouth like a boiling teakettle and he carefully put his hands out on the wall next to the window.

He heard some mumbled cop talk then, "Sir, put your hands on your head, slowly." The voice was deep enough to send primordial shock waves into Keenan's back, and he did what the nice police officer told him.

"This is my house, officer." The words didn't sound convincing even to Keenan.

"Stay where you are. Don't move or I *will* shoot you. Do you understand?"

That warmed Keenan some; rivulets of sweat trickled down both his sides. He nodded, but couldn't get his mouth working.

A few seconds later, he saw more red and blue lights reflecting off his house. They played eerily over the broken glass in the window. It sounded like two more cruisers pulled up.

When the first voice sounded right behind his ear, he jumped a foot. "Lace your fingers on top of your head, sir."

Keenan complied, but by then he was shaking like a leaf.

A hand wrapped around the first three interlocked fingers sending pangs of pain through his arms and into his head. He couldn't have budged from the spot to save his life. Something cold clicked around Keenan's right wrist. The officer gripped it tightly, bending the wrist forward until a new kind of pain joined the first. Not letting up on the pressure, the cop pulled the right hand behind Keenan's back until it nearly reached his neck. That third pain completed the ensemble. The cop repeated the process with Keenan's left hand and a second cuff zipped into place. Cold metal pinched his wrists, cutting off his circulation, but Keenan didn't complain.

Turning his head side to side, he spotted the two other officers flanking him. They stood back with deference to let the first cop do his job. Without ceremony, that one twisted Keenan around and one of the other cops blinded him with a flashlight.

Keenan felt hands the size of catchers' mitts on his shoulders, around each arm, chest, back, ass, and down each leg. When they got there, the hands stopped, apparently realizing Keenan was naked under that coat, and a snorted *huh* came floating up to his ears.

Without even an *excuse me*, the cop unbuttoned Keenan's coat and opened it wide, apparently to do a visual search for weapons. Hot cauldrons of embarrassment suffused Keenan's face and neck, warming his skin instantly. *Perv* flickered through his skull, but he didn't make a sound.

When the cop seemed satisfied, he re-buttoned the coat and pulled the change out of Keenan's pocket, then slipped it into a clear Ziploc bag with *Evidence* neatly printed across it. He seemed upset when he didn't find anything else on Keenan to join the change.

As Keenan's eyes recovered from the glare of the flashlight, the cop said, "What's your name?"

The officer towered a good head above Keenan and filled the dark blue uniform out very well. At eye level, Keenan focused on the intricate Portland Police badge that was shining dully in the sparse light. The man could have picked Keenan up and folded him into origami.

"Keenan Swanson. This is my house, sir."

"Sergeant Thompson. You got any ID?"

Keenan had no idea how he was going to explain this, so he dug into a reserve of brilliance he rarely used. "My cat…"

"Huh?"

"He got out. I chased after him and the door closed. Locked myself out. I swear this is my house."

Sergeant Thompson wrinkled his nose at him suspiciously and rubbed his chin, giving Keenan enough time to wallow in uncertainty. Keenan's artistic instincts chose that moment to kick in; Thompson would have made a great model: tall, muscular, an Adonis god with rugged manly features. A guy Keenan was certain could shake the fillings out of his teeth.

They chattered when he said, "You can check with Smith next door. He knows me."

As if on cue, the porch light on the house alongside Keenan's puffed away the darkness. The front door opened a slit. He could see the pulsing red and blue lights reflecting off his neighbor's glasses and nervous white steam escaping into the night.

Phil Smith was a royal pain in the ass and a prissy little fellow, but they were on a forced cordial basis, so Keenan hoped he'd ID him.

Thompson nodded to one of the officers, but before he could move, Phil closed the door to slide the chain off the latch then opened it quickly scooting outside before a draft could break into his warm house. Wrapping his arms around his shoulders, he crunched his way across the icy grass in his slippers and stopped well away from them. Looking like an avenging accountant, he eyed Keenan as if he were a serial killer.

Thompson hooked a thumb in Keenan's direction. "You know this guy?"

Phil took off the frameless glasses and rubbed them against the sleeve of his robe, elongating the torment. When he put them back on, he peered at Keenan and nodded.

"Absolutely, officer. That's my neighbor Keenan Swanson. Has he done something wrong?" The question was spontaneous, gleeful, and it made Keenan sore.

"Good night, sir," the officer said. "Go back home. We'll take care of this."

"I always thought he was a little shifty...crazy too." Smith was relishing the experience and Keenan made a mental note to have one of his posse scare the bejesus out of him later.

Thompson pressed a button attached to a wire on his shirt. "7-2-2 clear. Stand down from alert." He turned to the other two officers and pulled a key out of his pocket. "Thanks, guys. I'll finish this up." The two nodded simultaneously and headed for their cruisers. Thompson turned Keenan around with one quick push.

As the patrol cars pulled away, the cop fitted the key into the cuffs and turned it, releasing Keenan's hand, and then scowled at the loitering neighbor.

"Good night, sir." This was an order and a good one. Smith turned on his heel and flitted back to his house in a heartbeat, slamming the door behind him.

When Keenan was loose, Thompson surveyed the house by running his flashlight over the structure, stopping at the broken window. "That the only way in?" he asked.

"Yeah." Keenan had no idea what was on the cop's mind and didn't like it much.

"Meet me at the front door, sir." Thompson slurred the title apparently still not trusting Keenan. Without preamble, the large cop pulled out the rest of the glass and slid through the open window disappearing into the darkness. Keenan made his way to the front porch.

After an agonizing series of long seconds, the front door finally opened and Keenan scooted inside. The heat felt good but didn't take away the weakness in his legs.

Thompson's jaw was so tight Keenan could barely see his lips.

"I'll need to see that ID. Where is it?"

"Uh…" Keenan's brain went on break and it took him a moment to locate the memory containing his wallet. "It's in my jeans in the bedroom."

"Come with me, sir." Thompson didn't wait for a reply, and Keenan was an obedient shadow behind him as they made their way through the house.

When they got to the bedroom, Keenan flicked the light switch, but it didn't work. He tried the hall light and it flared on but didn't send much in the way of illumination through the door.

He scurried through the darkness to find his pants and pull out his wallet, crunching glass under his rubber soles. Disentangling it from the inside-out jeans with shaking fingers took forever, but it finally gave with a good tug. The stuffed old leather overflowed with cards of all kinds, some expired, some not, along with lots of miscellaneous junk. Buried in the back somewhere, it took Keenan a few seconds to extract his driver's license from the tight wad.

When he handed it over, the burly man in blue rumbled at the ID under his flashlight and finally handed it back. That was when he leveled a stern look at Keenan. He played his light over the broken glass, disheveled bed, and scattered remnants of Keenan's personal life.

"Would you care to explain this?" he growled.

Keenan did some dancing.

"Mice," he said. "Big ones."

Apparently, Officer Thompson had no sense of humor since he didn't even crack a smile. He tucked his flashlight into his belt, then put one hand on his holster and the other on his nightstick, obviously trying to figure out which he should use first.

Keenan put up his hands and tried to smile. "Kidding…sorry. Chasing the cat…"

Thompson shook his head and turned for the door. Keenan barely made his way past the officer to show him through the house.

When Keenan led him to the front door, the officer gave his house a professional once over with his eyes and left without saying another word.

Keenan closed the door carefully, turned his back to it, and slid to the floor. This had been one hell of a night.

Chapter Five

Apparition Advice

When Keenan was twelve his mother married husband number six, Jack, a brute of a man who worked as a longshoreman on Swan Island. Jack wasn't like a lot of the others; he was mean right down to the bone. A yeller by trade, Jack sat on his ass more than he worked. The only exercise this guy got as far as young Keenan was concerned was a daily workout that involved smacking the boy around the room. Keenan got to the point where he thought everyone heard ringing in their ears.

On a very dark November night a day after his fourteenth birthday (which was only noted as a black scribble on the calendar hanging on the fridge), Keenan got home from his job at the bread store to hear a loud shouting match coming from his house. He stopped on the sidewalk and contemplated just turning around and heading back to work another shift, but his hunger proved a stronger impulse. He thought he could sneak in and just grab a quick bite first.

The row was nothing unusual; hell, the two went at each other pretty much every night lately. When he walked through the door, before he even hung up his backpack, a loud slap and a thump echoed into the kitchen followed by his mother's scream.

What Keenan did next surprised the hell out of him. It wasn't that he and his mother were exactly close; he spent hours figuring out ways to avoid her. It wasn't even the fact that she was his mother. What goaded him into action was something ingrained into him by her from the day he was born. A man *never* strikes a woman.

He found himself charging straight for the son of bitch at full speed. Another *smack, smack, smack* got his legs moving even faster. Keenan wasn't a big boy at fourteen, but he had hit his spurt early so he was tall and what his mother used to call gangly. Six hours kneading bread at the store every day for the last two years had given him a healthy set of arms and shoulders.

When he reached Jack, Keenan grabbed him by the back of his shirt, twisted his hands in the fabric until Jack's arms were pulled almost straight back, and lifted him off his feet. The smell of cheap gin, cigarettes, and sweat added fodder to his anger.

Jack countered the action by bringing his head back and hitting Keenan hard on the collarbone. It hurt like hell and Keenan let go. When Jack turned around with a solid right, Keenan ducked, but not very well. The fist caught him squarely on the side of the face, and he went flying. He hit the wall at full speed, but fortunately, his backpack took the brunt of the impact.

Jack didn't wait for him to catch his breath. He charged at young Keenan with fists curled, teeth bared, and a roar of alcoholic rage. The booze was making Jack sloppy or he would have figured out what Keenan would do next. When Jack was almost on top of him, Keenan lifted both of his long legs from the ground and caught Jack right in the stomach. Jack doubled over Keenan's feet and Keenan pushed with all his might. Jack's body hit the far wall at full impact. He crumpled into a heap on the floor groaning.

Keenan got up off the carpet and bent over to get air back into his lungs. His mother jumped up and for the first time in years, he thought she was going to hug him. He was wrong.

When his mother reached him, she hauled off and slapped him across the face. "You son of a bitch! You hurt him!" The gin-drenched words permeated every inch of his awareness and cut his heart in half. She ran to her drunken husband and cooed over his misfortune.

Keenan didn't stay. He pulled the front door open with such force he heard glass break on the wall behind it. He didn't care. Leaving the door open, Keenan disappeared into the night.

Why that particular recollection happened to snap into his mind at that moment was beyond him.

He had had an entire night to get his tangled nerves to behave, but it was no good; he just couldn't get it out of his head and had been too exhausted to stay at home and confront his broken bedroom anymore. Keenan had finally stumbled to the Bagdad Theater Saturday afternoon for popcorn and a micro-brew, his favorite comfort food. But the movie was as listless and depressing as his mood, so he left early.

As he passed the yuppie shops on his way home from the theater, the memory of Jack stood up between his ears like a marauding bear. It made his stomach cringe and usually he pushed it down as quickly as it came up, but now it was stark against the inside of his eyelids. He forced his mind to think instead about what happened later that night.

He was so enraged, young Keenan started to walk. The pounding of the sidewalk was all he was aware of for hours. It barely registered, but as he moved along, each streetlight he passed went dark, some in a shower of sparks. Something wrong with the electricity, maybe, but he didn't care; heartsick and numb, Keenan finally decided to let his feet take him wherever they wanted to go. Where he ended up startled him at first, but it eventually made a kind of sense.

Laurelhurst Park was an oasis tucked in the middle of southeast Portland. Thirty acres of lush stands of green, expanses of well-tended lawns, and a huge pond that housed hundreds of swans, geese, and ducks, the park had been a mainstay of Keenan's childhood. His best memories were of chasing the squawking birds and throwing pieces of stale bread to feed them.

His feet apparently knew something he didn't because when they finally stopped it was at the edge of that same pond.

Keenan figured it must have been midnight. Low clouds had snuck in while he walked, obscuring the stars, the moon, and anything else that might have been in the sky that night. He had never been to the park this late; it was pitch black except for the far away lights on the street that surrounded it.

Apparently, the birds had all gone to bed because there wasn't a sound except the swish of the water as it lightly lapped the shore.

He sat down on the bank and finally let the tears come. It was only the second time in Keenan's life that he allowed grief to take over his self-control. The first had been when his mother had forgotten him when he was four and no one could find her. She appeared the next morning all sunshine and apologies, but even at that ripe young age, Keenan knew she had spent the night at the bar... or somewhere even more unsavory.

The tears on this particular night were abundant; they washed over his heart until everything trembled into sobs. He wasn't sure how long he sat there, but finally the tears dried up and he was able to breathe without the waterworks. A kind of euphoria settled over his shoulders that spun the matter between his ears. He felt better.

With a final deep sigh, he focused on the water, uncertain what his next move should be. A mist had gathered over the lake until it hung in a sheet of white that illuminated the trees around him. Keenan was impressed; he had never seen fog this thick.

It was only then that something caught his eye... something that shouldn't exist.

The clouds parted and out of the water rose a black woman in a ratty blue housedress with large curlers all over her head. She had no legs that he could see, and he could just make out the lake *through* her. It was very disconcerting and Keenan couldn't make any sense out of it.

Apparently, there *were* geese on the water because all of a sudden the air exploded with their noisy squawks, their wings flapping like crazy, their necks thrust out toward the opposite shore as they churned little yellow legs as fast as they would go.

Keenan got to his feet not believing what it was he was seeing. When she smiled at him, everything went loose and he wet himself.

"Hello, honey. It's a beautiful night, don't you think." It was the second time Keenan had seen a ghost, but the first time one had actually talked to him. He began a journey that would take him to worlds few living even knew existed.

* * * *

When Keenan got to his house, he unlocked his front door, balancing what was left of the large popcorn he had brought with him from the theater. He heard a familiar voice drifting in from the living room and smiled. Constance was back.

He was never happier to see her drifting there surrounded by a dozen other ghosts. The conversation took an abrupt halt as soon as he came into view.

"Kee…" Constance floated across the room, fading out and in as she went.

"Where the hell have you been?" The voice coming out of Keenan's mouth was unsettling. It sounded mad.

Constance stopped a few feet from him and put translucent fists on phantom hips. "Well that's a fine howdy-do." She shooed the rest of the ghosts away and followed him to the couch. Her normally joyous face crinkled with concern. Keenan swallowed hard against the fear creeping up his gut.

"Sorry I disappeared last night." She hovered above the coffee table, her curlers bouncing up and down every time she moved. When she looked down at her hands, she said a little sheepishly, "She wasn't too rough, was she?"

Keenan rubbed his eyes and rested the popcorn container on his knees. "I'm fine. Just a little shaky. Reggie told me about her last night. He says she probably won't show up again."

It was hard for him to keep the disappointment out of his voice and even harder to admit he had actually enjoyed it. Something deep inside him wanted more of what happened last night. Wanted it so bad, it was suffocating his normally cautious responses. That scared him...it was just too creepy. He sat back, took a handful of popcorn, and stuffed it into his mouth.

Constance folded her arms and pulled back her chin. "Something you not tellin' me, child?"

The last thing Keenan was going to do was discuss his sex life with Constance. He had enough problems talking to her about his regular life. "I just want to forget about it, Cee," he said through a mouth of popcorn.

"You need to be careful, Kee," she scolded. "The more she touches ya, the harder it'll be ta walk away. What if she comes back tonight?"

Keenan shrugged and counted the kernels on the top of the tub. "I don't know. I'll figure something out."

"She's dangerous."

"I know."

"She can kill you."

"I know that too."

Constance's ample bosom rose and fell in a very audible capitulation. "All right, have it your own way. I looked up one of the old ones last night. He told me a little somethin' about this one."

Keenan put the popcorn on the table and brushed his hands. "Look, she'll probably never show up again, Cee. I told you I'm all right. Quit hovering."

She moved over to stand next to him and her face softened. "That's what I'm here for, Kee." Lifting a vaporous hand, she circled his face without touching him. "No matter what, ya need to know I'm here t' protect you. Even when things don't seem quite right. You understand me?"

Something in her face sent a strange premonition through his guts. "Sure, Cee." But he wasn't really sure if he did.

She stood straight, licked her plump lips, and squared her shoulders. "You need t' hear what the old timer said."

Keenan rested his neck against the back of the couch. Putting his legs up on the coffee table, he decided it was probably best to humor her. More Creole mumbo jumbo, he was sure. "All right."

"Her name is Dabria. She was a lower angel of the nine choirs up 'til 'bout five hundred years ago. A Muse, some say. She was on earth to work with her mentor, Amos, one o' the principalities.

"Princa...what?"

"Didn't ya *ever* go to Sunday school, child? I swear what you don't know would fill a library." She clicked her tongue. "Seventh of the nine choirs assigned to guide humans."

"Oh," was all Keenan could manage, vaguely remembering something about the nine choirs. He'd look it up later.

"Anyway, while on earth, she fell in love with a human, an artist from Florence, name of Luciano Moretti. It was a trap set by one of the fallen, Azazel..."

"This is just Catholic horseshit, Cee. There's no such thing as angels or demons..."

"There was no such thing as ghosts a few years ago, remember?"

That stopped him cold. She had a point. "Oh, yeah. Continue."

"Thank you," she said tossing her head. "Anyway, Azazel killed the man and enslaved Dabria, turning her into a succubus. She escaped the demon, but was bound to this Earth to live out her days as a creature that had to seduce men to survive." Constance's eyes dimmed for a moment. "I kind o' feel sorry for the poor thing, truth be told. Weren't her fault... love can be mighty powerful, even for angels." There was a sadness in her eyes that Keenan had never seen before and it bothered him.

"You okay, Cee?"

She looked up and smiled. "Nothin' t' fret on, boy." She moved to the other end of the couch and scanned the room. "Maybe you should leave, Kee."

Keenan leaned forward and put his elbows on his knees. He didn't want to leave. In fact, he hoped she would come back. It was tying his stomach in knots.

"I'm not leaving my house, Cee," he said.

Constance glided to the other side of the room and turned her head to him. "Do what ya think is right, Kee. Once she's here, we can't be there for ya. Maybe ya can get through t' her, maybe not. If ya try, remember she was an angel once who loved a man. There may be something left of her heart." She shimmered in the light briefly then disappeared.

Chapter Six

A Haunting Refrain

What woke Keenan a few hours later was a hiss in his ear. He forced his eyes open and blinked at the nature show droning on the TV in his living room. After rubbing them, he focused on the myrtle wood clock hanging behind it. Midnight on the nose.

Dozens of specters filled the room. Some were floating, some sitting, or standing, or lying, or other "ings" that were decidedly wrong on many, many levels. Keenan stood to stretch and took his time with a deep, satisfying yawn. Midway through it, the lights, and the ghosts, snapped off. The room went dark, silent, and empty.

He choked on the yawn and bent over with a coughing fit. When it was over, Keenan banged his shin against the coffee table and swore at it.

"Okay…this isn't funny," he yelled at the living room. "Reggie, if that's you jacking with me, I…"

The words caught in this throat when a shadow traveled in front of the two large windows facing the street. Headlights came through it in glistening stars as it moved toward him.

Fear started as a hot ice pick shoved into the base of his neck and settled over his face.

He took a step back but hit his legs against the sofa and fell, landing with a thud on his ass. The shadow flitted back and forth in slow, even movements, giving Keenan enough time to get his feet on the floor and his butt off the couch.

Scuttling to the right, he found enough empty space to turn and run straight into his dining room table, smashing his right hip against the very solid fine oak.

He stopped breathing long enough to let the endorphins kick in and rubbed the injury fast to move them along.

The succubus materialized in front of him. She was even more beautiful than she had been the night before, though her face still hid behind an enticing mist. Keenan reached into a spot he didn't use very often—self-discipline. It was the hardest thing he ever had to do. His resolve was paper-thin.

He put up his hands and backed away from her, knowing he'd have to talk fast, before he surrendered.

"Look, as much as I loved last night...and believe me, I did...you have to understand that your visits are probably not very healthy for me. I'm sure you're a very nice...entity and all, but honestly, I think once is enough."

The form hovered in front of him as if thinking, the hair flowing in liquid wisps around her head. Keenan edged toward the front door.

"I'm sorry." His voice came out a bit shaky, but not bad, all things considered. "I really am." And he really was. "But, there's this woman I'm seeing and, well, I don't want to hurt her and..."

All hell broke loose.

A high-pitched sound, almost like a scream, filled the house. Windows exploded outward. All the smoke detectors went off at once. Everything in the room not tied down lifted into the air. It swirled together until the stuff formed a cyclone that swept through the darkness.

The stunning shadowed spirit swelled in front of Keenan until her head hit the ceiling and her body crammed the room. Waves of what Keenan could only describe as jealously saturated his skin. He was terrified.

"Dabria, right?" he shouted in desperation. He wasn't even sure what he was saying, but it was the only thing he could think of.

It worked; she stopped growing and held still.

"Dabria," he repeated, taking the moment to move his back against the dining room wall. "Isabella is very special to me. I really want a chance with her." He swallowed hard, not knowing if the succubus would kill him now or do it after she seduced him. Who could blame him if he hoped for the latter?

"I...you're very nice and last night was wonderful, but...please...I think you know what it means to be in love. At least I hope so." The words came out in a rushing flood of babbles. "I don't want to betray her...I mean, I don't really even know her and you're so...oh man, I want you in the worst way, believe me. You are so...hot..." He cut off the word but it tumbled out of his mouth unsupervised. Squeezing his eyes tight and melting into the wallpaper at his back, he waited for the fatal strike.

It didn't come.

He opened one eye a slit to find out why.

The shadow deflated in one swift whoosh and the whirlwinds came to an abrupt halt, sending everything crashing to the floor.

When he heard Reggie's voice in his ear, his heart stopped. He shot a glance at his transparent friend floating next to the open door. "Run, you idiot. Do you want to die?"

The succubus shrank away from them, and Keenan, ping ponging looks from one to the other, took the opportunity to bite his lip before taking Reggie's advice. Stumbling past the shadow, he jumped for the front door and darted outside. Without closing it or even looking back, he leapt down the steps and headed for the sidewalk.

When he rushed by Smith's house, he thought he saw the mousy man staring out the large front window, his mouth open, talking on his cell phone.

Keenan headed down Thirty-Second Street, turned left onto Hawthorn, and ran like an antelope with a lion biting its tail.

When he hit the crowd outside *Taps* at full speed, he came to a crashing halt and sailed to the ground, taking down two brawny beer drinkers, their respective girlfriends, and an innocent table that was sitting there minding its own business. Four obviously full pints of stout flew through the air and the contents rained down on the struggling quintet in a dark brown shower, soaking all of them. Two of the empty pints hit Keenan squarely on the back of the head, one after the other.

The tangled pile of human beings and beer began to disentangle itself, but Keenan's head was spinning wildly. So wildly, in fact, that he didn't feel himself roughly yanked to his feet then off of them, or see the swollen fist appear out of thin air until it was too late. All he heard was a distant *son of a bitch* and the sound of meaty flesh striking cheekbone.

The sparklers that gleamed in front of his eyes reminded him of the Fourth of July on the coast. He found himself down on the ground again.

"...you stupid prick!" The words soaked into his stupor and he squinted up to see six-foot-six of angry male mountain, a pleading red head attached to the man's arm.

Not that it would have stopped another blow, but Keenan forced his hands into the submissive position and tried to find his voice. "Oh, man..." he said to the mountain. "I'm really sorry. Are you all right?"

That seemed to do the trick. The man stopped and dislodged the girl from his arm. "What the fuck?"

"I didn't see you," Keenan said. "I was running from..." He feebly motioned down the street and the guy leaned against one leg, folding his arms.

"What?" he said.

"Some guys hijacked my car about five minutes ago." It was feasible. There had been a rash of car thefts in the neighborhood. The mountain's face softened. He looked concerned then greedy. Keenan took the opportunity to struggle to his feet. His spinning head was talking to his stomach, and not in a kind way.

"Really? Where?" The words were a little too anxious.

At a guess, the man and his buddy had probably been drinking since eight, so Keenan did the math: a pint of beer, say, every half hour for four hours...eight beers. Yah, pretty drunk. It looked like they were both pitching for a fight. Keenan gladly diverted their ambitions away from himself.

"Down on Twenty-Ninth, just south of Hawthorn. I was at a stop sign and the sons of bitches broke my window and pulled me out of the car. I was trying to find a phone. It sounded like they couldn't get the car started again. There's a trick to it. They may still be there."

The other man stood shoulder to shoulder with his buddy and rubbed his knuckles. "You girls stay here. We'll be right back."

A dark shadow appeared behind them and Keenan took a step back.

The two men took off down the street, and Keenan ran the other way, the protests of the two women mingling with the wind in his ears.

Taking a risk, he ran across Thirty-Fourth Street. When he looked to his left, he saw a car bearing down on him. It just missed him, honked its horn, and sped on past with a muted *asshole!* coming through the glass. When he looked over his shoulder, he could see the spirit dodging in and out of parked cars on either side of the street, almost playfully. Keenan put some fire into his feet and sprinted down the sidewalk.

Ancient houses zipped by him on either side, but thankfully there were no people around. He hadn't been up this way before but didn't stop to investigate. It was like most streets in the Hawthorn District; crowded with nicely remodeled turn of the century houses on small lots.

As always, the streetlights flashed and went out like Roman candles whenever he got within twenty feet of one, eventually making the sidewalk almost invisible. It's why he never took a walk when he was angry.

In the darkness to his right, the houses turned into a large open area. *A park?* He darted into the darkness and sprinted faster. That is, until he ran into something protruding from the ground right at testicle level.

Except for the landing, no Olympian could have executed Keenan's tumble through the air with more grace. He counted at least two flips, a half turn, and a twist, wondering when he would hit the ground. It wasn't long before a tree broke his fall. Every last molecule of air flew from his overextended lungs in a rush, and he landed in a crumpled heap on top of its roots.

Shock set off alarms inside his eardrums and settled into his face, making it heavy and hot. There wasn't any pain...yet. It wasn't ghosts he saw before his eyes, only stars, fireworks, and every shade of red known to man. Then everything went black.

He must have only been stunned, because when he opened his eyes, they filled with the vision of the succubus leaning over him. When he tried to move, agony blossomed through every nerve in his body.

The creature tilted its head and reached out to touch him. Keenan mustered enough energy to get him moving, but it was only to his hands and knees. It was undignified, but he didn't have much choice. He crawled like a baby toward a wall to his left.

The ground under his hands shifted from grass to what he assumed was asphalt; it was slightly sticky with tiny rocks that buried themselves in his palms. When he reached a brick wall and leaned his back against it, his strength gave out. The succubus rose as a dark shadow in front of him.

"Look," he breathed, closing his eyes and lowering his chin. "Take your best shot, doll. Just leave the coroner something to bury, ok?" The words were very jagged.

Radiating warmth took the chill out of his breath when she came nearer. Keenan braced himself for the inevitable. What he got instead, was a hot blanket of air that wrapped around his body several times and lifted him to his feet.

When Keenan opened his eyes, all he could see was black. A wide ribbon of heat curled around his neck, up along his scalp, and then melted down his face in slow, easy eddies. Every muscle relaxed inside the gentle cocoon. His shirt and coat opened to let it touch his chest and his pants fell around his ankles so that his legs, ass, and privates could experience it too.

Strands of supple warmth coated his body, from the top of his head to the bottoms of his feet. Keenan became suddenly weightless, buoyant, suspended above the ground, defying gravity and common sense. It was like plunging into a hot cloud, held firmly in place but freely floating. Sexuality had nothing to do with this; that was the last thing on Keenan's mind. Instead, it was immensely peaceful.

Like being in the womb.

The thought meandered through his head along with a thousand other soothing images. There wasn't the least bit of pain anymore.

A sound started as a quiet hum in the back of his neck. It took him forever to figure out what it was. Keenan couldn't strain to hear it since that would require effort. Instead, he relaxed and closed his eyes again, waiting for the sound to unfold.

It wasn't long before the music became distinct, a light humming, a faint melody, a woman's voice lilting through his brain. The sound wasn't like anything Keenan had heard before; it was exhilarating and yet sadly haunting at the same time. It went straight to his heart then to his eyes. He couldn't stop the tears despite his macho instincts. The effect was profound and life changing. He had never been so at peace, so certain, so alive. The urge to float inside the music forever dominated every other aspiration.

The shadow shifted around him, squeezing tightly, like a hug, then it released.

All of a sudden, the night poured back in on him, and he landed with a thump right on his naked ass. The pain from earlier and this new one ripped out through every pore. He groaned. Cold rushed in on him, stealing the heat and the moment.

Strangely, when he looked down, his cock was rock hard. When he looked up, the succubus was gone, replaced by the looming figure of a man. Everything collapsed immediately.

Keenan blinked in the brilliance of a flashlight shining on his face and shaded his eyes with his forearm. That's when he saw the gun. It was dark gray and looked like it meant business.

"You again." The words were gruff and gut wrenching. "Hands out to the side. Get up."

Keenan complied and his heart sank when he realized who it was. A meaty hand spun him around to face the wall.

"Spread your legs. Hands on the top of your head. Lace your fingers."

Keenan's hair was wet with fear, but he tangled his fingers together and pulled them tightly against his scalp. He heard the snap of rubber gloves, and the whispered jingle of metal against metal. When cold surrounded his right wrist, he knew he was sunk.

"Listen, Sergeant Thompson, I know this looks bad, but..."

"Save it."

The hands throwing his wrists together were experts. Click went the other handcuff.

Without a shade of embarrassment, Thompson turned him around, reached down, grabbed Keenan's jeans and shorts, and pulled them over his hips, zipping the fly and buttoning the button. He dragged his shirt closed and buttoned it as well. The blue-gloved hands were cold and humiliation flooded every inch of his skin followed by sheets of goose bumps.

When he was done, Thompson roughly turned him toward the brick wall again and thoroughly searched him. As he did, he reached into each of Keenan's pockets, removing everything: wallet, cell phone, change, and keys. Keenan could hear the distinct zip of another evidence bag. He wondered vaguely if he'd ever see his stuff again.

Pulling a frustrated sigh into his lungs, Thompson patted him down one more time.

"Mr. Swanson, I need to read you your rights..."

"Oh, God, no... It's not what it looks like." Hot pins of fear were making Keenan dizzy. He couldn't believe Thompson was arresting him.

"You have the right to remain silent. Anything you say can and will be held against you…"

"Honestly. There's a good explanation for…"

"Right," Thompson barked then whirled him around to face him. "You have the right to remain silent. Anything you say can and will be used against you in a court of law." A laminated card had appeared in his hand. "You have the right to talk to an attorney and have him or her present while you are questioned. If you cannot afford to hire an attorney, one will be appointed to represent you at no expense." Thompson tucked the card into his pocket and leered down at Keenan. "Do you understand these rights?"

"Really…I wasn't doing anything…"

"Do you understand these rights?" Thompson repeated with restrained anger.

The smell of freshly eaten sausage blew from the officer's mouth, and Keenan saw a splash of seaside on a summer weekend in his head. Over Thompson's shoulder, Constance, Reggie, and a score of other ghosts floated just out of the light. Constance was shaking her head.

"Yes…I guess…but I wasn't doing anything. I was just taking a piss, got light headed, and fell. That's not a crime, is it?"

One side of Thompson's lip and the opposite brow curled up. He nodded and played his flashlight above Keenan's head. When Keenan turned around, his heart fell into his guts and boiled there.

Just above his eyes, in neat silver letters splayed evenly across the red bricks, were the words *St. Angelo's School for Girls*. The Catholic cross hung straight and true beside them.

"Mr. Swanson, you are being charged with public indecency, a Class A misdemeanor. I strongly suggest you cooperate. Sorry, buddy," Thompson added with a huffed laugh. "You're looking at maybe a year in jail and a six grand fine. Tough break."

Sergeant Thompson yanked Keenan's arm once to get his legs moving toward the parked police car.

The red and blue lights throbbing above the snow-white sedan blurred through the sweat in Keenan's eyes. He had never even gotten a ticket, let alone been arrested. It all just seemed so bizarre.

His ghostly friends congregated just outside the throw of lights and started to disappear one by one. Reggie and Constance remained just long enough for Sergeant Thompson to slam the front door behind him and start the engine. The prostitute sitting next to Keenan in the back seat pointed at him and chortled. It took him a second to realize she wasn't alive. He concentrated instead on adjusting his hands so he could get feeling back into them. He wasn't very successful.

Keenan's imagination was ruthless, creating scenes of the local constable dragging him through the streets while citizens laughed and threw things at him. It was giving him a headache. Thankfully, Thompson shut the lights off once he got the car going.

When the car jolted into the street, Keenan's eyes and cheeks went hot and the rest of his face went numb. A black shadow materialized in the headlight for only a moment and then disappeared into the night.

Chapter Seven

Ghost in the Cell

Charles J. Murray was the biggest asshole at Portland State University during Keenan's freshman year. Keenan had trouble with bullies all his life. Over the years, he had developed excellent ways of coping. Running mostly, but his ability to ignore insults reached a genius plateau by the age of fifteen.

However, Charles J. Murray was a bully of extreme discipline. The junior football player had terrorized the campus for three years, and most students considered him pitiful at best. Not that any of them would say that to his face, mind you.

For whatever reason, Charles had developed a special affinity for tormenting Keenan. Names like numb nuts, faggot, and dumb shit all rolled off Keenan's back, as always, but this just pissed off the giant fullback. The initial pranks were mostly embarrassing, but when they turned increasingly dangerous, Keenan got on a first name basis with terror. Try as he might, he could not get away from Charles. He even moved off campus, but it took Charles less than a day to find him, probably torturing one of the housing student aids for the information.

In November, right before Thanksgiving break and a rather nasty incident involving dish soap coating his kitchen floor and a concussion, Reggie told Keenan he had had enough. The vindictive ghost hatched a plan that was not only diabolical, but could rid the school of this tyrant forever. It was the first time Keenan had seen Reggie's really sinister side and it bothered him. But since Reggie promised no real harm would come to Charles, he reluctantly agreed.

Keenan had never bought pot before. It wasn't that he hadn't tried it; he smoked it only once when he was about twelve. Unfortunately, he was allergic to the stuff and ended up in the hospital. He told his mom, and the doctors, that he had smoked a clove cigarette. His medical record still stated he was allergic to cloves.

The next morning, he approached one of the *dealers* someone told him about. Keenan was certain some undercover cop was right there watching his every move, ready to call in a dozen squad cars to bust him. Reggie had to bolster him all the way through the transaction, telling him exactly what to say. Feeling a little like a puppet and shaking like a leaf, Keenan gave the guy the twenty-five bucks, snagged the plastic bag, stuffed it inside his jacket, and then took off, staying to the shadows so no one would see him.

That night he knew Charles and his roommates would be at a game. Following Reggie's careful instructions, Keenan managed without too much difficulty to pick the lock on the frat house door and get inside, again amazed at Reggie's expertise in yet another fine art. Finding Charles's room was easy; it was the grossest one in the house. To this guy, rotten was a lifestyle. Keenan planted the pot under Charles's mattress and left to make an anonymous phone call to the police from one of the campus payphones.

The next day the headlines read *Heisman Hopeful Arrested on Drug Charges*. In actuality, Charles got off with a slap on the wrist, suspension from school for two weeks and had to sit out of football for the rest of the quarter. But the scheme worked; Charles was a pussycat after that. Apparently, his few days in jail taught him some valuable lessons about playing with others. He went on to the pros after college for one season, but was busted for steroid use and kicked out of the league.

Keenan still felt pangs of guilt every time he thought about what he had done to Charles. Now he realized karma must have caught up on her *to-do* list and finally gotten around to him.

When they arrived at the precinct, Sergeant Thompson drove through a huge door at the front. The cruiser moved into what looked like a garage, except it had rolling doors on both ends. The one on the other side was closed. Once the door behind them shut, Thompson opened the car door, unlocked Keenan's safety belt, and pulled him from the vehicle. Without batting an eye, Thompson marched Keenan through a heavy metal door he opened with a round electronic key and escorted him inside.

On the other side was a small cement and metal area with two identical holding cells. Each consisted of a concrete bench with lead pipes bolted to the wall at sitting height and a silver toilet bolted to the floor on the other side of the cell. Circling these luxuries were four blank, cream tiled walls.

As Thompson pulled Keenan to stand to the left of the cell door, he murmured, "You're going to cause me a whole night of paperwork, my friend. You better sing nice and pretty when we come back to talk to you. Understand?"

Keenan nodded and Thompson made him take off his shoes before he pulled Keenan into one of the cells. Once they reached the bench, Thompson roughly un-cuffed one wrist and attached the business end to the steel pipe, telling Keenan to have a seat.

"I might be a while," Thompson said over his shoulder closing the heavy door behind him. The beep of the electronic lock made Keenan's ears pound.

Rubbing his wrists as best he could, Keenan inspected the small room. Except for the toilet and bench, it was empty. Well, of accoutrements, anyway.

A strange little Asian man sat in one corner, eyeing him suspiciously and rubbing his chin. He was nearly transparent, except for a pair of shining black eyes and a red goatee.

"Got yourself in a real jam, didn't you?" The specter's voice was very old.

Keenan ignored him and searched the room. He was certain they had it bugged. Spending the night in jail was bad enough; a week on the psych floor, however, was not his idea of a good time.

"You don't need to talk, young man," the apparition stated. "I'm an attorney...or was before I died. Constance sent me to give you some advice and maybe get you out of this."

That brought Keenan up short and he thinned his lips at the ghost, not caring if anyone was listening. "Constance?" he whispered.

"Sure." The Asian man rose from the floor and drifted to float above the toilet. "Don't talk, just listen. Name's McGillivray, but you can call me Mac."

Funny, he doesn't look Scottish. A little smile tugged at Keenan's lip, the first one of the evening. It made him feel better.

Mac replied, "My father was Scottish, my mother Chinese."

Keenan could not get his wits wrapped around any of this. The whole situation was only confirming his suspicion that maybe he really *was* crazy and the last to hear about it. *Makes perfect sense.*

Mac assumed the lotus position above the toilet and put on a spectral pair of glasses that materialized out of the air. Resting them on his nose, a large leather bound book appeared on his lap. Opening it to somewhere at the center, he poured over the contents while water poured down Keenan's sides and back. It was getting very warm.

"Let's see..." Mac wrinkled his nose up and down several times and ran a finger along the page. "*163...163...* Ah! *163.465 Public indecency. (1) A person commits the crime of public indecency if while in, or in view of, a public place the person performs. . .*" Mutter, mutter, mutter, and then, "*(c) An act of exposing the genitals of the person with the intent of arousing the sexual desire of the person or another person. Public indecency is a Class A misdemeanor.*" He pursed his lips and regarded Keenan gravely. "Oh, that's very bad. And in front of a girls' school too. Don't suppose you knew where you were, did you?"

Keenan shook his head then watched his hands fold themselves together on his lap. The room was getting hotter and he reached to take his coat off. It was only then he realized he didn't have it on.

"Good. I'm afraid you're in for a night in jail, son." Mac regarded him gravely. "Normally, they just give you a citation and send you home. You must have pissed this guy off. You may need to get in touch with someone to come up with bail."

Bail.

The word was the first that actually took on some significance for Keenan.

Someone to come up with bail.

Keenan had no family in town, no friends, not even close acquaintances he knew well enough for him to go to for money. There were several ex-girlfriends, but he was certain they'd all just hang up on him. The only people he could think of were his next-door neighbor (fat chance) and Mike, the other graphic designer that sat in the cubicle next to him. Since Keenan had less than forty bucks in his pocket until Monday, and even less in the bank, Mike would have to do.

Just then, the door opened and a man in shirtsleeves and slacks sauntered through it. Under his arm was a clipboard with a yellow tablet attached to it. He was tall with pale skin, fishy eyes, and rumpled dishwater hair. He looked about as threatening as a sponge.

The man leaned on the wall across from Keenan and pulled a piece of paper from the back of the clipboard. Keenan didn't say a word while he examined it.

"Keenan Swanson, right?"

Keenan nodded and the man tucked the clipboard back under his arm.

"Sergeant Thompson read you your rights, correct?"

Keenan nodded again, but he couldn't look into those bulging eyes anymore, so he bowed his chin toward the floor.

"Good," the man continued. "I'm Detective Johnston, Mr. Swanson. Before we start any questioning, I need to know if you would like to waive your right to have an attorney present during an interview."

Keenan blinked back at him and didn't know what to say.

Mac floated to stand next to him and turned to the detective. "Tell him you'd like your phone call."

"I'd like my phone call," Keenan repeated dutifully.

Johnston put his lips to one side and gave him a single nod. "Okey, dokey. I'll check with Thompson." He ambled out the same way he came in and locked the door behind him.

Keenan was convinced he'd never get that phone call, but five minutes later, Johnston reentered the room without comment and handed Keenan his own cell phone, then leaned against the furthest wall, watching him with bored, half-closed eyes.

Keenan stared down at the familiar instrument as if it were some kind of poisonous snake. He had no idea what Mike's number was. All he could remember was the office number. Reflexively, he dialed it. The two rings didn't give him any time to think it through.

You've reached General Graphics and Designs. Our normal business hours are 8 a.m. to 5 p.m., Monday thru Friday. Please leave your name, number, and a reason for the call, and someone will get back to you as soon as possible. Have a wonderful day.

Keenan had one second to think of what to say before it beeped into his ear.

"Uh…" More sweat trickled down the left side of his neck. "This is Keenan Swanson and I'm trying to get in touch with, uh, Mike Albertson. I am at the…" He threw a panicked look at the detective.

"Southeast Precinct, Forty-Seventh and East Burnside," the man mumbled.

"Southeast Precinct, Forty-Seventh and East Burnside," Keenan repeated. "I've been arrested, but it's all a mistake. I need him to come down and bail me out." He fumbled for an additional explanation, but it evaded him. Instead, he stammered, "Th…thank you." It was brainless, but that was the state of his mental dexterity at the moment.

Without hanging up, he handed the phone back to the cop.

When the man left, Keenan buried his face in his hands. He was very tired.

"All right, son," Mac said. "Let's work out a strategy for your defense."

Keenan lifted his head and cocked it to one side. "Just leave me alone. I've had all the help I can stand for one day."

"Sure thing." Mac slammed the book shut. "I was only trying to assist." Keenan heard the faint *swoosh* of the man disappearing.

He closed his eyes and let his mind slip into exhaustion. It was going to be a long night.

After several hours of silence and staring at four blank walls, Keenan convinced himself he would be there forever. *Had they forgotten him? What time was it? What day was it?* The stress from the night before and no sleep was making him twitchy. Various apparitions floated through to pay their respects, make fun of him, or ignore him completely. Keenan didn't mind; without the distraction, his brain would have been on its own. That was always a dangerous scenario. He occupied most of his time trying to figure out what would come in next in the parade of specters.

Finally, he heard the buzz at the cell door and turned around.

A stout little man crossed the cell to remove cuffs then wiggled a finger at him. Keenan followed him out the door where the cop stopped him, indicating Keenan's shoes with a nod. Keenan slipped them onto his feet.

"Come on," the officer said, motioning Keenan to another door.

Three specters slid through the cell door and waved goodbye to him and Constance, who cropped up right in front of him, waved hello. She searched him up and down but said nothing.

The short man led Keenan down a long hallway with empty offices on either side, passed a break room, and along a short hallway with a door at the end. Keenan thought he was taking him to get fingerprints, photos, or something, since they didn't do that the night before, but to his astonishment the man moved through the metal door out into a spacious lobby where Keenan blinked against bright sunshine coming through high windows.

Keenan stopped dead in his tracks and his blood turned to ice. Standing in front of a glassed-in reception counter, looking like an angel in sweats, stood Isabella.

"Fuck," whispered Keenan.

"You're free to go," whispered the cop.

"Oh, honey," whispered Constance.

Chapter Eight

Spirited Away

Isabella turned to regard the two of them, and Keenan was amazed she was smiling. She gave him a wink, shook her head, and looked down to finish signing something. The little man grabbed Keenan's arm and propelled him toward the girl. On the way, he snatched the "Evidence" envelope from the reception desk and pressed it into Keenan's arms. The familiar jingle of his car keys gave him little comfort.

"Thank you, miss," the receptionist was saying when they came up. "Just make sure he stays out of trouble."

Keenan saw a mischievous grin lighten Isabella's face when she said, "Absolutely. I intend to make certain he behaves himself. I'll see to it personally."

As if handing off a wayward dog, the man gave Keenan a little push and Isabella grabbed his arm.

Keenan was too numb to resist her insistent pull as she led him through a glass door and out into a crisp, bright morning.

He tried to speak once they were on the sidewalk, but she beat him to it.

"Sorry, Keenan." Isabella let go of him and fished her keys out of her purse. "There was no way to get word to you that I was coming over. I was checking messages early this morning when I heard yours. I thought it best if I came over to get you out myself. No need to get another employee mixed up in all this."

Mortification saturated every muscle turning Keenan's knees into blocks of gelatin. His heart sank. *She's protecting the company. I'll be a laughing stock… if I'm still gainfully employed.*

"Look," he said running his hand through his hair. "I didn't do anything last night. It was a terrible mistake. I never…"

"I know." She clicked a button on her keychain toward a waiting sedan parked at the end of the lot. The tinny beep grated against his throbbing head.

"You know?"

"Sure…they told me they weren't pressing charges. Said one of the other cops wanted to teach you a lesson." She opened the passenger door and motioned for him to get in. "Said they didn't have enough to keep you. Lucky."

Keenan's mouth fell open, but nothing came out, and Isabella gave him another one of those special smirks he was starting to like. She slammed the door, glided around the front, and got into the driver's seat. Sweeping pretty brown eyes at him, she put the key in the ignition and started the car.

"Don't worry. This is between you and me. It never happened."

"I'm really sorry. I appreciate your taking me home. I'll never darken your doorstep again…"

"Not on your life, mister." She barely glanced at her side mirror when she turned right onto Burnside, cutting in front of another driver, who honked his horn. "You and I had a date, remember? You owe me breakfast."

What with his house demolished, his life threatened not once, but twice, and the arrest, the date had completely slipped his mind. Her nonchalant acceptance of the situation floored him. It had to be a mistake…or he had died and gone to flasher heaven.

"Listen, you don't have to…"

"You're not worming your way out of it, so get comfortable. You want to go home first to change?" She watched the road and Keenan watched her. The silhouette of her jaw line made him almost forget the last twelve hours.

"Yeah," he replied absently.

"Great. I'd love to see your place. I've never been to the Hawthorn District. I've heard the old houses are awesome."

That brought him back to reality with a jolt. His house was a war zone and he knew he couldn't explain it. He thought as fast as his idiot brain would allow him and said, "On second thought, maybe we can skip the house tour today. It's a mess. How about I take you on one later this week?"

Her amused look was difficult to read... a cross between smug and embarrassed. It took her face beyond the beautiful range and brought it up a notch to magnificent. Keenan fought back the urge to touch her.

"Deal," she said and looked behind her to slide into the left lane.

She just missed three other cars as she sped through Southeast Portland like a maniac. Keenan grabbed the "oh, Jesus" bar until his knuckles went white. Isabella swerved around another car that obviously wasn't going fast enough for her tastes and said, "Don't worry, Kee. Haven't killed anyone...yet."

The nickname startled him and he tightened his grip with purpose. "Okay...Is," he said pointedly. "Promise me I won't be the first and I'll let go."

A frightening chuckle escaped her lovely lips. "No promises, my friend. Hang on!" The car careened through traffic and Keenan closed his eyes. His hand stayed put.

When they arrived at *The Hotcake House*, the lot was packed, but there were still a couple of slots open, so Isabella shoehorned the car into one. Keenan knew if they could get into the lot, they could get into the building and have breakfast. The place was one of the most popular in Portland and had been the size of a shoebox for fifty years, despite that. The owners had no interest in expanding.

Keenan opened the door for Isabella and a waft of pancakes, syrup, bacon, and chatter closed in around them.

"Two?" a young woman asked.

"Yes."

A flush of embarrassment ran through Keenan's arms when he looked down at his clothes; they were wrinkled and dirty from the previous night's adventure. In a sudden panic, he realized he didn't know where his wallet was, but then remembered. He opened the clear envelope still clutched in his arms and saw it snug inside, along with his keys and cell phone. With nimble dexterity, he pulled them out and tucked them into his pockets. The rubbing bulges felt good, familiar, the first normalcy of the day. When he tossed the empty evidence envelope on the reception counter, the hostess gave him a patient nod. Obviously, she had seen it all.

She escorted them to the front of the building next to an immense plate-glass window facing Powell and handed them menus. The menus were a single laminated sheet with food items on only one side; all they served were eggs, sausage, bacon, hash browns, toast, steaks, hamburgers, french-fries, and the best hotcakes in the country.

When the woman left, Isabella leaned across the table and touched Keenan's hand. The heat of her fingers went straight to his core. All his muscles, except one, relaxed at her touch. That one was doing aerobics.

"Are you all right?"

He placed his hand on top of hers and a flicker of satisfaction spread like wildfire through him. Despite everything that had happened the last twenty-four hours, none of that mattered when he was with her. He surrendered without a fight.

"Fine," he said, examining the soft features on the back of her hand. "Just tired." He searched her eyes and had to smile. "Sorry I've been such a pain in the ass."

"Apology accepted. Don't worry, Kee...my lips are sealed."

I'd love to seal your lips.

Keenan shook the thought out of his head and sipped his coffee.

"You're good," he said. "If it were me, I doubt I'd take the risk on a relative stranger. I really appreciate it."

"Oh, I think if I were busted for exposing myself you'd be the first in line." Isabella's eyes softened and Keenan's mouth fell.

"Naughty girl."

The enigmatic smile that dusted her lips made her look like a goddess in the early morning light. "Oh, much worse than that. You'd be surprised."

"I guess so." Was there a hidden hot cauldron of desire buried under that professional façade? Keenan only hoped. "Why'd you do it?"

Isabella took in a deep breath of coffee fumes and tilted the cup. Watching the clouds of cream swirl through the dark liquid, she wrapped both hands around the cup. "Not sure," she said, and Keenan thought he saw a moment of regret pass through her face. "I'll lose my job if they find out. Not exactly professional to bail out an employee, even if I ended up not having to. I'm supposed to report it."

"They'll have to torture the truth out of me," he said gallantly. The sound of Isabella's laugh was like a drug.

"You'd probably like that."

Another surprise. Keenan loved surprises. "Torture's a little over the top. A short beating usually gets my attention."

"I'll remember that." There was that twinkle in her eyes again. Her smile faded and she sat back. "Seriously, you need to be careful. The company has a strict policy against being arrested. If the cops had actually pressed charges, I'd have to report it. I'd hate to do that, especially to someone I really like."

Alarm bells (*or was it bird song*) went off in his head followed by a waitress sidling up to the table.

"Good morning, folks. What'll you have?"

"I'll have a short stack," Isabella said, handing the waitress the laminated sheet.

The woman took the menu and nodded. "And you, sir?"

"Same, thanks."

The woman gave him a quick smile, took his menu, and scooted back to the open kitchen.

"You like me?" Keenan tried not to sound anxious and failed miserably.

"Can't stand you. I bail out every man who asks me," Isabella said with a saucy tilt of her head. "Honestly," she added with a huff. "Not very bright, are you? I've been trying to get you to ask me out for two weeks. I was beginning to think my womanly wiles weren't going to work on you. Thought maybe you might be gay." She paused. "You're not, are you?"

"Nope. Flaming heterosexual."

"Thought so. Anyway, this was a golden opportunity I just couldn't resist. I took the chance you weren't a serial killer or something. Surprised even me, to tell you the truth. I've never done anything like this before."

Bewilderment was a two by four smacking him in the back of the head. He couldn't speak.

"You know what this means, don't you?" she asked.

"What?"

"I saved your life. You're my bitch now."

This was just getting better and better. Funny, Keenan was sure this was going to be the worst day of his life. Just goes to show, you never know what's going to happen. He knew the shit ass grin on his face was coming across as desperate, but at least it was honest.

"Oh, great mistress," he said, bowing low over the table. "I am your humble slave. Do with me what you will."

She paraded those brilliant white teeth at him and raised an eyebrow. "Trust me...that's exactly what I had in mind."

Keenan's cock jumped up and did the happy dance all by itself under the table. *Oh, boy! Oh, boy! Oh, boy!* The rest of his body followed right behind.

"Check please," he said to the room. Isabella laughed.

It was just at that moment that the pancakes, and Reggie, appeared.

The pancakes were silent, but Reggie broke the mood with, "Just had to see it with my own eyes. What a lovely creature."

Keenan had never been more irritated. He tossed his napkin on the table and said to Isabella, "I'll be right back," then headed for the john. Skating through the tables, he made his way to the door and slammed against it with both hands to open it. Fortunately, the john was empty.

"What the fuck are you doing here?" he asked Reggie who was floating in front of the urinal swinging a phantom walking stick back and forth.

"Where are your manners, boy? I just came here to tell you something." He laughed and twirled the stick over his head. "I can't for the life of me remember what it was. That girl just took it clean away. Maybe I'll get *her* to try to feel me…"

"You stay away from her, Reggie." The words came out with force and Reggie's smile deepened.

"Much too good for the likes of you," he teased, but there was something simmering behind his eyes that Keenan didn't like.

"Look…," he replied, trying to keep his temper. "…just leave me alone right now. I've got a real chance here and I don't want to blow it. I'll do anything you want, I promise."

The glare in Reggie's eyes was almost tangible now and it gave Keenan the willies.

"Anything?"

Keenan hesitated before saying, "Yeah. Anything. Deal?"

A huge grin split Reggie's lips and with a flip of his hand, everything disappeared, except his lips. "Deal." They blinked out of the room. Keenan splashed water on his face before leaving.

When he got to the table, Isabella had a good start on the pancakes. He loved a girl with a healthy appetite.

She lifted her eyes and said from around a mouth of food, "That was fast. Nerves?"

Keenan sat down. "Nerves?"

Swallowing, she dabbed her mouth with the corner of the napkin. "Thought maybe you were crawling out the back window to head for the hills. Sometimes I have that effect on people."

Keenan drowned his pancakes in syrup and said, "Not me. There's just something special about girls who rescue me, a kind of glow."

"So, this happens often, does it?"

Keenan put his elbows on the table, leaning in to get closer to her. His shirt was probably soaking up the syrup, but he didn't care. "Nope. First time."

Her voice turned serious when she shifted her gaze to the food. "Well, I hope that's true. I'm in big trouble if not…in more ways than one."

"I'll bet you're in trouble a lot."

The quip created an unexpected effect. Isabella's lips curled down and a visible quiver rushed over her shoulders. "Sometimes," was all she said.

Keenan frowned and again touched the back of her hand. "I'm sorry, Is. I was just kidding."

Her face melted into a pleasant softness. "It's nothing. Just have a past with an attitude, that's all. When I was younger, I got in big trouble and still have to live with it. It haunts me every day of my life. You know what I mean?"

"Absolutely," Keenan said, tracing the fine hairs on the back of her fingers. The sensation was sending sparkling needles up both his arms, down his sides, and into his cock. He had never felt like this before. "Something happened to me when I was a kid too, something that changed my life. I won't bore you with the details."

A kind of sharp curiosity lightened her eyes and she put her fork down. She smelled like exotic spices, and the heady scent fell through Keenan's inhibitions like solvent.

"I'll show you mine, if you show me yours," she whispered.

He took his hands away and leaned back against the booth seat.

"You're kidding, right? Deep, dark secrets are nothing to fool with, young lady. You'd own me outright if I give them up. I'd have to be awful motivated."

Keenan picked up his coffee cup to take a sip, wondering if she'd take the bait. He wasn't going to tell her his real secret, of course. But he was quick on his feet and could come up with something special, if he put his mind to it. He loved this sort of game and Isabella was the perfect player. Obviously, she loved it too, since her eyes were flashing like opals. She sat back and licked her lips. He had never been more jealous of a tongue.

"All right," she drawled out slowly, "tell you what, you give me one of your dark secrets, and I'll give you one of mine. First to chicken out loses, okay?"

"Let's make it interesting," he replied, letting an ember of innuendo warm his voice. "How about a little truth or dare. The first person to fail to answer the question or refuse the dare loses and has to do whatever the winner says. We have to be completely honest. You game?"

Her jaw moved back and forth, and her lips pursed so close to a pucker Keenan could hardly contain himself. Isabella looked doubtful.

He allowed a slow knowing smirk to screw up his face before saying, "What? My tough little woman going all girlie on me? Afraid to play with the big boys?"

She wrinkled her nose at him and picked up her fork. "Deal. But I get to go first. We go until one of us cracks."

"Fine by me." Keenan toyed with his pancakes while Isabella searched for a question.

Her face lit up like a Christmas tree. "Truth or dare? Have you ever had a homosexual experience?"

"Amateur," he snorted. "Truth. Yes, when I was six. My friend Dave and me, back of the barn on my uncle's ranch in Montana. We touched each other, screamed, yanked our pants up, and ran in opposite directions. Never talked to each other again."

"Did you enjoy it?"

"Hey, that's not in the rules."

"Sorry. I just got caught up in the moment."

"Behave yourself or I'll call default and show you what a real man does to naughty girls."

"Ooo…" she purred, rubbing her arms and exposing her cleavage to its best advantage. "I'm all aquiver. Pig. All right, big boy, your turn."

"Well then, truth or dare? Have you ever gone naked in public?"

"Truth. Yes," she said without elaborating. Keenan was disappointed, but liked this game more and more. "Truth or dare," she continued without waiting. "What happened to you when you were a kid that changed your life?"

That one took him back a bit, but he regained his aplomb instantly. "Truth. I saw a ghost."

Apparently, she wasn't expecting that since she sat back and angled her head to the side, sending him a puzzled stare. "Really? We said we had to be completely honest, you know."

"I am." Keenan took a sip of coffee. He knew the unadorned answer would make her crazy, so he didn't embellish. Two could play at that game. "Truth or dare? What happened to you that got you into trouble?"

This time, Isabella didn't even hesitate. "Dare," she said firmly.

Keenan really wanted to know what this incredible woman could have possibly done to get her in so deep she couldn't recover. After all, she was perfect. There was a kind of injustice when perfect people got in the headlights of bad news. Especially ones this charming.

"Well?" The coquettish lilt to her voice was playing handball with his heart.

"Give me a second. I want to savor my victory before delivering the fatal blow." He knew what he wanted to ask her to do, but it was probably too soon and he didn't want to lose her. The urge to kiss her was overwhelming. "All right, I dare you to take off your jacket."

Apparently, Isabella knew what Keenan really wanted too, since she sniffed, "Wuss," and gave him a wicked laugh.

Without preamble, she unzipped her jogging jacket and stripped it off. Underneath was a baby blue running halter that looked tantalizing against her dark skin. Dark mounds of flesh peeked over the top and the deep cleavage was almost black. The exhibition made Keenan's mountain gorilla instincts come out. He wanted to pound victory against his chest.

"Wow," was all he could say.

"Eyes up here, buddy," she said pointing.

Keenan obliged by putting one elbow on the table, resting his chin in his hand, and staring into her eyes. "No place I'd rather be."

"Oh, my. He's charming too. My turn, hot shot." She pushed her lips to one side and closed one eye in concentration. Her face lit up. "Truth or dare? What happened right after you saw that ghost?"

He knew that was coming and hoped the dare wouldn't be something that could get him thrown back into jail. He wouldn't put it past her. Pulling a sigh into his lungs and giving up to the inevitable, he gave her a plaintive, "Dare."

A look of pure evil came over her face when she placed her napkin on the table. Standing up, she sidled along the end of the table and leaned against the bench seat. "All you have to do is hold still."

Before he could say anything, she was on top of him, straddling his lap, with her arms wrapped around his neck. That heavenly scent clouded out just about everything else. He instinctively placed his arms around her very slim waist and pulled her closer. His cock was doing what it did best when she sat down hard and brought her face within inches of his.

"Pucker up, big boy."

Isabella leaned into him and gently pulled out his upper lip with her teeth. She ran her tongue along it once, shutting down most of his reality receptors. The initial touch of her lips was so soft he could only feel the heat at first. He gladly let her play. Moving slowly, she increased the pressure until she had him in an expertly executed lip lock; it was obvious she had done this before.

Ecstasy burst through his skull like time-lapse flowers blooming. When her small tongue entered his mouth in search of his teeth, the sweet taste of maple and coffee went straight to his head and the entire restaurant exploded in catcalls, whistles, and overall chaos. He wasn't one for exhibitionism...and usually avoided it like washing dishes…but at the moment, it didn't bother him a bit. The only thing in his universe was a pair of delicious lips going to town on his, large hard nipples crushed against his T-shirt, and his cock begging to be let into its new favorite playground. Everything else was a blizzard.

After what seemed like next week rolled around, she broke the seal, sat back on his lap, and breathed hard. "Wow," she whispered.

"Yeah."

Their eyes locked and he got lost for good. Having her there in his arms, her hot breath roasting the top of his lip, and her chocolate colored eyes filling his vision, Keenan felt at home. He pulled her close until her chin rested on his right shoulder and held on. Closing his eyes, he let the contentment fall like honey through his senses. It nourished him more deeply than twelve stacks of hotcakes.

Isabella squeezed him tightly and sat back, touching his cheek with one hot thumb.

"Now that's what I call a dare," she said, beginning to disentangle from his arms. He was having a problem moving them. They dislodged reluctantly.

"Yeah," he repeated, not remembering any other words.

Isabella slid back to her seat opposite him, and the place settled down to a gentle roar, but not until after some very colorful suggestions from the crowd.

Before the dust settled in his stomach, refills on coffee and Constance appeared simultaneously. Keenan's love soaked mind had a problem sorting them out for a second. That is until the latter said, "You need t' get outta here, honey. I think it's coming t' kill you."

Keenan could feel his smile turn to slush, but he didn't say anything. Instead, he concentrated on smearing butter on his cakes and floating them in more syrup. Fortunately, Isabella's food was distracting her. Keenan shook his head at Constance when Isabella wasn't looking. *Go away,* he mouthed at her.

"Sorry, child, but you got t' come with me. There's something looking for you."

Keenan lifted the napkin off his lap and put it on the table. "I'll be right back," he said to Isabella. He stood, mustered a wide mouthed grin at her, and headed for the men's room a second time.

"You're walking funny," she called after him, which elicited additional comments from the crowd. Keenan ignored the advice and made his way through the sea of tables.

When he got to the john, he locked the door and shouted at Constance, "I can't believe this! You guys are driving me crazy! Are you out of your mind? This is the first time in probably two years I've been on a date and you, of all people, show up to spoil it."

Constance screwed up her face and physically bloated with anger. The strain was clear in her voice. "You need to listen t' me, boy. There's something after you...it's coming this way."

That put a cork in Keenan's irritation and he focused in on her. "What do you mean?"

Constance deflated a bit. "Don't know what it is, but it's something bad. And it ain't that succubus neither. Been watching it for about an hour. Something evil, kid. Something big. It was outside your house for the longest time." Her eyes changed color. "It's coming this way. You gotta get out of here."

Keenan ran his hand through his hair and a deep rage settled over his exhaustion. "You know what? No. I'm tired of this, Cee. All I ever do is run from this stuff. Forget it. I'm going back to my date and that's the end of it. It can't hurt me if I ignore it. I'm tired." It wasn't very rational, but it was the best he had at the moment.

He yanked the door open, threw his hands in his pockets, and headed back to his table, not even looking to see if Constance was following.

When he got back there, Isabella was licking the syrup off her fork. Her tongue was pink and smooth, like school erasers Keenan had used in his art. Her plate was clean.

"So," she said, "too much for you?"

Keenan pushed his own plate to the edge of the table and folded his hands. "Not on your life. But I gotta ask... haven't you heard the rumors? I mean, why would you want to go out with someone like me?"

Isabella brought her eyebrows together in irritation. "Those damn office gossips," she snarled. "I hate it when people blow something completely out of proportion. So you talk to yourself. You want to know a secret?" she said, leaning into him and putting her hands on top of his. "So do I. Hell, it's much more productive to talk to yourself than to those idiots, don't you agree?"

Keenan chuckled and twined his fingers through hers. "Amen, sister."

"Besides..." She fingered a curl on his forehead. "...I like a man who has some idiosyncrasies. I have a few of my own... they like the company."

"I gotta warn you," he said to her seriously, "mine play rough and it can get a little dicey sometimes."

That special glare flared again in her eyes. "Ooo." She lifted her shoulders a fraction and wrinkled her nose. "I like the rough stuff," she whispered.

That was when he saw it through the window behind Isabella's head —a large black cloud rolling down Powell Boulevard. It was so huge it was blocking out the light. Sparks of lightning skimmed off the surface.

A cold chill ran up Keenan's back. Probably not a good idea to stay in one place. Constance was right; he had to get out of here. This was a hell of a lot bigger than the succubus and probably much more dangerous.

"What's wrong?" Isabella asked. The blush of the conversation made her cheeks glow red.

"Look," he said, leaning across the table and squeezing her hand. "I need to leave."

The pain that cascaded across her face stabbed him in the heart. "Oh," she said softly, taking her hands away. "I see."

"No, no, no," he stammered, glancing again at the advancing menace. "Something's come up."

"Yeah," she said quietly.

He wasn't sure if it was the pain in her eyes, the throb that was making his heart sing, or just the exhaustion, but he did something then that he regretted almost instantly.

Keenan took Isabella's hands again. "This has nothing to do with you. You're going to think I'm crazy...hell, I think it myself...but I need to tell you something. I like you. In fact, I really like you and if we're going to go where I think we're going to go, I don't want to keep secrets from you. I'm very serious about how rough it can get. I need you to like me for who I am. No secrets."

Isabella tightened the grip on his hand, her face awash with fear and, if he didn't know any better, exhilaration. "No secrets," she whispered.

Keenan looked out the window behind her to check the mass's proximity to the building. It was just hitting the parking lot. The smell of burning electricity stung his nose and static buzzed against his eardrums. This was going to be bad.

"Isabella, I see things..." He stopped, searching her eyes and clearing his throat for courage. "Dead things...the dearly departed...people who have..." He hated the stammering but hadn't told anyone in a long time, so he was out of practice. The creature was almost at the building. "Do you understand? I see ghosts. Lots and lots of ghosts. Every day, all the time. I have since I was thirteen. I talk to them. Hell, they live with me."

Isabella slowly extracted her hands from his and stood up. He had seen that expression before, too many times. Tears welled up in Isabella's eyes. She took a step back from him. Keenan knew that look so well; she thought he was crazy.

Well, so much for romance. His heart broke.

Just at that moment, the cloud burst through the windows. Keenan jumped up to yank Isabella out of the way and dived to intercept it before it reached her.

It was very brave.

It was also very stupid.

It hit him like a semi doing a hundred down a hill. Air left his lungs in a rush and he found himself flying.

Fortunately, the kitchen wall was there to stop him. The impact took what little was left in his lungs then it all went black.

When Keenan came to, the cloud…and the girl…were gone. The waitress' face was close to his when she got him to his feet. Her hands were shaking.

"What happened?" he demanded, but the words made his head spin.

"You just jumped into the wall for no reason," she said, backing away from him as if it were contagious.

"Where's the girl?"

"She left. Ran out the door. Probably to China by now. Sorry, kid, but I think you need some help. How 'bout I call someone for you?"

He took his wallet out of his pocket, pulled out a twenty, and pressed it into her hand without saying anything.

Running out the door, he searched the lot. Isabella's car was gone.

Unable to stop it, Keenan fell to his knees, balled his fists until they went numb, and screamed up at the heavens, "Fuck!"

Chapter Nine

A Friendly Soul

When Keenan was ten, he was friends with an older kid named Riley McDougal. Riley was the kind of kid most respectable parents would have slammed the door on if he came along looking for a playmate. He didn't look threatening; thick glasses magnified his eyes so much it was hard to look at them long. He was tall and willowy with hands two sizes too big. But Riley had a special gift; he could spot trouble blind folded with his ears full of wax. He honed into it like a shark on its next kill.

For some reason he warmed to Keenan instantly and took him under his tutelage, for a fee, of course. Keenan had no problems giving Riley his lunch money every day; it was the least he could do for all the adventures they shared. Everything from stealing the neighborhood bum's booze (which Riley always insisted they pour into the gutter for his own good) to coasting down Forty-Seventh and Halsey at about thirty miles per hour on their bikes, usually out into traffic. Truancy picked him up so many times he was on a first name basis with all the officers. The lessons Keenan had learned at this dubious friend's knee served him very well through life... don't be afraid to take risks and best friends smack you hard to knock sense into you. Sympathetic friends were worse than useless.

Keenan thought about Riley on his way home from *The Hotcake House*. Cold penetrated his light shirt and sent uncontrollable shivers through every pore. Keenan liked the pain. It focused his anger, smacked him hard to knock sense into him.

He stomped the pavement, ignoring the blisters forming on the bottom on his sockless feet and the ringing in his head. Reggie and Constance weren't the target for his rage. The bull's eye was smack dab in the middle of his chest, pounding out fury with each accelerated beat.

What the hell was I thinking?

For some idiotic reason he thought that once, just once, he might find another human being he could share his own special hell with. In a way, he was grateful Isabella ran away. He wouldn't wish this life on anyone.

It was two miles to his house and he could have called a cab, but the walk helped him get his thoughts together. It was hard to keep the anger intact. It eventually melted into a deep depression. Exhaustion and loss left him dry in the biting cold.

From behind him, he heard something he had been expecting. The quick crack of the siren didn't even startle him.

Mustering an attitude, one he thought he was due, Keenan stopped, tightened his lips, and gave into the inevitable. He clamped his hands tight against the top of his head and closed his eyes.

"Go ahead…make your day," he said to the sky.

He heard a door opening and then a gruff voice. "Get in," it said.

Surprised, he turned around to see Sergeant Thompson sitting in his cruiser with the front passenger door open.

Keenan stood on the sidewalk and gaped at him. "Well, what do you know? Three for three. You arresting me?"

For the first time, Keenan saw a glimmer of humanity shift through the large man's face making it look almost placid. The expression was so out of place, it was like looking at a Salvador Dali painting.

"You want a ride or not? Just get into the fucking car." Thompson frowned up at him.

Keenan wasn't sure why, but he tucked himself onto the passenger's seat and closed the door. The cruiser was deliciously warm. Keenan fought the urge to bask in it.

Without thinking, he buckled his seat belt and couldn't resist saying, "Let's ride."

Thompson grunted a non sequitur at him and pulled into traffic. The roar of the V8 from the Crown Vic sent waves of thrill through Keenan's legs. He suppressed the excitement by clamping his arms over his chest.

Thompson pressed the button on the wire around his neck. "Dispatch, this is 7-2-2 on 7 for 30. 10-63. Over."

"Roger, 7-2-2. Copy your 7 and 63." The voice came over another radio under a laptop at the center of the dash.

He released the button and sent an angry look Keenan's way. "Are you trying to get yourself arrested? What kind of stunt was that back there? I should take you someplace where they can lock you up for good."

Keenan exhaled and pressed tighter on his chest. "I don't need a one-way ride to the seventh floor at Providence, thanks. Been there."

Thompson pulled into another lane. "I got to be out of my mind," he muttered. "If I had any sense, I'd whisk you off to the loony bin without a second thought."

"So, why don't you?" Keenan snarled. "I think we both know that's where I belong. I could use the break."

Thompson eyed him quickly and then concentrated on driving. "Don't know why, but I like you, son."

His familiarity made Keenan sit up and rail a bit against the "son;" hell, the cop couldn't have been more than a couple years older than him.

"I saw something last night," Thompson continued. "Something I can't explain. You got some real problems, don't you?"

Keenan didn't like the sudden turn in their relationship. It gave him too much leeway to feel sorry for himself, so he said, "No more than any other red blooded American boy, officer."

"Cut the crap, Swanson," Thompson said. "You got about thirty seconds to tell me what the hell happened last night."

That surprised Keenan. "What do you mean? I told you…"

"No." The sudden calm in his voice actually soothed Keenan a bit. "I've seen lots of things in my lifetime," the cop stated slowly. "Fought in Afghanistan, Iraq. Saw some stuff that'd curl a sane man into a ball they'd roll right into the nut house. Seen stuff in this neighborhood too. It's old, you know, really old. One of the first Portland neighborhoods around. I've investigated… some pretty strange things over the years. Sometimes there's a logical explanation, sometimes not." He shrugged and flexed his right hand. "But these… events seem to stick to certain folks. You know what I mean?" He stopped at a red light and leveled experienced eyes at Keenan. "Folks like you. What I saw last night…" He shook his head. "It's been making me crazy. I pulled a second shift to ask you about it."

That really startled Keenan. "You've…you've been looking for me?"

"Since this morning…I just missed you at the precinct, so decided to cruise around. Went to your house three different times. By the way, your front door is open."

"Thanks," Keenan said absently, not focusing on the traffic in front of them. His voice was almost as numb as he was.

Thompson stared ahead and pulled through the intersection when the light turned green. "When I heard the call over the radio about a man screaming outside *The Hotcake House*, knew it had to be you. So…" He tightened his grip on the steering wheel. "So I gotta ask…what did I see last night?"

Keenan didn't answer immediately, knowing he was sliding on pretty thin ectoplasm right then. He knew his answer could land him in jail again, or worse. He tried lying. "You didn't see anything. Just a drunk guy taking a piss who couldn't keep his balance."

"Try again," Thompson said, shooting Keenan a glare that could melt ice.

Keenan stared out the window watching the world rush by as they moved along Ninth Street. It began to rain.

"You...you wouldn't believe me," he whispered.

"I'm not saying I will." Thompson's jaw tightened as he watched the traffic. "Before I picked you up last night, I looked everywhere for a...I don't know. Magician? Mirrors? Anything to explain what it was. Came up with zilch. I just need to know that a man cocooned in a black cloud, suspended three feet above the ground has *some* explanation. I need you to give it to me."

Nodding, Keenan took a deep breath and it lightened his heart. There was something in Thompson's demeanor that eased the muscles in Keenan's neck and a kind of relief settled in over his eyes.

"It's a long story," he said.

"We got time."

Keenan swallowed hard. "It started when I was thirteen..."

He couldn't stop the words from gushing out. He told Thompson everything... the ghosts, the succubus, the entity that attacked him at the restaurant, everything. When he was through it was like the words had washed away every ounce of strength he had left in his body. Deep fatigue soaked his skin and he closed his eyes. The world got very quiet.

"So," he said. "You going to take me back to jail or to the ward? If I have a say, I'd vote for the hospital. Much more relaxing and better drugs."

"Shut up. I'm taking you home."

"Really?"

"Really."

"You don't think I'm crazy?"

"Oh, hell yeah."

"Then, why..."

"'Cause if you are, then so am I. I know what I saw."

"Oh." Keenan touched the dashboard and concentrated on the road ahead.

"Can I give you some advice?" Thompson was having problems with this big brother stuff by the sound of his voice, but Keenan appreciated the effort.

"Sure."

"I wouldn't go around telling this to just anyone…"

"Believe me, I don't. You're the first one I've ever told the whole story to."

"Good," Thompson replied simply and turned right onto Hawthorn. "If it were me?" He searched behind him before moving into the left lane. "I think I'd ask these ghost friends of yours a lot more questions, especially that lady one. Like, for example, why is it only you see them? Why are they picking on you? More important, can you ask them to leave? But that's just me."

The revelation hit Keenan between the eyes with the force of a rock hammer. As far as he knew, he had never asked them to leave. He'd asked them to leave him alone, to stop what they were doing, to shut up on a daily basis, but couldn't think of one time he had asked them just to leave. It had never even crossed his mind. It suddenly dawned on him that maybe, despite the fact that they drove him insane, he just didn't want them to. There was a perverted kind of comfort in having them around. The realization lodged in his indignation and left a bad taste in his mouth.

"Wow," was all he said.

"Yeah." Thompson turned onto Thirty-Second and stopped the cruiser. "We're here."

The house was pretty much the way Keenan had left it the night before, except that he didn't notice any glass on the ground. He was sure the succubus had busted out every window in the place.

The passenger door seemed to weigh a hundred pounds when he opened it. He got his feet out and stretched when they hit the street. Thompson got out on the other side and put his hand on his holster, scanning the house with his eyes narrowed. He said brusquely, "You stay here," and headed up the sidewalk to the open front door.

When the cop pulled his weapon out and approached the door cautiously, a cold prick started at the base of

Keenan's skull. He stayed put behind the police car and even crouched a little. Thompson disappeared around the side of the house.

In a few seconds, Thompson frantically motioned Keenan to get down. He complied without question.

"Dispatch, this is 7-2-2. We have a 1-5-7, personal prop."

"Roger your 1-5-7. What's your 20?"

Thompson gave Keenan a cool look. "What's your house number?"

"My what?" Numbness crawled through his thighs as he squinted at his surroundings.

"Your house number."

"Umm..." Keenan was having problems focusing. His mind wandered through the fog; he forgot he had no numbers on his house. The mail lady... uh, person hated that and left him nasty notes all the time. "1402."

Thompson turned away from him and spoke into the radio. "1402 S.E. Thirty-Second. Swanson, Keenan. Looks like they got it all. I'll need K-9 and backup. Put ICS on alert."

Keenan had no idea what all of that meant, but apparently it was serious.

In a matter of minutes, six cruisers, including two K-9 units roared to his street, some parking in front, some down the street, and some around the corner. Keenan was a little embarrassed when neighbors he hardly knew began to peek out of their windows. A few of them came out on their porches to watch, sipping coffee, but didn't get any nearer.

Thompson stayed on the grass in front of Keenan's house but silently ordered several officers to spread out around it with hand signals. They obeyed immediately. Keenan found himself impressed by the skill and precision of their actions. Whatever was going on, the bases were covered.

When the men and women were in place, someone replaced Thompson, freeing him to speak to one of the K-9 cops. Keenan couldn't hear what they were saying, but Thompson was motioning to the house and the other cop nodded. The brown and black German shepherd he had on a special harness looked excited, but in control. It didn't make a sound.

Moving slowly up the stairs, the K-9 cop pulled his gun and put it up close to his shoulder, watching the door the entire time. The dog slithered up the steps close to him. When they were on the porch, the officer squatted down and talked into the dog's ears. They stood up like pylons. The cop grabbed the dog's collar, undid the leash, and pointed him toward the open door. The dog darted through it.

Once inside, Keenan could hear the dog barking frantically. The click of claws on his hardwood floors echoed out the door.

All at once, the barking and the clicks stopped. There was a long pause then a piercing whine from the animal. In less than a second, the dog erupted out of the door like a bullet, rushed passed his handler, and took the cement stairs in one leap.

"Charlie, get back here!" The cop took off after his partner who was half way to Hawthorn by then.

Thompson scowled after the duo and quickly motioned to the other K-9 unit waiting outside a cruiser down the street. The officer missed the first signal, watching instead the retreating pair, but then caught the second one. He pulled a huge black lab out of the back of the patrol car.

The performance with this second canine was about identical to the first. Encouraging words, over enthusiasm, frightening barks, and those hard nails on even harder floors. Then silence, a loud growl, and an even louder yelp. This time the dog knocked his partner over before taking off down the street.

Keenan couldn't stop the smile trying to make its way around his lips. He knew what was happening; it was the funniest thing he'd ever seen. At least the ghosts were good for a few laughs.

Thompson's nose widened angrily when he glowered at Keenan, but one side of his lip went up when he apparently realized that maybe, just maybe, Keenan was telling him the truth.

He snarled and four officers gathered around him. The next orders were quiet but quick. They each pulled their weapons, made their way carefully up to the porch and lay flat on either side of the door. Keenan could only imagine that there were several cops at his back door to keep whoever was in there, in there.

"We're coming in! Put down your weapon or we will shoot," yelled the cop closest to the door. Keenan knew the cops were only hearing silence in return, but he heard the chaotic chortles, boos, and rude comments bursting out of the door; the ghosts were having a field day. He wished Thompson could hear them.

One by one, the cops tucked themselves into the house, guns pointed forward.

Keenan heard *clear* shouted from man to man, as they moved deeper into his home. The inside probably looked like a frat house on Sunday morning; the cops must be thinking that war had broken out in there.

The voices faded and then went silent. A minute later, the lead cop came out and swept four fingers to the group. Thompson touched the radio button.

"Dispatch, this is 7-2-2. The property is clear."

Without preamble, he crossed to Keenan, grabbed his arm angrily, and propelled him toward his house. "That was some stunt with the dogs, asshole," Thompson snarled under his breath. "If anything happens to them or my officers, you're dead. Do you understand me?"

"But I didn't…" Keenan had the protest shaken out of him.

"Shut up," Thompson snapped. "Not a word about the ghosts." He shook him again. "I mean that."

"Ok."

Keenan's knees turned to warm pudding as he approached his front door. The sidewalk leading to the house seemed to elongate as he moved forward. The glances from the police were sympathetic at best. He was terrified.

When he entered the house, he stopped dead.

The house wasn't the disaster area he originally thought it would be. Everything seemed to be in place, the windows were intact, and, except for stuff that was always in disarray, it all looked normal. Well almost normal; something seemed to be missing.

"Dispatch, this is 7-2-2. We'll take victim through the house and then release for investigation. Give us about ten minutes."

There was a hiss then, "Roger, 7-2-2."

Keenan walked over to the gaping hole where his TV used to be and scowled at the entertainment unit. All of it was gone: the 37 inch TV, the DVD player, three video systems, all his DVDs and CDs, even the old VCR.

"Don't touch anything," Thompson said with authority. "Just take me on a tour and let me know what's missing."

Panic gripped at Keenan's chest and he ran to his office, Thompson on his heels. The desk looked naked. They had taken not only his Mac, but the laptop, printer, and everything else. The dangling cords looked crippled and destitute. His stomach did a flip, and a good one. There wasn't a single piece of artwork or design packet on his desk. They had not only taken all his stuff but several pieces of original artwork, one of a kind photos, and irreplaceable negatives from his clients. They had left nothing. *Oh, God, I am so fired!* Even his incomplete paintings were gone.

Urgency pushed adrenalin through his blood and he began tearing through the house, searching every room. There wasn't a single thing of value. They had taken it all.

Keenan finally sank down on the couch and buried his face in his hands.

"Don't worry, son," Thompson said from behind him. "I'm bringing in a team. We'll find your stuff." He shook his head and touched Keenan's shoulder. "You have the worst luck."

That didn't help at all.

Chapter Ten

Giving up to the Ghost

After the circus of cops left his home, Keenan stared at the empty space that used to be his TV.

They had asked him a million questions, dusted the place for prints, and searched into every private area Keenan possessed. The robbers missed his stash of porn, but the cops sure didn't. There were many, many embarrassing moments. He felt more violated by the cops than he did by the crooks.

Thompson stayed at his side the whole time and made sure none of them got too close to the truth. Keenan had few live friends and the last thing he expected was to find one in the vet turned cop that had harassed and arrested him the night before.

Was it only last night?

Things were getting decidedly bizarre.

As he stared blankly at the vacant stand, Keenan could feel the sides of his mouth touching his chin. He got up to inspect the kitchen again. When he rediscovered the poor state of his cupboards, he shuffled back into the living room and fell down on his couch. At least they hadn't taken it.

Fatigue wound around his face until his eyes closed on their own. It wasn't long before he fell asleep.

* * * *

Isabella was in what must have been his bedroom, standing in one corner, counting loose change onto his dresser. She was naked except for a pancake that dangled from her right ear.

Her body was the most glorious thing Keenan had ever seen. Black areolas circled two very hard nipples and her breasts were the size of oranges. They crowded together on her chest and bounced nicely when she counted the change. His cock stiffened with each movement.

The slim waist and hips beneath them framed a flat, smooth stomach and a black triangle of curly hair beneath. That churned his juices, and he tried to move over to her, but he was stuck. He looked down at his dream self and noted with interest that he was tied to the bed with paper napkins that all had "Hotcake House" imprinted on them. His erection was the size of a bratwurst. He couldn't move.

"Isabella?"

He knew it was his voice, but didn't think he had opened his mouth. She looked up from the change, smiled, and put a finger to her lips.

"Shhh. I'm counting," she said and went back to it. "Don't look at me or I'll have to torture you."

He tore his eyes away, but not before one more languid inspection.

To fill the time, Keenan checked out the room. He was right, it was his bedroom, yet in a way not his bedroom. There were cubicle walls all around him instead of regular walls, a gaggle of ghosts with their faces pressed to the window glass from outside, and a cop car parked over by the bathroom. Thompson was asleep in the cruiser, snoring like a chain saw.

When Keenan looked back, Isabella had moved to the end of the bed and was standing there staring at his cock. The attention made his ass squirm and his already aching erection harder. When she licked her lips, he almost came.

Crawling very slowly over the end of the bed, Isabella's breasts dangled darkly over his legs. He saw her black eyes when she glanced up at him, and the mischievous expression produced an even deeper anticipation. Keenan's butt clinched without any help from him as she moved forward, spreading his legs as she came.

Sinking down until her nipples tickled the inside of his thighs, Isabella rubbed them in gentle circular motions against his legs. Her hot flesh elicited a loud moan, but not from her. Keenan's guttural groan seemed to please her, because she lowered her head and began to lick the inside of each thigh. That really got his mouth going. He almost lost his voice with all that screaming.

When she reached his balls, Isabella stopped and Keenan groaned.

You can't stop. Not there!

She shook her finger at him three times and, without warning, took one of his balls into her mouth. The sensation was torturous and magnificent. He shouted again despite his laryngitis.

In mid scream, a shadow solidified against the far wall. When it materialized completely, Keenan's voice caught in his throat. The succubus, in her full glory, appeared behind Isabella.

"Isabella, watch out!"

Isabella looked behind her, and all Keenan could see was the top of her head as she confronted the apparition. Then she did a very strange thing. She laughed. It scared the shit out of him.

Without preamble, she turned her face back to him, wrapped her hand around his already engorged cock, and gave it a tight squeeze. The heat from her grip was almost painful, but it sent shards of rapture coursing through every blood vessel. Smiling sweetly, she wrapped her lips around the swollen head and sucked it into her mouth. The sudden sensation forced his eyes closed and he howled.

When he got his eyes open again, Isabella was working her mouth and hand in slow in-and-out motions down his shaft. But what took his breath away, beyond the exquisite feel of her hot mouth against his cock, was what the succubus was doing behind her; she was rubbing Isabella's back, making her writhe against the ghostly hands. Her ass rose into the air.

Keenan watched in fascination as those strange hands moved down to Isabella's ass and spread her wide open. With a single finger that she made sure Keenan saw, she opened Isabella's moist pussy lips and thrust it into the hot slit to the knuckle.

The succubus extracted the finger and bent her head down to run her tongue along Isabella's pussy, slopping up her juices.

Isabella moaned against Keenan's hard member, the vibration deepening the ripples of bliss running through him. The entity thrust that long tongue deep into Isabella's wet folds, first slowly, then stroking faster. Isabella's mouth tightened down on Keenan with each thrust.

With a stifled scream, Isabella broke the seal and threw her head back, arching her spine until her soft belly hit his legs. The trembling climax that shook her body sent waves of movement through his legs, his chest, and into his head. It was as if the climax had liquefied the air.

Keenan's hands were suddenly free, but the girls had the show so he let them continue. The succubus grabbed Isabella's hips and turned her around so she was lying on her side facing away from Keenan. He adjusted himself until he had her between his legs. His cock stood at full alert near her open pussy. The succubus lifted Isabella's leg and draped it over Keenan's. His cock was throbbing with anticipation.

Keenan wrapped his arms around Isabella's irresistible body and pulled her as close as she would go. As if on cue, the succubus grabbed his throbbing cock and guided it to Isabella's hot moist opening.

Without an invitation, Keenan slid the swollen muscle into her heat. It was dripping wet and so tight he had to move in measured thrusts to get it all the way in. He didn't mind. When the bottom of his shaft became soaked with her juices, he pulled it out a bit then slid it back in. Cradling her breast, he pinched the hard nipple between his thumb and index finger until Isabella's deep moan resonated from her chest and she moved her hips against his pelvis.

The succubus floated above the couple in an almost protective stance. When they found their rhythm, waves of lust flooded Keenan's blood. With each hard thrust, their bodies seemed to melt into one another.

Keenan watched from behind as Isabella's body undulated against his when he drove into her hard. The succubus then lowered her head, stuck out that long tongue and began to lick Isabella's clit as Keenan plunged his cock into her. The entity sucked the tiny bud into her mouth and Isabella bucked violently. For several precious moments, the entity tortured Isabella with her lips as Keenan buried himself inside her. The hot tongue and mouth that occasionally whisked onto his swollen muscle made it jerk inside her. Keenan was ready to burst.

Isabella screamed and ripples of pulsating muscles gripped Keenan's cock until he lost count. The climax came in great waves of pleasure and Keenan forced his eyes closed to savor it. The waves grew in size and intensity until Keenan's world shook violently.

* * * *

"Hi."

The voice echoed against the dream and he snapped awake in an instant to two almond shaped eyes staring down at him. He could just make out his reflection in the warm brown.

"Hi," Isabella said again.

Keenan bolted up and placed his hands as stealthily as he could over the bulging hard on that was making a lump in his pants the size of New Zealand. When she glanced down, he was pretty sure it didn't work.

"Dreaming about me, big boy?" Isabella's tantalizing lips parted and she actually licked her lips. Keenan covered up by rubbing the still warm dream images from his head and the bright red blush residue from his face.

"Look." Isabella sat on his coffee table, knee to knee, her chin down, twirling the ends of a crimson Indian scarf in her fingers. Jeans and a white peasant blouse had replaced the running suit. A thick shawl hugged her shoulders. "I'm sorry about this morning." She lifted her face to him and looked very serious. Keenan preferred the happier face. "But you scared me. Can we talk?"

"Uh…" Words eluded him. He was still trying to get his wits wrapped around the fact that she was there. "Sure."

But his confidence sloughed away leaving him exposed, as if his skin had fallen away from his ego. Isabella's beauty was a distraction. He hopped up from the couch and headed for the bathroom.

"I'll be right back." As he moved through the house, he had never felt emptier. The house was silent, his insides twisted into icicle swirls, and for the first time in his life he began to doubt his own sanity.

Leaning against the sink, he pondered his reflection in the mirror. It would take discipline to get the chaos to melt around his cerebral cortex, so Keenan took his time, sorting everything out as neatly as he could.

He liked Isabella. No, he *really* liked Isabella. There wasn't another time in his life he had fallen so hard or so fast for a woman. Sexual attraction aside, there was something about her that made him want to give up everything to be with her. It was almost like an addiction… a wonderful, mind-altering drug that sent his hormones into overdrive and played Twister with his emotions. Every time he got near her, problems, stress, even monotonous routines fell away like melting chocolate. He wanted to move in and shut the world outside.

But there was that troublesome problem again; he saw things. No doubt. But lately the thought that he might actually be crazy began to beat the hell out of his confidence. Maybe they weren't real.

Like Thompson said, maybe Keenan needed help. A lot of help.

The only consolation from that thought was that he hadn't actually cheated on Isabella… kind of. He shook his head, trying to force the glaring contradictions to get a grip on themselves.

Keenan focused on the water swirling down the drain. Was his life doing the same? Did he really want to put this wonderful woman through it all, drag her down with him? That gallant thought fought long and hard against the overpowering desire to be with her.

In the throes of that debate, Keenan made a decision and headed out to the living room.

Isabella was stretching (and very nicely too) to look closely at one of the few of Keenan's paintings the thieves hadn't taken. It was a portrait of a little homeless kid that lived in the underground beneath Keenan's flat in Florence. Big blue eyes looked through black locks of hair like a puppy in a cage.

"His name was Anton." Keenan crossed to the couch.

Startled, Isabella jumped back and whirled around. "Sorry. It's magnificent, Kee. I had no idea how talented you were. If you can paint like this, why are you doing layout work?"

Keenan shrugged. "Fine art doesn't put food on your table or pay the electric bill, unfortunately. You need to be or have a good businessperson to sell art these days. I know about as much about business as I do about raising pigeons."

Isabella lifted one slim eyebrow and the opposite side of her mouth. "I know about business."

Keenan appreciated the proposition. It added another check mark on the pro side of his growing list. The con side of the same list only had one item, but it was a damned big one.

Keenan let the silence ride and Isabella changed her tactics.

"Your place is very— how can I say this delicately— minimalist, isn't it?"

"Yeah, apparently when the crooks were doing their eeny meenies, my house came up a moe."

Isabella grimaced and gave him a sad frown. "Sorry."

"Hey…" Keenan plopped down on the soft cushions and Isabella joined him. "Just another day in the sunshine."

In a graceful gesture, Isabella lifted her hand to his face and stroked it with her thumb. "You poor darling. It's been a hell of a weekend for you, hasn't it?"

Knowing he was probably making the biggest mistake of his life, Keenan pulled away from her and scooted a little further to the right. "Isabella…"

"I know," she said, folding her arms across her chest. "I'm moving way too fast. Occupational hazard. I'm sorry, Kee. I'll slow it down a little."

Wondering for an instant why moving too fast would be an occupational hazard, he put that aside and got to the meat of the thing.

"It's not that." Keenan turned his knees away and laced his fingers together. "Not to sound too cliché, but it's me." The words took on a life of their own then, animated by lack of sleep, jumbled nerves, and stale adrenalin. He didn't have the heart to look at her. "I like you. I like you a lot. Probably too much. You are the most amazing woman I have ever met in my life. I'm probably one of the biggest suckers of all time for saying this, but..." The air in his lungs went a little sore. "...I have some slight problems. Maybe not so slight." It was only then that he cinched up his sinews and looked her in the eye. "I need some time to sort things out. It's going to be one hell of a journey. One I can't possibly ask you to take with me, feeling about you the way I do." All of it was coming out so pitiful, he was sure Isabella was going to bolt out the door. Then he said the eight most devastating words in the history of the human existence. "I think we need to just be friends." He watched Isabella's face shift under them. "For a while, anyway," he added quickly. "Until I can get this all worked out."

Isabella unfolded her arms, placed her hands on her knees with unhurried accuracy, lifted herself off the couch, and threw the right end of her shawl over her left shoulder. Keenan braced himself for her departure.

What he got instead set his emotions reeling.

"I know you're getting off on being all noble and everything, but I have a few words of wisdom to impart before I go." She threw her shoulders back and got her hands moving, generations of Italian heritage rearing up on its indignant haunches.

"First of all, I think I should be the one to decide whether I want to journey down any roads with you, you macho son of a bitch."

Well, he probably deserved that one; it was a little pretentious to think she would want to go anywhere with him.

The pink flush in her cheeks was adding brilliance to her eyes the angrier she got. It was making Keenan very uncomfortable.

"Second of all; where do you get off thinking you are the only one with problems?" With a grand hand gesture, she swept it past all humanity. "We all have problems, buster... all of us. Normal people get through them with help... not on their own!"

"That's what I was saying..."

"Shut up! I'm not finished."

Keenan sank into the couch more dazzled by Isabella every second.

She leaned into him and got one sneakered foot up on the couch to get closer. "I like you, too... always have. But I will beat you bloody before I see you succumb to your own life. You want joy, love, freedom, all those wonderful things we humans fight for but usually fail to reach? Then you have to quit feeling so fucking sorry for yourself and kiss me!"

With that, she straddled his lap, slammed her mouth against his, and sucked away thirty-two years of hesitation, self-loathing, doubt, and fear. Time went away...

...and all at once, so did Isabella.

Something yanked Isabella from his lips. When he opened his eyes, she was almost out the door, pulled by a gray-black tendril of smoke. The cloud entity filled every window outside his house and in an instant, Isabella was gone. When he jumped up to follow, everything went black.

Chapter Eleven

Wild Ghost Hunt

When he opened his eyes, Reggie was crouched next to his head, staring directly into his face. Keenan could see the clock hanging on the wall right through him. It read 12:30. Everything in and out of the house was pitch-black.

"You busy?" Reggie asked.

Keenan shut his eyes tight, trying to figure out where he was. It all shot through him in an instant.

He jumped to his feet.

"Where is she?"

"It took her downtown."

"What? What's going on, Reggie?" If he could have shook his old friend he would have. He settled for wringing his hands instead.

Reggie was floating crossed legged above the coffee table. "Don't know, old bean."

"Damn it!"

Keenan rushed to the open door, but it slammed in his face. When he tried to open it, it wouldn't budge. He stepped back. It was the first time any of the ghosts had done that and it scared him.

"What the fuck, Reggie?" he screamed.

Reggie nodded to the couch without moving. "Have a seat, my friend. We need to talk."

Keenan tilted his head toward the door. "You did that?"

Reggie looked at his fingernails and brushed them against his lapel. "Of course."

Keenan couldn't keep his bottom lip from trembling. He backed away from the specter and caught himself on the dining room wall.

"What is this?"

He had known Reggie almost as long as he had Constance. The Englishman had been with him for nearly every adventure, had advised him countless times on life, love, and the pursuit of happiness. Reggie had been his best friend when he couldn't find a human one, had guided him on his choice of jobs, houses, cars, and even girlfriends. In essence, Reggie had seen him through everything.

That thought now made his arms cold and his guts ache. He gaped at the floating spirit.

"Oh, come on, old boot." Reggie leaned forward. "Just because I don't use my…abilities, doesn't mean I don't have them. Many of us do, you know."

Keenan maneuvered himself away from the wall, not knowing exactly what to think. It was scaring the shit out of him.

"You said you would do anything for me, remember?" Reggie continued with arrogant nonchalance. "There in the restaurant. I'm here to collect. You owe me, brother."

"I don't owe you jack shit!"

"Au contraire, mon frère."

The glimmer of intensity lighting up Reggie's ghostly eyes was making Keenan very nervous. He searched the room for a way out.

"Only you can save her."

Those words tightened the vise suffocating Keenan's responses. "Isabella?" was all he could manage.

"Of course not. You have to help us."

Keenan tried to shake the strange words out of his ears and frowned. "What the hell are you talking about? You're not making any sense. Where is Isabella?"

"Isabella is meaningless."

"Not to me, asshole!"

"If you want to save one, you have to save the other. Don't you understand?"

"Hell, no! This is crazy, Reg."

"More than you could know. It's all up to you, old boot."

"Me?" That got everything inside to stop at once. Keenan was having a hard time breathing. "What the fuck can *I* do?"

Reggie chuckled and the front door banged open. "You'd be surprised. Coming?"

Without waiting for a reply, Reggie floated towards the door. For some reason, Keenan followed.

"Where are we going?" he asked, double-checking for his keys.

Reggie put his hands in his pockets and headed out the door. "To church." Then disappeared into the night.

Chapter Twelve

A Grave Miscalculation

When Keenan was thirteen, the only girl who would even talk to him was Sally Rae Wikowski, his best friend. Partnered a couple years before for a science project that involved a dead cat, a set of scalpels, and balls of steel, the two of them had bonded over thirty-five feet of intestines and bad dead cat jokes.

Keenan's thirteenth summer was spent with Sally's family at Diamond Lake where the two of them chatted for hours about God, the universe, and everything, paddled for countless hours over the silky water, and road bikes around the forested shore. Monday of the third week, on one such ride, they decided to get miles off the trundled path. In retrospect, it was probably not one of Keenan's better choices. Five things happened on that day that changed his life forever.

The first was when they found an old dilapidated cabin and decided to explore it. Rotting timbers barely held up a sloping roof, the fragile walls crisscrossed in ruins, and what they could see through the gaping door was inky. Sally was reluctant to go in, but Keenan bullied her into it, calling her a girl. That did it. She marched into the cabin with determination.

When they got inside, Keenan remembered the waterproof matches he always kept in his pocket and struck one. In the flare of the fire, they could make out decaying rough built furniture: a table, a single chair, and a cot lying close to the ground. On the cot was a bundle stretched the length of the small bed. Keenan's baser instincts kicked in when he saw it and he moaned at Sally, "Oooooo, ooooo." Apparently, Sally didn't appreciate it since she hauled off and landed a good right hook to his shoulder. He behaved after that.

After exploring the small cabin and the third match (a matter of only a few minutes), Sally wanted to leave, but Keenan's curiosity twisted his arm and the second of the four things happened. When he pulled the cover off the bed, a crumbling skeleton stared back at them. Both froze and took a step back in unison.

Then the third thing happened. A faded man rose from the covers to hover above the dead body. In the sparse light, his ghostly grin sent panic racing through Keenan's every nerve. He dropped the match and flames roared up as if someone had doused the place in gasoline. Grabbing Sally's frozen arm, Keenan pulled her toward the door and ran as fast as he could. They didn't even stop to get their bikes.

Several thousand feet away from the cabin, when his breath gave out, Keenan threw himself to the ground. Sally was right beside him. When he looked back, black clouds were filling the forest behind them. The woods were on fire.

That's when the fourth thing happened. Without warning, Keenan suddenly found his arms full of Sally, crying and trembling. He was never sure why he did it; it may have been the adrenalin from the scare, a deep-seated desire sparked by panic, or just an instinctive comfort reflex. Grabbing her face, he pulled her into his arms and kissed her deeply. It was at that instant their friendship died.

Sally, apparently caught up in the moment, returned the kiss with passion, giving Keenan his very first taste of a girl. The kiss set off adolescent crescendos through every hormone in his body. It was the first time he had a hard on outside his bed.

When they broke the kiss, Sally looked up at him in complete surprise. He blinked at her, uncertain what else to do, and held her out at arm's length. Guttural words escaped his moist lips, but that was all.

That's when the fifth thing dawned on him; the forest was on fire and he had absolutely no idea where he was. They were completely lost. His stomach sank into his hips when he screamed at Sally to run.

Rangers got the fire out in time and rescued the kids, but Keenan had never been in more trouble in his life; he spent the next four summers working to make up some of the loss. The trip back to Portland with Sally's family was completely silent. That fall, they moved away and Keenan never saw her again.

Keenan rolled that incident over in his mind as he drove. Those emotions were playing a repeat performance behind his eyes now: passion, happiness, stark terror. He was thirteen again; gangly, out of control, knowing that each decision was worse than the last. Confidence slipped away, replaced by a doubt that was so tangible Keenan could feel it as a knot in his stomach. Who was he to rescue Isabella? He should call the police. But, with the exception of maybe Thompson, no one would believe him. That one truth was something he had to live with; whatever needed done he would have to do himself. There wasn't anyone else.

At Reggie's instruction, Keenan aimed his car at downtown Portland.

He knew the old church Reggie told him to drive to. Condemned several years before, the historians wouldn't allow the city, or the new owners, to demolish it. The court battle went on for years and the church fell into ruin.

He was afraid to ask Reggie too many questions. There was something decidedly edgy about his friend. It was completely out of character for the ghost and Keenan didn't like it. Reggie was uncharacteristically quiet. He lounged in the backseat, his eyes closed. Keenan knew he hated riding in the jeep. He wasn't sure why Reggie didn't just meet him there.

Keenan concentrated instead on his own motivations. He had no intention of helping Dabria. He would grab Isabella and get her the hell away from ghosts, entities, succubi, or any other creature that got in his way. They'd live on an acre of forest so far away from civilization you'd need a compass and helicopter to find them, have fat laughing babies, and live happily ever after.

He didn't owe that creature anything. She had attacked him, taken advantage of him, had actually raped him. His macho pride was having a hard time getting that particular piece of information to register properly. He eventually labeled it seduction and left it at that.

Keenan wasn't sure why *he* had to rescue the succubus. Couldn't someone else do it? Hell, there were hundreds of ghosts and who knew how many other ethereal creatures out there? Weren't there? Why couldn't they do it?

The Wrangler swerved to the right when he took a corner a little too quickly and he compensated by steering to the left. The answer that followed the adrenalin rush startled him.

He couldn't help it; he did want to help her. Wanted it more than almost anything. Keenan wondered if that was self-motivated. Maybe somewhere in the back of his mind he was thinking about that night in his bedroom. No, it wasn't that and that's what surprised him. He wanted to do it because of what she did the next night.

The memory of that warm touch on the school's brick walls had done something to him, something profound. Dabria had changed him that night, made him somehow stronger, happier. Keenan had no idea what exactly that meant, but it was true. The music from that embrace still lingered in his heart. It was there when he was in jail, during the precious time with Isabella, and even when he stepped into his home to find all his belongings gone. In everything that had happened over the last two days, it was the one thing that made it almost worth it. He focused on the road when the streets turned dark.

The city was Sunday-evening deserted when he hit the Morrison Bridge and rushed over it to downtown. The only people he saw were the night creatures, living and dead, walking hand in hand with disillusionment, the wash of despair paling their already drained faces.

Keenan hated downtown; it was where the really old ones hung out, the spirits who had lost their spirituality. No *respectable* ghost would be caught dead downtown...like living like dead, he guessed.

The church loomed at the end of the street, a shadowed sentinel in the midnight sky.

When he got to it, Keenan pulled into the driveway, only to confront a chain link fence with a heavy padlock intertwined through a set of impressive gates.

It hadn't even dawned on him they would lock up the place.

Dummy, he said to his head. "Great," he said to the gate.

He put the car in reverse and began to back out.

"Ram it," Reggie piped up from the back seat. Keenan thought the ghost had lost his mind.

"Screw you! I'm not ramming a locked gate with my jeep."

Reggie's voice was strangely compelling when he said, "Go through the gate!"

Just for spite, Keenan slammed the jeep into first and hit the gas pedal as hard as he could. The heavy wrangler went through without a hitch, but the noise probably woke everyone in a twenty-block radius. The gates bounced off the fence and banged back to smack the Jeep's rear end. Keenan grimaced at the thought of how much damage they had done to his precious baby.

At any moment, he expected to hear sirens, but when he rolled down his window to listen, the night was silent except for the roar of the freeway a few blocks away.

He drove the jeep through the lot and stopped just outside massive church doors. When the jeep rattled to a halt, he lifted his eyes to the structure filling his windshield.

Despite the decrepit condition of the old stone building, it was still outstanding. A wall made from rough square cut blocks rose three stories above Keenan's head. On each corner was a tower with a conical spire at the top.

At the front of the building, one rose twice as high as the others. The intricate stonework that climbed up those spirals reminded Keenan of cathedrals he had seen in Venice and Florence. The memory provoked a familiar guilt that he swallowed. Not the time to play hardball with regret. The church was impressive.

Of course, now the stone was almost black with city soot and crumbling everywhere. Steel plates or bars sealed the windows, and a padlock barred the massive wooden doors against intruders. Graffiti and gang signs dotted the walls wherever a hand could reach and even above that line in places. It made Keenan heartsick; this was such a waste of architectural perfection. A craving to fix the building leaked out of his desires.

Looking behind him to make sure the cops weren't coming, he got out of the car and circled around the side of the building. Halfway down the sidewall, well away from the street and prying eyes, was an open door. When Keenan turned to speak to Reggie, the ghost was gone.

Cursing, Keenan approached the small entrance. He was furious he hadn't thought to bring a flashlight but then remembered he had one of those little safety lights on his keychain. Digging into his pocket, he pulled it out and tested it by blinding himself for a second. When his eyes cleared, he turned to the door and took a deep breath.

The smell coming from the building caught in the back of his throat. It was an odd blend of cheap motel, rat droppings, and stale incense.

The light was a step above useless, but at least he could see a few inches in front of him. Not that there was a lot to see; the door led to what he thought was an old church kitchen. They had removed all of the cabinets, appliances, and a lot of the floor, so it was mostly a huge room with a giant stone grill at one end.

Broken tiles, rusting nails, and old rotting wood covered the floor. Keenan took his time, knowing that a fall would shred him. He could only imagine what was happening to his sneakers. He stopped in the middle of the kitchen.

"Isabella?" he called as loud as he could and then listened as a series of echoes returned. After several seconds, there was no other sound.

Once on the other side of the littered floor, Keenan found a broken door that barely hung from its hinges. When he pushed, it crashed to the floor sending echoing thunder through the building that answered itself a few moments later. It was only then he realized he was alone. Completely alone.

In this wreck of a church, it caved in on him in one frightening realization. There wasn't a ghost, specter, mist, shadow, or anyone else, physical or otherworldly anywhere near him and hadn't been all evening. A hot rush of fear froze his heart. It was like someone had taken the blood out of him. The solitude hollowed him out. He couldn't move for a moment.

"Reggie?"

He hoped his friend would swoop in and scare the hell out of him; that it was all a joke. But the reverberating name came back to him unaccompanied.

Keenan forced his feet to move with a veiled threat and made his way through the door and into a huge open space. He tried to shine the little light into the vast chamber, but the dark sucked it away. Sending another uneventful *Isabella* into the void, he strained to hear her voice, but it was hopeless.

The small flashlight was giving up the ghost. It flickered and Keenan gave it a good shake. Using its feeble last rays, he found two tables, one on either side of the entrance. A thick woven blanket of dust covered one, but the other looked like someone had cleaned it recently. At the center of the table sat a camping lantern and a box of wooden kitchen matches. He figured the renovators used it, but Keenan doubted the matches worked. He tried one. Miraculously, the match struck on the first go and the lamp flared to life. *Nothing better in the world than kitchen matches!*

He held the lantern up and the size of the chamber startled him. It was huge. The area in front of him was obviously the nave, but it was bigger than any he had ever seen. There were raised galleries on both sides and hundreds of broken pews running the length of the chancel. Many of them were missing, the rest askew or overturned. A fine blue mist of dust illuminated by the lantern lay suspended in the air. The full effect was like looking into a sunken ship. Rustic brown boards obscured high windows from the outside, but Keenan could make out dull stained glass in each. Dust had turned the colors gray; it was like seeing them in a black and white photo. They must have been phenomenal when they were at their full glory.

Keenan made his way to the center aisle where the debris was less tangled and chewed over his next move. He had no idea why Reggie had disappeared and without ghosts to talk to, he was left alone with his own resources, which were sparse. His macho instincts wanted him to run through the building screaming Isabella's name until the dust sloughed off the rafters. The other, more sensible instincts wanted him to run out of the building like an idiot. Middle ground, somewhere between desperation and almost heroic tendencies, was quiet destitution. When he screamed her name into the gaping open, the words echoing back to him were pathetic. He wanted to throw up.

A soft moan echoed through the chamber and Keenan froze.

"Isabella?"

The moan was indistinct. It could have been coming from anywhere. Keenan closed his eyes and listened until his ears rang, but the sound eluded him. Flipping a mental coin, he decided to head toward what he assumed would be the altar.

As he moved, his stomach was doing the mambo and he had to force it to stay still by squeezing hard. That fixed it. The thought of going deeper into this eerie ass church did not appeal to him, but he was committed, even with the primeval part of his brain screaming *run, you idiot, run for your life!* Try telling that to shut the fuck up.

When he got to the front of the nave, darkness and more rubble greeted him. Piles of broken stone covered the floor. He looked up and saw why; directly above the rubble the roof had caved in and rained debris onto the church floor. Water splashed from the hole and caught Keenan full on the face when he looked up. He stepped back sputtering.

Two ornately carved doors stood at attention on either side of the back wall. He moved to one and heard the moan again. It was definitely coming from behind one of them. He pulled on the first and tried to turn the handle. Locked tight.

Moving to the second door, he couldn't stop the lady or the tiger feeling sneaking up his spine. That mixed with the cold water on his face added a macabre tinge to the scene. It was like walking through a Vincent Price movie. He expected wax monsters, pendulums, or psychopaths to jump out of every shadow. All he wanted to do was find Isabella and get the hell out.

The second door opened with a loud scrape against the floor.

Keenan put the lantern in first, just so the light could take care of any unforeseen adversaries. He needn't have bothered.

The sanctuary was about half the size of the nave, but much more ornate. It was obvious no one had been in there since the closure. Everything was intact, from the dozen or so crooked oil paintings on the walls to the richly worn oriental carpet that filled the floor. Except for a thick coating of dust and long stringy cobwebs on everything, the room looked as fresh as yesterday.

Hundreds of lit candles cascaded down both sidewalls, filling the chamber with flickering lights that bounced against the expensive chandelier high above Keenan's head and the saint crowded stained glass windows surrounding the arced ceiling. The chandelier was the most amazing thing Keenan had ever seen; the intricate web of wrought iron, braided wires, and hundreds of glistening crystals were outstanding. It belonged in a palace, not a church.

At the other end were three things Keenan had a hard time getting his senses wrapped around.

In the exact middle of the back wall was a big table with something dark on it. To the right of the table was a giant glass bubble. Swirling kaleidoscope colors filled every inch.

On the left, a looming black and gray cloud hung a few feet off the ground. It was very odd: a still photo of violence, caught in suspended animation. The only movement came from a yellowish glow that radiated along its edges. Keenan recognized it instantly as the thing that had attacked him at the restaurant.

He stopped cold.

The moaning was louder now and coming from the table. Keenan could just make out a dark figure lying there.

Cursing his curiosity, he found himself moving through glue as he approached the table.

When he got close, he stopped and took a step back.

This time he didn't give a shit what his curiosity told him to do.

The succubus was a black shade writhing and moaning against the stone. A veil wrapped tightly around her obscured her features. He thought she was suffocating. The agony in her voice pulled at his heart and almost made him brave. Keenan didn't move.

He tore his eyes away to study the clear balloon to his right. It wasn't glass exactly; it was more like a giant child's bubble, flexible, with prisms of color running over the surface where the candlelight hit it. Inside what he thought were swirling colors was something else completely.

The ghosts, what must have been all of them, crowded behind the transparent material, each fighting for position, their hands, elbows, heads, pushed out against the soft material leaving it lumpy and moving. At the very middle staring down at him in profound sadness was Constance. She was speaking, testing the translucent wall with her hands, pleading with him, but he couldn't hear what she was saying. He scanned the mass of spirits trying to find the one who had led him here. Reggie was decidedly missing.

The succubus's voice was growing louder. Keenan barely got his legs moving. Terror was a new sensation he couldn't get a handle on. Sweat soaked his sides, back, and neck; a hot blaze of fear made his heart a jackhammer; his hands shook.

Casting a suspicious eye to the lifeless cloud on the left, he took the two steps up to the altar and watched the creature groaning on top of it.

She was smaller than he remembered, barely five feet, he would guess. Without her magic (or whatever) she seemed tiny and almost human…but she was definitely not human.

Keenan could see the undulating skin beneath the shroud, the unnaturally long fingers, and thin waist. In this state, without her allure, the succubus looked distorted, twisted, like a woman stretched thin by some machine. It made his stomach do a flip.

The creature stopped her writhing and tried to move her arms toward him, but the shroud was a cocoon prison. Keenan reached to touch her and a deafening crack of thunder filled the space around his head. The next thing he knew he was soaring through the air.

Finding himself sprawled several feet away and the lamp shattered next to his ear, Keenan lifted himself onto his hands and shook his head. He could feel bruises rise on his left arm and hip. They hurt like hell.

Struggling to his knees, he looked up at the succubus then the cloud. It was glowing with more intensity.

"Keenan Swanson." The booming voice filled the entire chamber and he had to throw his hands over his ears. He wasn't sure exactly where it came from, but assumed it must be from the cloud. An idle thought went through Keenan's head, *a voice from the burning bush*. A throbbing headache, aided by the recent spill, made the pain unanimous. Everything hurt now.

"Let them go!" he heard himself say. The ground shook under his knees.

There wasn't an immediate reply, so Keenan took the time to get up. His feet weren't sure whether he was staying or going, so they took a neutral position, turning him sideways. A high-pitched noise tickled his nose.

"They will stay." The voice had better control. That statement just made Keenan a bit nauseous.

"Yeah?" He sounded weak against these bizarre circumstances, and he figured it all had to be a dream anyway, so thought he might as well go for broke. "You can suck my dick!"

There was a rumble that sounded almost like laughter. "Do you want to save them?"

For a moment, Keenan wasn't exactly sure what it was asking. How the hell was he supposed to save them? Not exactly his forte.

"What does that mean?" he asked.

"You can save them all. All it requires of you is a sacrifice."

Keenan scowled at the response, not liking the direction the conversation was taking. "What kind of sacrifice?"

"A sacrifice of flesh."

Keenan didn't like that either. It sounded painful. "I don't know what that means, asshole. You want to clarify it a bit?"

"Your soul you keep, your flesh you give to me."

Well that cinched it. He needed his flesh, enjoyed it on a daily basis. Besides, it was where he hung his clothes.

"What happens if I tell you to go screw yourself?"

There was another distinct rumble/laugh noise. "Then the seraph and the spirits descend to hell."

That made his heart stop for half a beat and he had to gasp to get air to it. "You can't be serious."

"I am."

Keenan shook his head, trying to get his brain to work. It was becoming more and more difficult. "What are you going to do with my flesh...uh, my body?" he asked, trying to buy some time to jump-start his thinking. "I mean, it seems all this puny bit of skin would do is slow you down. You're an entity, for Christ's sake. What do you need me for?"

"I need you to father a new world."

"Oh." Keenan humored the thing, not exactly sure what the hell it was talking about. He scanned the frustrated ghosts in the bubble, the writhing beauty on the table, and the open doorway behind him. The light from the entity was enough to drown out the candles now. It threw Keenan's shadow against the back wall. All Keenan wanted to do right at that moment was get the fuck out of there.

"I want to talk to my friends," he shouted at the chamber. He wasn't sure, but he thought he saw a kind of pulsation from around the cloud's still form.

"No," the voice said. "Decide...now."

The pulse got stronger and the creature's voice sounded almost nervous.

"Give me a break," Keenan shouted back. "Can't I at least talk to Constance?"

"Decide now!" The voice was decidedly nervous now, shaking.

All at once, as if it had blown off a tight restraint, the cloud exploded to almost twice its size. It darkened to deep gray edged with black and scared the shit out of Keenan.

He didn't even realize he was doing it, but he suddenly found himself stumbling to the door and out into the darkness down the long aisle of the nave heading toward the kitchen. Not even sure what happened, he risked a look. Behind him was pandemonium.

Bright lights glowed from the open door accompanied by screams, shouts, and curses. Keenan didn't stick around to see what came next. As fast as his feet could carry him, he was through the kitchen, out the side door, and yanking on the Jeep's door handle with both hands. While he fumbled to get the car keys out of his pocket, the gray mass rose from the back of the church, casting blackness out from its folds that dimmed the distant streetlights.

Keenan gave it a fleeting look, crammed the keys into the ignition, got the jeep going, fastened his seatbelt out of sheer habit, and drove away like a bat out of hell.

Chapter Thirteen

A Bat Out of Hell

He was doing seventy, but the storm kept coming. Keenan was terrified he'd hit some poor homeless guy crossing Morrison. Fortunately, the streets were vacant except for him, the cloud, and a single police cruiser with its lights and sirens at full blast.

Keenan had no idea where he came from. Thompson was bringing up the rear trying to keep up. At least he hoped it was Thompson. All he could see was a large silhouette in the car.

Hitting the Morrison Bridge at about eighty, the car bounced, caught air, and came down with a thud. Sparks flew. The seatbelt throttled him good. His chest shouted at him madly. Keenan was thankful the airbags didn't deploy. The cloud was still gaining. So was the cruiser.

The grates on the bridge hummed a thunderous melody against his teeth and ears, numbing his face as he sped past.

Keenan knew he had to find open road, somewhere he could outrun the creature. Clamping his teeth against the stupidity of his actions, he cleared the bridge and took a quick left onto Grand, a disregarded red light steady against his guilt. The tires screeched and the car tilted toward its side. Keenan instinctively leaned to the right. Thank God for American engineering and cast iron Jeep frames. The car righted and banged against the street nearly running into several parked cars.

The turn cost him. When he looked into his rearview mirror, the creature filled it. He couldn't see the pulsating blue and red lights anymore. Getting his thoughts together with a shake of his head, he floored it, catching a possibility straight ahead.

He so suddenly took the freeway exit, the creature had no time to turn; it went right past him.

The next part was tricky; taking a thirty mile per hour curve at seventy was not an especially good idea. Keenan figured he had nothing to lose, so cranked the wheel and hoped for the best.

Providence had to be with him that night. The car didn't flip over, he managed to miss the side railings, and he had a clear straight road in front of him. He floored it again and hit a hundred before he left the ramp.

He mustered enough courage to peer into the mirror again. The creature was still behind him, but now the cop was between them. Before they went out, the bursting glow from the streetlights illuminated the cruiser's windshield and Keenan recognized Thompson immediately. He was so relieved to see the gruff cop he could have kissed him. Thompson was furiously pointing to the right, trying to get him to pull over.

Fuck that, Keenan thought. He wasn't about to give this thing the "sacrifice" it wanted; joining his ghost friends for eternity wasn't exactly what he had in mind as a way of life.

A pang of remorse traveled through his chest when he glanced back at the frantic officer. The cloud was catching up with the cruiser and Keenan had no idea what the thing would do to Thompson to get to him. None of the alternatives appealed to him. It was one thing to condemn a bunch of ghosts and a succubus to hell; it was another to be responsible for a cop's death. Especially Thompson's.

On impulse, he saw a wide section of turnout and stood on his breaks to make it.

Gravel flew up on all sides of him. He heard something go *bang*. The jeep careened back and forth for several hundred feet, raining more rocks onto his windshield, and bouncing him around a like a Bozo Bop Bag. A shower of sparks suddenly covered the hood. They flowed over the windshield like a river. When the car came to an abrupt stop against something at the side of the road, the airbag burst open and smashed Keenan's skull into the headrest. Stars ignited behind his temples followed by a crushing throbbing in his chest.

The pain was brief and the bag deflated quickly. Something hot and liquid poured out of his nose. Keenan could taste salty copper in his mouth. The buzzing in his ears mingled with the siren whining behind him. Blue and red lights pulsated in a fuzzy confusion. Black then orange shimmered in front of him; he smelled burning rubber. Everything else spun wildly. He wanted to throw up. It took him several seconds to realize someone was shouting at him.

His door burst open and a pair of hands reached passed him to grab the seatbelt. When it opened, Keenan slumped forward, unable to keep his body upright. The same hands caught him under the armpits and dragged him from the wrangler.

What seemed like a mile of being drug through gravel went by and a kind of warmth spread from Keenan's head to the bottom of his feet. When the motion stopped, he heard a massive explosion and someone folded him into the ground.

Tiny pieces of gravel imbedded themselves into his forehead and right cheek. Smoke made his eyes water. It was irritating as hell. The smell of electricity and gas filled the air.

There was that shout again. He thought it was saying his name. He wished it would just go away.

Reality rushed back into him all at once. It brought with it agony, confusion, and the rugged face of Sergeant Thompson suspended above his head. He had never been happier to see a cop before.

"Swanson," Thompson was saying. "Can you hear me? Are you all right?"

Keenan groaned and tried to sit up. A big mistake. His head caved in. He put his forearm over his eyes and tried to stay still so his brains wouldn't fall on the ground and his insides wouldn't explode.

"I'm ok," he said. "You?"

"You stupid son of a bitch," Thompson growled pressing something against Keenan's nose. "You could have killed both of us. I..."

There was a terrible sound...an otherworldly shriek. Thompson suddenly disappeared from Keenan's side.

Adrenalin pumped expediency into Keenan's unprepared body. He sat up and scrambled as best he could to his feet. His legs weren't very cooperative and he fell to his knees.

Suspended in front of him was the entity. Lightning now covered the roiling mass of fury, sending tendrils into the night in every direction. It looked pissed.

Keenan scanned the scene to get his bearings, trying to figure his best route of escape. Flames completely engulfed his Jeep. A pang of loss hit him as he watched his baby burn. The smoke traveled down the highway away from them. The cruiser sat parked and still running close by. Spinning lights reflected off the gray mass eerily, but the sirens were now silent.

On the ground next to the cruiser lay Thompson. He wasn't moving.

"You son of a bitch!" Keenan tried to get up, but his surroundings were full of angry rain cloud. He couldn't move. Several wisps of electricity snaked out of the mass and wrapped around his body. The jolt contorted it and took the breath right out of him. His vision blinked out and shut down.

Chapter Fourteen

Angels and Demons and Ghosts...Oh, My

Keenan must have been a baby. The image of his dad, long gone by the time he was born, loomed above him. Shadows of the bars on his crib tattooed across his baby chest like restraints. The rotating plastic fish above his head moved softly in his father's cold breath as he leaned into the bed. Keenan knew so little about Sam Swanson. An auto accident had claimed him before Keenan was even born. Yet here he was, staring down at him, a wispy smile playing against his pale face. Keenan cooed and lifted tiny fists to touch it, but they fell through like mist and instant pain forced howls out of Keenan's tiny body. The freezing touch hurt like hell. When the lights flicked on, the pale man faded. Keenan's mom put a bottle into his mouth and he fell asleep, the deep brown eyes of his father burned into his memory.

Keenan woke up from the dream. He couldn't move, but for some reason he was still aware of his surroundings, even if everything had gone black.

The pain was gone. It had disappeared with the light. He was standing... no, he was floating above a glowing floor of clouds. Wherever he was started to lighten. He realized with a jolt that he had to be inside the entity.

He wasn't scared. If anything, it was all slowing down. His heart didn't hammer anymore; his chest was rising and falling evenly. Even his hands were still.

At the base of his skull a single vibration started. It was as if someone had put a tuning fork on his neck. The buzz faded into subtle music. It reminded him of the night the succubus had embraced him. But this tune was different.

The sound did not make him calm and peaceful. On the contrary, it sharpened his senses making everything glaringly clear. Something forced his eyes closed so that all he was aware of was the music as it throbbed between his ears. Not singing exactly, but not instrumental either.

Someone spread a blanket of black in front of his mind and stretched it tight. At the center of the fabric stood four tiny people. He couldn't make out their features at first, but as the melody swelled they grew in size until he could almost reach out and touch them. They were frozen in place and looked faded and unreal, as if they were cut out of fifties cardboard. 3D fifties cardboard. There were three men and one woman. One by one, they clarified.

The first man was old and bent, but with a divine twinkle to his eyes. There was a kind of contentment in his face that Keenan immediately trusted. The man was wearing a simple long blue robe and sash, but instead of a shadow, he cast a glow. It was soothing to look at him.

Next to him was a young man dressed in a short green intricate tunic with a golden sash around his hips and long black stockings. He had a short cape over his shoulders and a flattened hat on top of his head. Otherwise disheveled, his chin sported a trim beard. There was a humorous twinkle in his blue eyes. Keenan had only his artist's eyes to confirm it, but he was pretty sure this was the most handsome man he had ever seen. He looked so familiar Keenan was amazed he couldn't figure out where they had met. Over the man's shoulder was strapped a bag with rolled parchments, brushes, and other primitive artists' implements. Keenan knew his history; from the clothes, this man had to be from the fifteenth century, around the time of the Renaissance.

On the other side of the old man was a vision. She was tall and lithe, nearly as tall as the young man. But the comparison stopped there. She was an exotic dark to his earthly light. Raven black hair, opalescent brown/black eyes, and skin the color of an Italian bronze goddess. Her ample breasts, lifted by a high tight waistband, rounded into dark cleavage. A braided golden sash tied her hair away from her porcelain face, which made her dark eyes gleam. The blue gown she wore accentuated her coloring until it was almost painful to look at. Keenan's breath caught in his throat.

The woman also looked familiar, but he couldn't place her. The sorrow in her eyes reached into Keenan's chest and pulled out his heart. It was obvious she wanted to be with the young artist, but a third man standing next to her held her arm.

This fellow was tall and lanky, handsome, confident, self-assured down to his fingernails. There was the look of mischief in his eyes that stimulated Keenan's baser instincts immediately. He was trouble, the kind of trouble that thrilled the male soul and left him begging for more; a creature that preyed on vulnerable spirits and made them enjoy taboo pleasures, despite their convictions, commitments, or promises. This was a man who made bad men out of good, introducing them to every sin a man craved...and forcing him to enjoy it to excess. He had coaxed self-destruction into an art form. The pusher, the pirate, the vagabond, the rascal men gravitated to because they lacked a similar courage. The tempter. He was the thrill of men and the secret desire of women. Keenan recognized him immediately; after all, he had been under his influence for decades.

The steely eyes staring back at him from the frozen apparition made him swallow hard and hate cloud his vision. His appearance had changed a lot, but those eyes were exactly the same; there was no mistake.

Reggie had never looked so good.

He didn't know what he was looking at, but when he tried to open his eyes they were stuck.

"Hello, young fellow."

Keenan about jumped out of his skin when the old man moved. The fellow leaned on a stick and crossed to stand in front of him.

"I'm here to tell you a story."

"Who the hell are you?" Keenan asked, but his mouth didn't seem to be moving.

"My name is Amos. I am an angel."

Something bumped into Keenan's memory and he had to shake his head to get it out. "Wait a minute. Amos. The succubus's Amos?"

When a grin curled the warm old face, Keenan fought not to return it. He had decided to hang onto his annoyance; afraid if he didn't he'd lose himself.

"Well, I am a friend to Dabria, if that is what you mean."

"Whatever," Keenan replied irritably. "What's going on? Is Thompson ok? Where's the entity? Where did you come from? What's Reggie doing here? How come..."

Amos lifted his hand and Keenan couldn't go on. The last words wedged in his throat.

"You ask a lot of questions, young man. If you will allow me a smattering of patience, I think I can appease your curiosity. That would make this much easier. I need you to understand quickly. He sent me to bring you back. There isn't much time..."

Keenan revved up his nerve and blurted out, "Who sent you? That... cloud thing?"

Amos's laughter filled the air. "I *am* that cloud thing, Keenan. He turned me into that when he captured me."

"You? Then why did you threaten me? What are you going to do to them?"

The angel shook his head and touched Keenan's arm. A flash flood of comfort soaked Keenan's senses and he went quiet. "Not me, son, him," he said nodding to the figure of Reggie in the tabloid.

Putting a finger to his lips, Amos closed his eyes and the scene around them changed completely.

Keenan suddenly found himself in Florence...fifteenth century Florence. He was walking down a dirty cobbled street, the woman and Amos in front of him. It was like watching a movie, only from the inside of one of the character's heads. Keenan's disbelief dissolved under the heat of the sunshine, and he felt like one of his ghosts looking out at the world. Settling back, he decided to let it play out… as if he had a choice.

Chapter Fifteen

The Ghost of Dabria's Past

Amos breathed deeply. The smell of baking meat pies and heady herbs poured from the villas as they passed, preparations for a noble man's lunch, most likely. The streets were crowded with the masses; from peasant to the elite, humanity merged their experience, their existence, and their scent like spice markets in the East. Amos pulled the smells into his lungs until they were full. He loved the humans more than what was probably healthy, but he didn't mind. They had entertained him for centuries.

"So who is this young fellow? Why have we been sent..."

"Quiet, child." Amos scowled at the charming creature walking beside him.

"Forgive me, master," she said, folding her hands and bowing her head. "This is my first divine request...I wish to please Him."

"As do we all, my dear." Amos adjusted his heavenly glow and winked out a cloud that had formed above their heads. "The young man is an artist..."

"Oh, I love artists. When I was a Muse, I used to visit..."

"Please, Dabria," he said lifting his hands.

A hot red flush of heat colored her cheeks making her even more beautiful. Her aura shimmered yellow, then gold, and Amos smiled at her impudence.

He toyed with the idea of calming her, but thought better of it; he did not want to rob her of the thrill of her first divine request.

Amos had selected Dabria specifically for this mission because she had been a Muse. She had just arrived from her final duties and was very inexperienced in anything else. Training her to be a guardian would take time, but Amos was very patient. After this one stop, he would return her to heaven so she could study her new craft. Amos loved mentoring and, as a rule, he had little opportunity for it.

"Suffice it to say we are being sent to guide the young man," he said. "He is painting frescos in the grand cathedral but it pleases Him to make certain he inspires another."

"Who will he inspire, master?" Her voice took on a demure obedience Amos appreciated but knew was a strain for her. Dabria had always been a wild spirit. It was what made her an excellent Muse. It had also made it impossible for her to reach her angel status for centuries; free will, over enthusiasm, and creative thinking were not always desired traits in an angel. They were there to obey.

"A young boy named Michelangelo. He will be a great artist one day."

"But what of our charge, master. Forgive me, but I wish to learn as much as I can. Knowledge will aid me in guiding him, will it not?"

Amos snorted an acknowledgement and motioned to a half-built cathedral. "We will see, little one. This way."

As they entered the busy construction project, workmen nearly ran them over as the men bustled back and forth, shoring up beams, laying stone, and carving great slabs of marble. All of them were half-naked, their sweat glistening in the spotted sunlight shining through the open ceilings. The handsome men were excellent examples of God's best work.

"Oh." The erotic noise escaped Dabria's lips and she touched them with her fingers to stop it.

Amos scowled at her but appreciated the conflict. As a Muse, Dabria had spent centuries learning the joys, pleasures, emotions, and dreams of her subjects. It had been her calling to read these things and find the spark that ignited the fire of their imaginations. Inspiration was not necessarily always revelation; it often came during an intimate moment, a quiet whisper in the ear, or the touch of a lover. The barrier between inspiration and sexuality was paper-thin. Pleasure was as much an influence as divine intervention at times; these were humans, after all.

At the back of the cathedral, sheets of paper hung from ceiling to floor. Amos led Dabria there and opened a slit in the paper so they could enter.

A handsome young man stripping off a painter's gown was arguing with a workman and did not notice them when they came in. He shouted above the noise.

"…for the love of God, man. How am I supposed to paint in all this chaos? There is marble dust in everything…my paint is ruined. These conditions are impossible. Tell your employer it is 1485, not 1285. When he can give me leave to paint without these outrageous conditions, I will return!"

When he turned angrily, he ran into Dabria. Without thinking, he wrapped his arms about her to keep her from falling.

For several heartbeats, he stopped breathing, as did Dabria. It was as if they had both turned to stone. Amos cleared his throat and bowed low.

"Signore Moretti, may I introduce my niece, Dabria?"

The artist did not let her go immediately and seemed to be having problems finding his voice. "My immeasurable pleasure, Signorina," finally tumbled out of his mouth. He then realized she was still in his arms and let her go abruptly. "My pardon, Signore DeMarche, Signorina. I was startled…"

"It is not an issue, sir. Dabria, this is Signore Luciano Moretti, the artist I am attempting to woo to our project. Dabria is a fan of your work, sir. She aspires to be an artist herself one day."

Ignoring protestations by the man at his back, Luciano took Dabria's hand and laced it around his arm to escort her from the building. "Really? I have never taught a female student, but it would be my pleasure to start with you, if I may be so bold. If you would like me to look at your work and give you some advice..."

Dabria touched his arm with an expertise that made Amos blush. "You flatter me, sir." She lowered retiring eyes and allowed the young artist to lead her from the noisy building. "It would honor my uncle and me if you could find it in your heart to appraise my work. But I am fearful it will disappoint you and diminish us in your view. My uncle's need is quite urgent. We desire your genius to paint our modest devotion to God. But I am afraid we impose dreadfully. Had I known you were already engaged, I would have insisted my uncle find another..."

"Nonsense. I now find myself between projects. It would be my great pleasure to service you...and your uncle." The force of his words apparently startled him since his mouth hung open a moment and Dabria blushed.

Amos had to smile to himself. In the span of seconds, Dabria's charms had already won the artist over. The ten-year-old Michelangelo had only recently started to loiter in the small church, awed by the sculptors. Amos thought it would be weeks before he would be able to get the two together. His mission was beginning nicely.

"Would you both dine with me tonight at my father's villa?" Luciano asked. "We have a passable cook and some nice wines. We can discuss the project and make arrangements to send my crew to the chapel to inspect it."

"It would be our pleasure, sir," Amos replied, bowing deferentially.

Luciano took Dabria's hand, turned it, and touched the palm lightly. "The pleasure is all mine, sir. Tonight." He bowed to them and rushed up the street, turning around several times to wave, singing and laughing as he went.

Amos was very pleased with the outcome of their brief visit, and delighted they would be able to return to heaven soon. He had been on a mission among the humans for years and it would be good to go home. Dabria would accompany him back to begin her training. Not a day too soon, as far as Amos was concerned. A Muse can inspire genius in men…but this Muse was inspiring more than that, he was sure. The sooner he got her out of here, the better.

He turned to walk to their temporary home at the chapel and Dabria followed him silently.

"You are suddenly so quiet, child. What troubles you?"

"Hmm?" She came out of her reverie and took his arm. "Nothing to fret about, Amos. That young man…he is very interesting, is he not?"

"He is a gift from God to the future, little one. His work will inspire many."

"Of course," she replied. "It is just…"

"What, child?"

"He is very talented, I am certain, but does his wife not suffer from loneliness when he is out upon projects all day?"

That question set off bells in Amos's head. "He is not married. Why do you ask?"

"For no reason, master. I am merely curious."

Amos grunted and led her to their rooms in the chapel.

* * * *

That night the dinner went splendidly. The food was excellent, as was the company, and before dessert reached the table they had their commission, their commitment, and their artist. Amos could not have been more pleased. They made plans to have Luciano start first thing in the morning.

The painter's father asked Amos to join him on the balcony for news from Rome. Amos was reluctant to agree, fearing to leave the two young people alone with one another. He had seen the spark at dinner, the covert glimpses, could feel the ardent flames rising. When Luciano's mother insisted on taking Dabria for a tour of her son's works in the house, Amos thought it would be safe enough. He left with Luciano's father.

The man turned out to be a brilliant conversationalist. Amos found himself entranced by him for several hours. When he looked to the skies, he was amazed at how late it was.

Excusing himself, he sought out a servant to show him where his niece was. After searching for several minutes, he dismissed the man and headed for the garden. He knew at once that something was not right.

Off in the distance, he could hear voices and laughter lilting through the tangled foliage. The scent of sage and thyme permeated the air. As he approached, he stopped at once, spotting them through hanging olive branches.

"Kiss me, sweet angel," Luciano was saying, holding Dabria tightly in his arms. "One kiss. If you reject me, then I will become a priest. No other kiss will ever satisfy me again."

"You are too bold, sir," Dabria whispered, but her voice was breathless and wonton. The sleeves of her gown were down around her shoulders and moisture glistened on the top of her half exposed breasts. "I will not surrender to your advances. You will steal the kiss then leave me to boast to your friends."

"Never," Luciano whispered and pressed his lips tenderly to hers. Dabria responded with resistance at first then passion, entangling her hands in his hair.

Amos was shocked and would have jumped through the branches immediately had a thought not stopped him.

What if he were to break this up now, embarrassing the young artist? Would Luciano not refuse the commission out of mortification? Would Dabria be less than useless to Amos, rejecting Luciano out of her sense of duty and devotion? She could not fight her nature, no more than the young man could fight his desires. Amos would find a way to end this without jeopardizing his mission. There was nothing more important. Without Luciano's commission, the young Michelangelo would not move on to greater accomplishments.

He backed away slowly, mindful not to make a sound. When he was well away from the couple, he cupped his hands and shouted, "Dabria? Are you out here? It is very late, we must return to the chapel."

A moment later, he heard her reply. "Yes, Uncle. I am coming."

When he saw her next, Dabria had taken care of her state of disarray and looked as she had when they arrived.

Neither she nor Luciano could hide the blush of love that brightened their faces, but they did well to keep their expressions solemn and proper. They were very civil to each other, but Amos could read their eyes.

During the next several months, the relationship that had flared between Dabria and Luciano apparently dwindled with time and Amos was content. Dabria was the perfect lady and barely spoke with Luciano when he was present. Amos sensed even a little animosity between them. His heart breathed a sigh of relief.

On the night before they were to leave for Rome, a great party had been put together to celebrate the dedication of the church, Luciano's brilliant artwork, and the departure of Amos and Dabria.

Amos fussed with the preparations for hours but had not seen Dabria even once. He sent a servant to fetch her, but when he returned he told Amos the lady had left the house. Thinking Dabria went to the market for last minute provisions, Amos threw himself into the arrangements, and the time flew by. When she did not appear by the time the guests began to arrive, he sent his servant to find her in the town.

At the end of the evening, the guests started thinning out and Amos made curt goodbyes. His mind filled with a dread that grew with each passing moment. Something was terribly, terribly wrong.

As he said goodbye to the chapel priest, Amos's man ran up to the house, panting fiercely.

"Please sir," he said catching his breath, "you must come. She has aligned herself with the painter."

The man tugged on Amos's arm and the angel found himself running through the night-darkened streets of Florence. He had to fight the instinct to use his powers to expedite their arrival. The world seemed to cave in around him as they ran.

At the center of town was the grand cathedral Luciano had been working on the day they met. Amos's stomach turned to knots when the now finished building loomed as they approached. The servant pulled him through an open door, along a corridor, and into a small sanctuary at the end of it.

On a bench, looking up at them, sat Dabria. Her face had changed. Dark circles marred her beautiful eyes. The angelic glow that normally radiated from every pore was gone. Tears stained her face in the muted light and Amos gasped. Muses did not weep.

Amos fell to his knees and his heart broke.

Next to Dabria, looking stern and deliberate, Luciano stood like a stoic statue, holding her hand next to his heart. Behind them was the cathedral priest.

"What have you done?" Amos whispered from the ground, knowing the sin would be more than he could bear.

"Forgive me, Amos." Dabria's voice was a harsh hush and more tears drenched her cheeks. "But I love him. More than anything…more than my immortal soul. We have consummated that love, taken vows to protect it, and on this night were joined in marriage. We are husband and wife."

"I wanted to tell you, sir…" Luciano protested, but Dabria stopped his voice with a glance.

Amos could not believe his ears. She had married a man. She was mortal. The punishment for her action was banishment and expulsion from heaven. The gap in his heart widened. He had to excommunicate her at once and condemn her to hell.

"Out!" he shouted, rising to his feet and confronting the priest and the painter. "Out of here, now!"

Luciano tried to raise his voice to object, but the servant and the priest wrapped their arms around him and forced him through the door. The priest's hands shook as he closed it behind him.

Brightness spilled from Amos's hands and feet, lightning burst with a loud clap from his mouth. The room grew small around him, the ceiling closer. He knew the angel he had become would terrify the young Muse; she had no experience with the vengeful hand of heaven. Amos had no choice.

But Dabria was not terrified. Indeed, she went to her knees before him and bowed her head. The pool of her gown made her appear to melt into the stone floor.

"You must do this, Amos," she whispered, her sobs getting the best of her voice. "I will not resist you; I go gladly, peacefully. Please know that I love you, Amos, but I could no more resist the pull of my love for Luciano than you could resist the pull of God. He completes me, fills me to the brink with joy. Except for this tragedy, I could finish my existence here and have no misgivings. I do not ask for your forgiveness, for I know what that would cost you. I only ask that you make this swift. I have no regrets."

When she lifted her eyes to him, Amos knew what he would do. The consequences ate at his heart. He loved her. He loved them both. If he forgave them, he would be condemned to stay in heaven for the rest of existence. He could no longer be a guardian. To return to earth after such forgiveness would put him in the hands of demons. They would hunger for his soul and make certain he never returned to heaven again. The thought was a bitter one. He loved the humans, had guided them since their inception. The thought of leaving them behind was simply too unbearable.

The light radiating from his body blinked out. He reached down, took Dabria's hand, and lifted her to her feet. Taking her into his arms, he cradled her head and whispered, "I forgive you."

"No!"

Dabria tried to cling to him, but he vanished from her arms.

* * * *

From heaven, Amos checked on the lovers from time to time. They lived their lives well. Luciano took many commissions that made his name well known throughout Italy. Dabria loved her husband and he loved her. Her nightly prayers to heaven reached Amos's ears and it pleased his heart. His duties in heaven were varied and enlightening, but he missed her companionship and the humans. He did not regret the decision, however.

Ten years passed and Dabria's prayers diminished. Amos fretted about the dwindling voice. He knew of nothing wholesome that would silence her prayers.

Finally, he petitioned the archangel to send another angel to be Amos's ears and eyes on earth. He needed to find out what had happened to his cherished Dabria. The master angel was loathed to grant him the favor, knowing that the creature he so loved had brought about Amos's shame. But he granted the wish with the condition that Amos could do nothing to assist Dabria. Amos agreed and went to his friend Gazardiel. She descended to earth that very night.

She passed into a small cottage at the center of town. As she entered the cottage, Dabria doubled over into the chair next to her and wept for a long, long time. Amos wished he could comfort her, but knew he was constrained by his promise. Instead, he stayed with her until the worst of it was over. He wished he knew what so troubled her.

When the tears ceased, Dabria sat up and wiped the moisture from her face with her apron. Determination lighted her eyes. She rose to cross to the door, grabbed a shawl from the hook, wrapped it around her thin shoulders, and left the house.

Gazardiel followed the woman through the streets of Florence, but the journey was short.

At the end of a hidden dark lane was a dirty tavern. Smoke poured from an open door along with the smell of cooking pork, cheap spirits, and the chatter of a gang of men. Dabria hesitated for a moment, tightened her grip on the shawl, and finally walked through the door.

When she was inside, she saw men of every type packed into the place: bankers, artists, politicians, workmen. The only women were scantily clad wenches who served ale, wine, and debauchery to the tavern's patrons. As she passed, she ignored the obscenities whispered to her by drunken men. Several of them tried to touch her, but she held enough of her previous spirit to stop them with a cool glare. In the muted light, Amos noticed how thin she had become, the dark circles under her eyes, and her sunken cheeks. The change appalled him.

In the back of the tavern was a murky corner filled with a large circular table littered with gaming pieces. Around the table were several men in leather and finery. At one end was Luciano with a vixen on his lap feeding him her breast. Another bobbed up and down with her mouth wrapped around his erected member under the table. Dabria stopped and tears threatened her eyes. She got them under control by tightening her lips and removing her shawl.

"Tell your strumpets to leave. Your wife wishes to speak with you," she said with force.

The crowd of men went instantly silent and the girls ceased their activities, rearranging their attire, and scuttled away from Luciano.

It was obvious he was very drunk. He adjusted his codpiece with difficulty and threw an insipid smirk across the room while he was doing so. Most of the men rose from their seats, gave Dabria a quick bow, and disappeared into the crowded tavern. One remained on the opposite side of the table, but Dabria only had eyes for her husband.

"My beautiful wife," Luciano slurred to his friend, "has come to retrieve me, no doubt. Go home, wench! You may service me later."

Dabria's mouth fell open.

"You are drunk, my fine artist," the man said, pouring him another splash of liquor. "Perhaps she is right. It may be time to go home. She is a lovely creature, man. Much better fare than this modest house can provide. Are you mad?"

Luciano gave the man a foolish grin and tipped the drink, spilling much of it on the table. "But my dear Reginald, she is a nag."

"I have told you what to do with nags, have I not?"

"I will not beat my wife," he replied, downing the drink.

"You never know, she may enjoy it."

It was only then that Dabria turned her full attention to his friend, obviously to lash out at his impudence. When she focused on his face, she gasped, took a step backwards, and almost fell over a chair.

Amos had not even glanced at the man. When he had Gazardiel do so, his blood ran cold.

"Azazel," Dabria whispered in terror. "Who let you out of hell? Why are you here, demon?"

That seemed to get the man's attention. He sat up and leaned across the table to inspect her more closely. Inhaling through his teeth, his mouth curved until straight perfect teeth shone out of the darkness.

"A Muse," he hissed. "And now mortal from the looks of it."

Luciano squinted over at his friend and murmured, "A what? What are you saying?"

Without taking Dabria out of his sight, Reginald touched his friend's face. "Sleep, my sweet artist."

Luciano slumped onto the table.

The man rose and came around the table to bow. "Forgive me, madam, but they call me Reginald now. I miss the old name. It is good to hear it again. Especially from such a lovely mouth." He made the word obscene.

Dabria took another step back, evidently preparing to flee, but Reginald jumped and caught both arms before she could turn. She fought him, striking his face with her fist before he got her under control, but the only thing it elicited was an indecent snigger.

"My God, you are exquisite." He ran leering eyes over her body with slow exactness. Dabria squirmed under the examination.

It made Amos sick to see it. He cursed himself for making that agreement with the archangel. There was nothing he could do for Dabria.

"I must have you," Reginald said, releasing her.

She turned to leave, but closed her eyes and clenched her fists. "What have you done to my husband?"

"I? Nothing. Luciano is a lecher."

Dabria whirled around her eyes blazing. "My husband is a good man. Release him from your spell." The laugh he gave her sent tremors through her body and her voice shook when she said, "Release him immediately."

"He may be too far gone, signora. His depravity is deeper than you think. Would you like to know what your... good man has done? I would be happy to share the darkness of your husband's soul. It took very little to convince him. A small push, nothing more."

"Monster!"

"Yes, well." Reginald stepped around her, wrapped his arms around her chest, and whispered in her ear. "Fornication is the least of it, I am sorry to say. May I tell you the rest?"

She took in a shaking breath and closed her eyes. "No."

Reginald looked disappointed. "Pity." He turned her in his arms and touched her cheek with his thumb. Her breath came out scattered, and he watched her bosom rise and fall, an ember of passion igniting his eyes. He touched the top of one bulging breast and she moaned, but not in protest. Reginald pulled her close and touched her ear with his lips. "But a sample of the delights awaiting you, my dear. I could fill your cup and then drink it dry."

Dabria regained her senses and freed her hands enough to push him away. "Pig!" she shouted. "Return my husband to me!"

Reginald leaned against the table and stretched his neck while he watched her. Pulling his head back, his face turned sardonic. "Your plight has struck me deeply, madam. Perhaps there is something I can do for him."

Her breath stopped. "What?"

He crossed to her with his arms behind his back, his black eyes never leaving hers. Dabria seemed confused. Without leave, Reginald grabbed a handful of her dark hair, breathed in her scent, and bent her head back. He played his fingers against her throat but she did not move.

"I can make this all go away. You have but to ask."

Furrowing her brow, Dabria struggled to get free. "Demons do not grant favors without compensation. What is it you want from me?"

"Only your obedience, sweet lady. Luciano will live out his life a changed man, sinless, free. You have but to give me your soul."

She lowered her eyes. "My soul is already forfeit or do you not know the price for my sin?"

Good girl, Amos thought. *If he does not know I forgave you, there is nothing he can use.*

"I do not wish to send you to hell, my charming Muse. I wish you to serve me here on earth."

Dabria blinked back at him. "How can I serve you here? I am mortal. My life will fade in a few years."

"I swear to you once the bargain is accepted, you will not die. But I promise you this, your husband will enjoy a special place in hell if you do not submit to me. Do we have an agreement?"

He let her go and she almost fell. Reginald caught her arm and sat her in a chair.

For the longest time, she watched her husband sleeping at the table. The tavern seemed to go quiet around them.

"Very well," she finally whispered, "but with a provision." She lifted her head to him and there were tears in her eyes. "You must let him live out this lifetime with me. You must let him know love until he dies. His soul will remain forever free of sin."

"Nothing easier."

Reginald held out his hand to her. It took her a long time to take it. As soon as they touched, the room grew louder and Luciano sat up abruptly.

"Go with your wife, friend. You do not belong here."

Dabria lifted her husband from the table and led him through the crowd as fast as her legs would carry her.

The next morning, Amos watched as Dabria made breakfast for her husband. Her eyes were very sad, but there was contentment in them too. At least she would have a lifetime with him.

Luciano stumbled out of the bedroom and spotted his wife at the stove. He crossed to her quickly and took her into his arms.

"My God, the things I have done to you," he said, kissing her neck, her face, and her hands. "Forgive me, my love. Forgive me. Forgive me."

"We discussed this last night, love."

"My apologies are boundless," he replied, lifting her off her feet and swirling her around. "You must forgive me again."

Dabria touched his face with both hands and looked into his eyes. "I have forgiven you already, but I gladly forgive you again. I love you." The passion in her words was deep and profound. She then laughed. "Now put me down. Breakfast is ready."

After breakfast, Luciano dressed and prepared to go out. He asked if Dabria would like to go with him.

"Where are you going?" she asked, clearing away the dishes.

"I am going to church."

Dabria stopped and tilted her head at him. "Church? You have no commissions right now."

"I do not go there to work, my love, I go there to pray."

A flow of relief colored Dabria's face and she smiled back at him. "You go along, my love. I will finish these up and meet you later."

He swept her up into his arms again and kissed her until they both laughed out loud. Luciano left the house whistling and singing.

A few moments later, screams and shouts came from outside and Dabria looked through the window. There was a crowd gathering on the street. She wiped her hands and left the house to investigate. Echoes of *runaway cart* and *he did not see it* spilled down the roadway.

Amos watched as she crossed the street to the milling crowd and knew that what she found there would break her. Amos did not stay around to see it. He did not have the heart. As he left, he had her screams to accompany him back to heaven.

Luciano was dead.

Chapter Sixteen

The Shade Turns

Keenan could feel sensation coming back into his hands first. They curled under his body, pressed into the road by his weight. He was lying on the ground. The smell of asphalt and grease advised his nose to shut down. It told them to go to hell. Shards of electricity crackled out of his elbows; at least that's what he thought was happening. It was all kind of weird. He waited to open his eyes. No need to rush anything.

"Get up, son." The voice was the same one he had just heard in his dream. *Curious.* Maybe he was still asleep.

"Come on. We have to return to the church."

That got Keenan's interest, and he cracked an eye without moving anything else.

"What just happened?" The words came out of the half of his mouth not stuck to the road. All he could see from that angle was black asphalt and greasy gravel.

Tempting fate, he rolled over on his back and looked up. Faint dusty stars glimmered above him and a figure appeared in his field of vision. It was Amos.

Keenan shifted his head slightly and then lifted it. "That wasn't a dream." It was a statement, but not a very firm one.

"No, son."

Keenan squinted up. "You're Amos."

"Yes. It was the only way I could convince you."

"Convince me of what?"

Keenan sat up and scanned the area. Everything looked exactly as it did before. In fact, it hadn't changed at all; the flames engulfing his car were absolutely still and the lights on top of Thompson's cruiser weren't moving. Everything was frozen. *Neat trick.*

When he saw Thompson still sprawled in front of the cruiser, he got up the rest of the way.

"Scratch that right now," he said. "Is Thompson all right?"

"He is asleep."

Keenan twisted his head to the angel. "Asleep?"

"We have to go now."

"Convince me of what?" Keenan repeated and crossed to the cop.

He wasn't sure what he was supposed to feel for, but placed two fingers on the side of Thompson's neck. A steady, slow throb pulsed against the pads of his fingers.

"Convince you to sacrifice yourself. To save them."

Keenan just nodded. Things were coming into focus and he was beginning to see some logic in what was going on. But his head was simply too full of holes to figure it all out. He decided to exercise his vocal chords, but they weren't cooperating either.

"So, Dabria is the succubus. I get that. Reggie is the bad guy. I get that too. And you're Amos, the angel. Reggie got you to come back somehow, right? Why?"

"Dabria escaped him two centuries ago. He needed me to lure the succubus out of hiding."

"How?" Keenan shot back at him. He didn't know what to think. As far as he was concerned this fellow could have made the whole frickin' thing up, Keenan could simply be dreaming, or Thompson had actually had him committed yesterday and this was all a fantastic drug induced hallucination. The bets were about even.

The angel didn't speak. Instead, he gathered up his arms and a lightshow came out of every orifice. Keenan had to shade his eyes. *All it needs is Led Zeppelin,* Keenan thought disjointedly.

"You doubt my validity?" the angel bellowed. Wind bellowed along with him, and Keenan suddenly found it almost impossible to stay on his feet.

"Fuck no!" he shouted back. "I just want to know why you came back to earth when you knew he would catch you!"

The lightshow stopped abruptly and Amos looked at his hands. "A fair question," he replied quietly. "Actually, it's a little embarrassing. He prayed to me."

That prompted a nervous laugh from Keenan who slapped his hand over his mouth to stop it. Amos looked irritated, but continued. "I thought it was Dabria. She was in trouble again. She said the demon had found her. Anyway, I panicked. When I couldn't get the archangel to grant me another visitation, I..." He looked at the bottom of his robe.

"You skipped out," Keenan said for him.

Amos' hot glare had little force and faded into a shrug. "Yeah." He zapped a small rain cloud above his head absently and then rung his hands. "He used me to lure Dabria back to him." Leveling his eyes just above Keenan's, he added, "To seduce you."

"Yeah, I got that. But why me? What does he want?"

"I'm not entirely certain of his motivation, but I know why he picked you. He needed the seed of a powerful psychic. He's using it to create the... ultimate being. I guess you fit the bill."

That made Keenan chuckle. "Son of a bitch," he said shaking his head. "Reggie told me in the bar, about you, Dabria, the Cambrian, all of it! Great. Me the father of the ultimate being. Man, did this guy get his wires crossed." Keenan put his hands on his knees and surveyed the lonely highway. "He said he wanted my flesh. Don't suppose you know what he wants with it, do you?"

Amos shrugged. "My guess would be so he can become human. Being a demon has its disadvantages. For one thing, you are incorporeal... not to mention invisible. That makes it difficult to function normally in the physical universe. I believe he wants to raise this creature himself."

"Yeah."

"You have absolutely no reason to, but you have to trust me, Keenan. We need you to stop him. And we need to find that baby."

"How am I supposed to do that exactly?"

Amos rubbed the back of his neck. "Well, by dying, to be honest with you."

Keenan pulled his head back. "Fuck that!"

"You don't know all of it and I haven't got time to explain. Suffice it to say that without your sacrifice, everyone's dead. You, me, your ghost friends, Dabria, and your corporeal friends too, in the end. If Azazel completes his plans, the earth and humankind is dead in twenty-five years, maybe less. It's all up to you."

Keenan wasn't convinced, but the urgency of the situation was nagging the back of his neck. The flames on the car were defrosting and he figured he was running out of time. Maybe he'd just go back and see what happened. God, he wished he could talk to Constance...or Isabella. He pulled in a deep sigh to relieve the pressure. It just made his ears crackle.

"Where's Isabella? What did you do with her?" he demanded.

"She's fine, son. Safe. I needed her to get you to come to the church. You've got to trust me."

Keenan didn't answer him and looked at the cop instead. "Can you help me get Thompson into the cruiser?"

Amos shrugged and turned back into a cloud. "Just leave him here and I'll take you back. It would be faster that way."

"Not on your life, buddy. Who knows, I might need rescuing later."

Keenan got his arms under Thompson's and lifted with a groan. The man was as solid as a rock. *Man! You need to lay off the weights, big boy.*

Amos disappeared and Keenan struggled to get the cop into the back seat. Thompson's position on the hard plastic bench was probably going to give the poor guy a stiff neck, but it beat the alternative.

Keenan got behind the wheel of the cruiser and sent one forlorn look at his Jeep. *Goodbye, old friend.*

Everything came to life at once and Keenan could feel the heat from the flames even through the windshield. He put the cruiser in gear and searched the road before easing it in. There wasn't a soul around…bodied or disembodied.

Chapter Seventeen

Descending into the Pit

It took him a while to figure out all the controls on the cruiser. Lights lit up the dashboard in flashing blues, reds, greens, and yellows. The soft dash lights were doing nothing to help him. It reminded him a bit of his very first car, a 1966 AMC Rambler with push button ignition and shifting. Futuristic, he had called it. This was more like the space shuttle.

Keenan had no idea what he had in mind. After failing to get his wits in order, he settled for just going along for the ride. The impulse to turn tail and run was stomped by his responsibility. It was a first for him. Maybe it was time to be a hero. He'd been just about everything else in his life.

When he got to the church, there were cops everywhere. He counted at least seven cars. Holding his breath they wouldn't look at the cruiser too closely, he eased on by without making eye contact. He drove three blocks away and parked it.

Thompson was snoring like a rumbling jigsaw in the back when Keenan pulled the keys from the ignition. Going to the back door and opening it, he tried again to shake Thompson awake, but it was impossible. Whatever Amos gave him had knocked him out but good.

Keenan slipped the keys into Thompson's breast pocket. He then searched the cop's belt for a flashlight. It came out of its sling without any trouble. Keenan stashed it in his coat pocket, grateful it was smaller than some he had seen on other cops.

Something caught his eye and an interesting idea blossomed in his head. Being a pacifist, he did something he thought he'd never do; after some finagling with the holster, he lifted Thompson's Glock and examined it.

It was a lot lighter than he expected and the finish was more like plastic than metal. When he found the trigger, he realized with a jolt that the weapon had no safety. Made sense, since cops needed their guns to shoot fast. *Just point and click.* The thought gave him a rush and he decided it was probably best not to think about it much. Macho had never been a requirement for him, but the touch of cold death in his hand made him feel like a man.

"Baby!" he said to the Glock.

Keenan stuffed the gun into the back of his belt. It was a little like a bad PI movie. Not that a gun would be any good against ghosts, demons, angels, or what have you; it just made him feel a little better having it.

He got back into the front seat and searched the dash for a way to turn off the lights. He finally found the button below the laptop and slid it to the off position. The lights blinked out.

The night was cold around him when he closed the cruiser doors searching the street for any sign of cops. His breath came out hazy white and the streetlights in the distance looked misty. Otherwise, the street was clear.

Keenan had no idea what he was doing. The thought of going back to the church sucked the life out of him. He was scared, but something else was niggling the back of his thoughts. *Dabria.* The story Amos told him had reached deep inside his guts and given them a hard twist.

He never thought of himself as much of a hero; hell, he figured a lifetime of hauntings got him out of *that* chore. But he was having distinct heroic feelings now. It was weird to find out that heroism and stark blind terror were so similar. Made him respect cops and firemen a whole lot more.

Winding his way slowly down the abandoned street, Keenan made out blue and red lights blinking in and out as he got nearer to his destination. By the time he got there, only two sets were still moving. The cops were leaving.

Standing behind a skinny tree that probably didn't hide him very well, Keenan waited until the two cops finished talking. The streetlights had all gone out as he passed, so he was hoping the darkness would conceal him.

The cops finally got into their respective cars and headed out, but not before the last one relocked the fence. They sped off down the street.

Keenan approached the church making sure there weren't any more of them lurking around. There wasn't a soul visible anywhere.

When he got to the fence, he was relieved to see that the cop hadn't fastened it tightly. Keenan was able to get himself through the opening, but only after he got stuck. Sucking in and pushing hard, he burst through and landed on his ass. Compared to the other pains of the evening it was slight.

Keenan pulled himself up, searched the street again, and slid to the side of the building.

When he got to the door, he found it locked and swore under his breath. Now what was he supposed to do?

Scanning the building, Keenan spotted an enclosed fire escape leading up to the roof. There was a locked cage around it, but he thought he could climb it. He pulled his cell phone out of his pocket and checked the time. 2:30 a.m. Swallowing his disappointment, he thrust the phone back into his pocket and whispered, "Piss." All he wanted was for this night to be over.

Scaling the cage was easier than expected. It was almost completely gone on the opposite side, and he was able to squeeze through the opening to get to the ladder.

The ladder was plenty difficult, however. The years had rusted through half of the rungs, but he didn't know which until he reached them. Twice he almost fell to the ground, once several hundred feet up. His arms and legs were weak from all the evening's abuses and his hands were giant slabs of meat against the rough rusted metal. He was sure his palms were hamburger by the time he reached the top.

Keenan had never been fond of heights. A fact, unfortunately, he had forgotten in all the excitement. When he hauled himself up and over the top of the ladder, he landed on a small platform protruding from the roof. It prefaced one of the stained glass windows. The smell of roofing tar soaked his senses.

He made the mistake of looking down. The faraway ground came rushing up into his eyes and his head started to spin. Keenan did the only thing he could think of. Falling to the rooftop, he curled into a fetal position until the dizziness passed.

Testing the roof with his foot, he forced himself to clamber across the slippery accordion tile riding it up then down. Several times he slid down the roof, twice almost going over the edge, but, except for the bruises trashing his arms, legs, and elbows, he was still in one piece when he reached the gaping hole in the roof and peered into the darkness.

Suspended just below was a large pipe about four inches in diameter. It had a big hole in one side where water poured out to the floor below. Moving his butt as close to the edge as possible, he touched the pipe with his foot and gave it a good push. It was as solid as rock.

Getting on his stomach, he inched over and pulled Thompson's flashlight out of his pocket. It took him a couple of seconds to figure out he had to turn the head to make it work. The crumbling tiles under his stomach were weakening. Thoughts of a long fall to his death were paramount in his mind, but he forced them back by putting tar-laced air into his lungs. All that did was make his head spin, so he gave it up. There was a kind of freedom in succumbing to the inevitable that made him feel better.

Shining the light down into the dark church, he followed the pipe along the ceiling and to the rear wall of the upper gallery. The pipe disappeared into the floor on the other side of the gallery, a good seventy-five feet away. There were no pews or seats there, from what he could see.

He cursed himself for even contemplating what he was about to do next, but he rubbed his hands together, secured the backend of the flashlight in his mouth (trying hard to not think about where that flashlight had been), and scooted forward until his feet were hanging over the edge of the hole. The swirling light dancing against the darkness was making him dizzy as he leaned in and wrapped his hands around the solid pipe.

He figured once he lowered himself down, either the pipe would give out and he would fall to his death, *it* would hold but his nerve would give out and he'd hang there until he lost his strength and fall to his death, or both the pipe and his nerve would hold long enough to get him to the upper gallery. At this point, he wasn't too concerned about any of the options. Praying to various gods, he tightened his grip and lowered himself over the edge.

When the weight of his body jolted him, he almost lost the flashlight, but he clamped down on it until his jaw ached. Hanging there to get his bearings, Keenan couldn't keep the image of dead pheasants hanging from the rafters in his uncle's barn out of his head. Maybe he would be gamey enough for a feast in a few days.

Keenan maneuvered the flashlight as best he could to look forward. From this angle, the gallery didn't seem that far away. Question was, how solid was that pipe where he couldn't see it? It was taking his weight ok; hadn't even moved when he lowered himself onto it, but what about swinging a hundred and seventy pounds to move along it. He tried to remember his twelfth grade trig. How many additional pounds per square inch would swinging along that pipe add to the stress on the rusty metal?

Not that it mattered. Keenan knew he was just putting off the inevitable. He had to move one of two directions, forward or down.

Tightening his grip and thanking his lucky stars for all that walking and exercise, he slid one hand forward on the pipe about a foot. So far so good. Making sure his hold was firm, he then lifted the back hand and swung it quickly in front of the other one. Then he stopped.

His heart was racing fast enough to make his eyes pulse through the sweat pouring into them. Keenan hadn't thought about wet hands, but the pipe was rusty enough to create its own friction. With a rush of adrenalin, he decided to go for broke and plowed ahead moving his hands one after the other to cover the distance to the looming balcony ahead.

Amazed at how quickly he was going, Keenan gave into giddiness as he moved forward. He could see his target, was almost there, could see himself passing the railing and gently releasing the pipe to stand in the gallery. He was so proud of himself.

Two feet from his goal, the pipe gave way.

Keenan suddenly found himself vertical, swinging toward the ground floor as the pipe snapped one bracket at a time above his head. He instinctively grasped it with his arms and legs, like a child clinging to its mother. The only sensation was the rush of falling wind, the slight *ping ping ping* as the metal straps broke one by one, and the sudden emptiness in his middle when he seemed to leave some of his insides on the ceiling. He slammed his eyes closed and waited to die.

Gravity and the strength of those last few brackets had other plans, however. Keenan swept within inches of the floor, the pipe caught on a beam way above his head, and stopped abruptly.

His balls, chest, and shoulder caught most of the impact, and he wished he *was* dead for a moment or two. When he looked down, he was less than a foot above the ground. Prying his legs and arms from the pipe, he slid the rest of the way to the floor, extracted the flashlight from his mouth, and then threw up.

It took Keenan several minutes to adjust to being alive. Despite the pain in his groin, he wrapped his arms around the pipe and kissed it. Sputtering, he wiped his mouth with the back of his sleeve and spit several times.

From somewhere behind him down the long nave he heard the rustle of someone making their way through the debris. He fumbled with the flashlight, amazed it still worked when he twisted the top, and played the light down the long expanse. There was definitely a shadow coming toward him.

"Who's there?" His voice resonated through the ruin around him, coming back muffled.

The figure stopped. "Keenan?"

Keenan couldn't believe what he thought his ears were hearing. He didn't reply.

"Keenan, is that you?" That wonderful voice made him go all loose inside.

"Isabella?"

The figure hurried across the open area and landed square in his arms. His balls ached where she landed, but he didn't mind.

"Oh my God, I thought I'd never get out of here," she whispered in his ear, holding him tight. The warmth of her body made the pain disappear.

He thought maybe this was another one of Reggie's dreams. At first he was so bowled over just to have her in his arms, he forgot that maybe he should be suspicious, or maybe even a little surprised.

"Are you all right?"

She stepped out of his arms and looked up at him. In the muted light, he could make out shining tears on her cheeks and a red nose. Dust covered her hair, her face, and her clothes. Even mussed and dirty, Keenan felt the pang of desire run through his blood when he looked at her.

"I think so, Kee," she said breathlessly. "Something grabbed me. I don't know what it was. I must be out of my mind." Her trembling shoulders vibrated against his hands and her eyes were wild. "I blacked out. When I woke up, I was here. Where are we?" The words tumbled out of her mouth in breathless abandon.

"It doesn't matter, Is." He turned her around to make sure everything was intact. "Are you sure you're all right?"

"No," she whined and buried herself in his arms again. "I heard you shouting and running, but I couldn't find you. Then I heard your jeep and tried to find the door, but it was too late. The police pulled in right after you left, so I hid.

They locked the door, Kee. They locked me inside. I've been scared shitless."

She pressed her trembling body tight against his chest and cried.

"You have to get out of here," he said into her ear. "It isn't safe. I'll get the kitchen door open then you need to go."

That elicited an abrupt stop to the tears and Isabella looked up at him. She pulled herself out of his arms and with an effort, got her emotions in check with a sniff and a shake of her arms.

"I'm not going anywhere until you tell me what the hell is going on. Why are we here? This is crazy."

It is crazy. A rush of fatigue ran through Keenan's body. *What was he going to tell her? What would she believe? Hell, what did he believe at that moment?* The questions were only gathering momentum.

He took her hand and squeezed it. "Listen, I don't have time to explain everything, but I will, I promise. There's something I have to do here, something important. I need you to trust me right now. You have to leave and I mean in a hurry. Sorry, Is."

Without waiting for her to respond, he pulled her into his arms, gave her a good stout kiss, and dragged her toward the kitchen. Isabella planted her feet firmly against the ground. She was a lot stronger than Keenan had anticipated.

"I'm not going anywhere without you," she said, getting her wrist from his hand and taking a step back. The words seemed to take her back a bit; she folded her arms and rubbed her shoulders. "I mean, I'm not going anywhere until I know what's going on. I've spent the last hour in this horrible place. You better start talking, mister. You said there wouldn't be any secrets, so start talking, stud." Isabella plopped down on the ground and glared up at him.

Keenan rubbed his eyes and glanced at the small chapel at the end of the nave. It was absolutely quiet in the church, and he couldn't see any light coming from under either of the closed doors. That startled him a bit. Again, without the ghosts around that lonely feeling gathered around his shoulders and sent a shiver down his back.

Joining Isabella on the ground, he stood the flashlight on its end between them. When he searched her eyes, he thought he saw something he hadn't seen in a very long time. For a split second, the love was unmistakable.

She lowered her chin in a quick movement.

Keenan was confused; they had only met two weeks ago, only gone out that morning. Sure he had a deep case of the lusts for her and, if he was honest with himself, there was something beyond that, something that had shocked him the first time he saw her. But this was different. In the instant glance, he read something much deeper in her eyes. What amazed him was he was sure his heart was echoing the sentiment with the same intensity. In that split second he was almost certain he loved her, too. It knocked the wind out of him.

"Why did you come to my house?" he asked her softly, for some reason knowing it wasn't to apologize.

When Isabella looked up there were tears in her eyes. She put her hand on his cheek and brushed it with her thumb.

"Hell if I know. Ever since I met you, I can't get you out of my head. I can't stop thinking about you, about being with you, about spending every minute..." The words stopped abruptly, and she yanked her hand away from his face. Even in the soft glow of the flashlight, the blush on her face was bright. "You're going to think *I'm* nuts."

Keenan nodded and touched her chin to lift her face so he could see her eyes. "Go on," he whispered.

"Well..." She rolled her eyes and shook her head against his hand, but then tightened her lips to muster some courage. "Keenan, I think...I might be in love with you." She curled the side of her mouth. "Sorry."

In response, Keenan wrapped his hand around the back of her neck and pulled her close to kiss her.

The touch of her lips against his sent bells off in his head. Whistles blew like fire engines. The world swirled around inside his skull like a carnival ride. His heart turned into a bagpipe and swelled with an emotion he had never known. The contentment expanded into his body, filling every nook and cranny with hope and a deep masculine desire to shield the woman in his arms and protect her from the vagaries of existence. The flashlight fell over when he pulled her into his arms to make her melt into his body. Voids filled in his life in an instant; holes he didn't even know existed overflowed. It was as if a missing piece of his life had been shoved into his hands.

The kiss lingered for an eternity and Keenan let it. For a long time, that soft mouth was the only thing in his universe.

When he couldn't breathe anymore, he pulled away from her face and buried it in her hair. The tangy scent helped him to focus. Keenan couldn't find words to say to her.

"I'm assuming that means you feel the same," she said breathlessly in his ear.

He pulled away, took her face in both hands, and kissed her again. "Yes," was all he could manage for the moment.

"Well…good," she said.

Isabella began to laugh and Keenan couldn't help joining her. The sound floated up from the two of them clasped in each other's arms, reverberating against the walls of the church and the rafters above their heads. It came back to them in a chorus of hilarity, filling Keenan's ears.

When the laughter subsided, Isabella smoothed his eyebrows with a dirty thumb. The gesture was so familiar it startled Keenan.

"Come with me, Keenan. There isn't anything here for you, do you understand? It's just an empty church. I'm real, I'm flesh, warm, a real living human being who loves you, who's always loved you. I know there's something you feel you have to do, but you don't. All you have to do is come with me now. Let's get out of here. Ok?"

Keenan watched her dark irises dilate softly. His outline in them was a silhouette illuminated by a beam of light and a deep desire. He touched her lips with his thumbs and pressed his mouth to each of her eyelids. The tears were salty against his lips when he licked them afterwards. There was nothing more important than Isabella. Almost nothing. He pulled her against his chest once more and whispered into her ear, "Ok."

Keenan grabbed the flashlight, Isabella's hand, and headed toward the kitchen without a backward glance.

When they got to the door, Keenan tried it, but the chain securing it was too tight. Even when he tried to kick it, the only thing it did was hurt his foot.

He ran the flashlight around the room until he caught sight of something just above his head to the right; a plain panel painted over to make it look like the walls in the kitchen. On a hunch, he tested the shaky counter and hauled himself on top to check it out.

The painted over glass must have been hidden from the outside by the ladder. With a quick flick of the back of the flashlight, it shattered outward and left an opening about girl size. He cleaned out the rest of the glass with the metal tube and peered through. The fire escape ladder was right in front of it.

"Give me your hand," he said reaching for Isabella.

The face staring at him didn't look too confident, but she let him help her stand on the counter. It teetered for a second, sending her into his arms again, much to his delight, but then stopped. He stomped down twice to make sure it was secure.

Maneuvering around him, Isabella peered out the window into the night.

"I think I can squeeze through here all right, but what about you?" she said testing the sides of the window.

"I think so. Let me lift you up."

He put the flashlight on the small window ledge and grabbed Isabella around the waist to lift her through the window. When her legs were out, she flipped onto her butt and Keenan could see that her legs reached the ladder without a problem. Gaining a purchase, she had her feet on one of the rungs and pulled herself out the rest of the way, holding tight to the rung just above her head.

"Come on," she said, holding out her hand to him. "I'll pull you out and guide your feet to the ladder."

Keenan moved his hand through the window and grabbed a lever he had seen earlier. Isabella scowled at him.

"I'm sorry," he said, grabbing the handle firmly. "You've got to get out of here. I'm not going to lose you, Isabella. Go to my house. Stay there. I'll see you later."

The last words were a little more ominous than he intended, but without hesitating, he pulled the lever down. The ladder, with Isabella holding firmly to it slid to the ground under the kitchen window and locked into place on the ground. The security cage surrounding it fell with it, blocking the window entirely with crossed bars. There was no way for her to get back in.

"What the hell are you doing? Are you crazy? You'll never get out!" she cried up to him. "I'm calling the police!"

"Listen to me," he pleaded, shining the light down on her. "There is something I have to do and, like I said, you have to trust me. Please." He put as much of his heart into that one word as he had ever into another. "Go to my house and stay there." He dug his keys out of his pocket and struggled to get the house key off the ring, then threw it to her. "If I'm not back by sunrise, call the southeast precinct. Ask for a Sergeant named Thompson. I love you, Isabella. Please trust me."

The expression on her face was a comic twisting of joy and frustration. Her mouth moved, but no words came out. Instead, she bit down on her lip and balled her fists at him. With a huff that could have very well contained a disdainful *men!* in it, she turned toward the parking lot and stomped off.

Keenan jumped down from the counter and sunk to the floor to bury his face in his hands.

He had never regretted anything more than leaving Isabella. She was what he had wanted all his life, what he had dreamed of as long as he could remember. More than solitude from the throng of the ever-present entities; more than comfort, satisfaction, or even peace; more than fame, fortune, or any other wisps of glory most men craved.

Isabella was his holy grail, his Mecca, his religion. He knew it down to the sinews of his soul. And he had left her behind.

His heart was screaming at him for being such an idiot, his head was lecturing him soundly about the odds of getting out of this alive, and his body was whining that it had had more than enough for one night, thank you very much.

But in the end, it was his devotion that silenced them all. Courage may make him a fool tonight, but he was going to give it that chance.

Standing up from that floor and heading for the chapel was the bravest thing Keenan Swanson had ever done.

Chapter Eighteen

The Devil in Mr. Swanson

Keenan stood in the center of the chapel. The environment had changed dramatically from a few hours before. There weren't any candles. The rugs had disintegrated in so many places all they consisted of were ragged tatters of reds and blues. High over his head, the stained glass windows he had thought were so beautiful were blackened and invisible; the chandelier was a web of hanging wires and dusty bolts. The room was as wrecked and broken as the rest of the church.

There was no alter, no shining bubble of ghostly friends, no storm cloud of Amos. All that remained was the musty smell of age and an even deeper void in his heart. They were all gone.

Even his voice sounded empty. "Hello?" It thumped against the darkness without even an echo to keep it company.

He had sent Isabella away and probably ruined his chances with her forever for nothing.

Flicking Thompson's flashlight over the room, something white caught his eye against a far wall. He walked as light-footed as possible so he didn't stir up too much dust. Sitting in one corner of the room was a pair of white gloves and above them a gleaming pair of unattached eyes. The rest of him materialized in slow motion.

"Reggie," Keenan whispered.

The apparition pulled out of the corner and floated toward Keenan. He took several steps back, not knowing what the demon would do to him.

Reggie seemed essentially the same; smart clothes, dapper mustache, swarthy irreverent sneer on his face, but his body had solidified—it looked almost living now—and his eyes had changed color. They were a deep black without iris or pupil, with no more emotion in them than a shark. The effect was profound; it scared the shit out of Keenan.

"Hello, old fellow."

It was probably Keenan's imagination, but Reggie's voice seemed a bit more sinister. Searching to see how close the door was, Keenan took another step back.

"I suppose the game is up, isn't it?" Reggie stopped and a long cigarette appeared in his fingers. He juggled it between them and popped it into his mouth. Clicking his thumb and forefinger, a flame shot out from one and he touched it to the end of the cigarette, and then blew it out. Keenan had seen him do this a thousand times before, but this time he could smell the smoke, could feel it brush softly against his face. This was no ghost. He took another step back.

"Don't be frightened of me, old friend." Reggie picked a piece of tobacco from his lip and flicked it out into the darkness. "I'm still the same old Reggie."

Keenan ran his flashlight around the room to try to buy some time. He had no idea what he was going to say to Reggie, if anything. His first inclination, and a very good one he thought, was to turn tail and run. Something inside that stupid new courage was keeping him from it.

"It is a bit dark in here." Reggie's smile only made the strange eyes more frightening when Keenan glanced at him. "How about some illumination?"

The room started to take on an odd golden glow that crept up from the floor and didn't look like it had any real source. The glow did nothing for the chapel's condition except lighten its decay. Without thinking, Keenan turned off the flashlight and put it back in his coat pocket.

He watched his friend. The ghost (er, demon Keenan guessed now) pulled the cigarette from his lips and threw it to the ground. Stamping it out with a dusty boot, Reggie folded his arms and searched their surroundings, clicking his tongue and shaking his head.

"This won't do. It just won't do at all." He winked at Keenan. "Needs a bit of cleaning up, what? I can do much better than this."

Reggie snapped his fingers again and a flow of rejuvenation started from the back wall that moved in a matter of seconds to the front. What was left was a new room Keenan didn't recognize.

Along every wall were now cases stuffed with old books, ancient artifacts, and international trinkets. It looked like a room from the Smithsonian.

Reggie stood behind a huge dark desk, probably teak or some other expensive wood. There was a red tucked leather chair behind him and another just in front of Keenan. Old, yet very well maintained lamps sent soft light up the walls, making it warm and comfortable. On the desk, beyond the normal office accoutrements, was a large cut crystal decanter containing some ruddy brown liquor and two crystal brandy snifters. Reggie had a pipe instead of a cigarette, and the brocade smoking jacket he had on looked very expensive.

When Keenan turned around to search the room, there were no doors or windows. He was trapped inside with Reggie.

"Please." Reggie pointed the stem of his pipe toward the opposite chair and sank down into the one behind the desk. Satisfaction melted down his face as he flexed his neck against the leather and adjusted his butt into the seat.

Reluctantly, Keenan sat down in the other chair. The leather was worn and as soft as a kitten, but he ignored the comfort.

"This was my office some years ago," Reggie began, picking up a golden tool to clean out his pipe. "Of course, it's all just an illusion, you understand. I thought you might be more comfortable here for our little—chat."

"Where are they?" Keenan's voice sounded a lot braver than he actually felt inside. Those eyes were creeping him out and he had to swallow hard to get over it. *Steady, boy.*

"Safe," was all Reggie said as he repacked the wooden bowl.

"What do you want, Reggie? I came back to get on with this."

Reggie puffed on his pipe to get it going and let the smoke fill the void above his head. Keenan had expected it to smell like tobacco, but when it reached his nostrils he almost gagged; it smelled more like burning flesh.

"Anxious, aren't we?" A soft gleam flashed in one of those animal eyes. "I suppose Amos told you who I was."

Keenan moved his chin slightly. "Not really. Some kind of demon, right?"

"Balls!" Reggie snorted and put the pipe down. "Give an angel a little leeway and all they can come up with is *some kind of demon.* I, sir, am the father of all incubi." He picked the pipe back up. "Azazel," he finished with an air of self-importance.

Keenan was unimpressed and said, "So I've heard."

That took something out of Reggie's prowess and he twisted his lip. "Obviously, you don't know what that means or you'd show a bit more respect."

Keenan grabbed his crotch and squeezed it. "Yeah—respect this."

The pain came out of nowhere. It was like someone had thrown a spear through his gut and given it a good twist. Keenan doubled over in the chair and couldn't breathe or even move for several pounding heartbeats. The pain stopped in a flash, not even leaving a memory.

When he sat up, he glared into an arrogant sneer on his ghostly friend's face. It was obvious Reggie could read the fear in Keenan's eyes because he started to laugh.

"God, that was rich. You, actually growing a set of balls. Never thought I'd see it, old corker. But really, it's a bit late in the game to get all heroic on me. Are you ready to listen or do you want to pound your chest at me again?"

Keenan sat back in the chair and gripped the arms until he could feel his knuckles go numb, but he didn't say a word.

Reggie took another puff on the pipe. "I know you think I'm all evil incarnate, my lad—and honestly, I think that's very sweet—but you really need to get the whole picture here." It was hard to tell from those soulless eyes, but Keenan thought he saw a fleeting urgency when Reggie asked, "What did Amos tell you?"

"Ask *him.*"

"I did. He wasn't very cooperative and I didn't have much time to, um, persuade him. So I'm asking you."

Keenan lifted his chin in an act of defiance and replied rather nonchalantly, "Suck my dick."

Reggie sighed and clicked his tongue.

Another wave of agony twisted Keenan in his chair, this time burning a hole in his chest. He screamed, but the sound came out muffled. When the pain subsided, the memory was much clearer. Keenan knew this would only get worse.

"That really is getting to be tiresome, old boot." Reggie stood up from the chair and poured some liquid from the decanter into one of the goblets. "I *could* torture you all night—if you were anyone else, that prospect would hold a certain charm for me—but I'm not fond of torturing my friends." He came around the desk and thrust the glass into Keenan's hands. "Will you at least give me the opportunity to explain my position before you start believing whatever nonsense has been crammed into that monkey brain of yours? Not everything is as it appears. Angels are not always the...angelic characters you would imagine. Nor are demons as evil as all that." He turned to the desk and filled the second glass. Taking a sip, he sat on the edge and stared off into space for a moment.

The aroma of the liquid coming up from Keenan's drink was doing something to him. As soon as it reached his nose, he had a powerful compulsion to drink it—all of it. Without thinking, he lifted the glass to his lips and tipped it up to spill the contents into his mouth.

The warm nutty liquid was like an organism inside his mouth. It instantly sent tendrils of pleasure through his face, neck, and chest. Nothing had ever tasted so good. The heat got into his blood and coursed through him with each beat of his heart. When it was distributed everywhere, it was as if his senses had exploded.

Reggie pursed his lips and blew a simple breath in Keenan's face.

When the wind hit Keenan's skin, it was a paradise breeze, filled with sandy beaches, palm trees, and the breasts of hundreds of beauties. The currents rippled against his cheeks like a rainstorm. The sound burned against his eardrums, humming a deep music that flamed directly into his soul. The sweetness of the liquor on his lips made him want to suckle the glass and lick away the sticky remains. Keenan had never experienced such rapture.

"From my personal stock," Reggie said. "Another?"

"Fuck, yes," Keenan heard himself say.

When Reggie poured, the room seemed to be crisper in Keenan's eyes, as if someone had turned up the contrast on a giant TV. The sound of the gurgling liquid mingled with his breathing and even (he thought) the rustle of the ancient volumes rotting on their shelves. He could read titles of books that were dozens of feet away, even the small imprints on the bottom of the spine. Details on an ornate Indian brass elephant were crystal, the intricate decorations as clear as day, though the animal couldn't have been more than two inches high.

"What did you do to me?"

Reggie finished pouring and handed the glass to Keenan. "This? A trifle. You'd be amazed by what other delights I have at my fingertips."

Keenan slammed the glass on the desk and got up from the chair. Pacing, he tried to shake the effects of the drink before they went too far, but it was useless. The waves of pleasure coursing through his body were relaxing every muscle, opening every inhibition like a drunken whore. In the part of his mind that he still controlled, he fought the intoxication, but knew he was losing the battle. Despite his best efforts, he was starting to feel absolutely wonderful.

Finally surrendering, he stopped in his tracks and turned his face to Reggie. The relaxed grin on his face seemed more natural than breathing to him now.

"Better," Reggie said and lifted Keenan's glass from the desk. He crossed to his friend and placed it back in his hand. "Go ahead. I think you deserve a bit of a break from all the turmoil."

Keenan looked down into the glass, fighting the urge to devour it, and nodded. "You're trying to seduce me."

Reggie's laughter filled the room and Keenan was beginning to think this demon wasn't so bad after all. "Seduce you? Hell, if I had wanted to do that you would have lost your cherry to me in college. I admit, you were an alluring piece of ass when you were younger and it was tempting," he added with a wink. "No, my friend. I only want you to relax a bit…we need to talk."

The liquor was dampening Keenan inhibitions, but he wasn't drunk. It reminded him of taking speed when he was in high school. He sat back in his chair and sipped at the second glass of spirits and Reggie took his seat.

Stapling his fingers against the desk, Reggie lifted those black eyes to Keenan and his face turned serious. "We've been friends a long time, Keenan."

"Yeah, about ten years."

One side of Reggie's brow went up. "Well, actually a bit longer than that, but we'll talk about that later. I'm certain Amos filled your ears with all sorts of stories about me, yes?"

"Sure." Keenan found himself fascinated by Reggie's face.

"Told you that I was, for lack of a better phrase, the 'bad guy'?"

"Uh huh."

"Well, I'm not." Reggie turned his chair until Keenan could see his profile in the soft light. Sharp angles creased the demon's chin making his face almost cavernous. It was hard to look at him long. There was something moving under his skin.

"You see…" Reggie swirled the dark liquid in his glass, "…I believe in man's right to choose his own desires, goals, or destinies. That there is an overwhelming need to have some frivolous god dictate a man's future fills me with disgust. Do you follow?"

Keenan tried to fathom what he was talking about, but it eluded him. "I guess I'm not sure."

"Of course not." Reggie turned the chair and rested his chin on his fingertips. "Let me ask you a question; do you believe you control your destiny or that it is controlled by something else?"

The leather in the back of Keenan's chair was contouring to his body, making him want to drown in the opulence. "At the moment?" he replied easily, "I think you're pretty much running the show."

Reggie smiled. "Touché, mon frère. For the moment I am, but otherwise, who controls your fate?"

Keenan shrugged. "Honestly, I think I control my own."

"Spoken like a true Homo sapiens," Reggie sneered lifting his glass in salute. "From my point of view, the truth of the matter is this. Humans were given the great gift of free will. In essence, the Father told them they could make their own decisions, good or bad, right or wrong; their fate was in their own hands. This royally pissed off our friends the angels, who have no such rights. Why, you may ask."

Keenan wasn't asking, but nodded anyway.

"Imagine, if you will, being told that the new guy they just hired to be your assistant is getting more money than you, a better office, and better benefits. You are told if you complain about any of it, you're fired. So, what are you going to do? I'll tell you; you're going to create a situation where the new guy looks bad every time he enjoys even one of those benefits. You're going to create sin."

As the liquid worked its way through Keenan's brain, his heightened senses seemed to be extending into his mental processes as well. What Reggie was saying to him made sense and he was able to follow without drooling.

"So what you're saying is the angels created sin to keep man in line."

Satisfaction spread through Reggie's face like a fire. "Precisely."

Keenan shook his head and downed the last of the liquor. "I don't buy it. Men created sins, the bible, all of it for men. We've created our own sins. The angels needn't have bothered."

"Yes," Reggie replied lifting an index finger. "But who do you think whispered into the ears of those men in the beginning, started them on that long path?"

"So you're telling me that killing someone is not a sin..."

"Not at all. Humans do it every single day, many of them under acceptable circumstances, but that's not exactly what I'm saying. Putting aside for the moment that man is reborn over many lifetimes and that death really doesn't mean more than living through another hellacious childhood, most "sins" are harmless. Take sex, for example. That lovely creature you care so much about. What's her name?"

A twinge of distrust hit Keenan's windpipe. "Isabella," he said.

"Yes, Isabella. Are you saying to me that you don't want to throw that exquisite creature over a stump, hike up her knickers, and just take her, whether she wanted you to or not?"

"Of course not!"

"You say that because you've been raised to believe it. But what does your body tell you?" Reggie's tone changed, softened, twisting its way into Keenan's ears. "When your cock is hard and aching for the hot touch of those moist lips and pulsating muscles, does it give a shit about proprieties? No. All it wants is to slam home inside her body. And I've got news for you, my friend; if that hot little vixen desires you, it's what she wants too. She doesn't really give a rat's ass about pleasantries, gallantry, or overtures. All she wants is for you to rip her clothes off and take her hard in a fit of passion. If she says otherwise, she's lying."

Keenan ignored the riot starting in his pants and narrowed his eyes at Reggie. "That's horseshit, Reggie. Sure, the sex drive is pretty strong. I'll grant you that. But you're forgetting about two things: respect and love."

Reggie blew air out of his mouth in frustration and wrinkled his nose. "Respect. Highly overrated if you ask me. But if you insist on love, then what about that? What if the object of your desire is with another man? Say... me, for example. Let's pretend for a moment that I'm not an incubus and just another Joe Schmoe like you. What if this Isabella had been with me?"

Keenan shrugged, still trying to figure out what Reggie was trying to get at. "Then I back off and hope things will work out later."

A glow gleamed in the demon's eyes and he licked his lips. "What if you didn't have to?"

"What do you mean?"

"What if there were no such rule? What if you and I could come to some arrangement? An understanding where we both could have her at the same time, with her permission, of course?"

The thought of an Isabella sandwiched between him and Reggie sent an unexpected pang of lust through his loins. The intensity of the picture amplified by the drink made Keenan squirm in his chair and Reggie's smile deepen.

"You see?" he continued without losing a beat. "There are many, many pleasures that you humans deny yourselves in the name of sin and retribution. My point is there is no retribution, only fantasies and legends created by jealous angels to punish human spirits because they got a better deal."

"You're talking chaos. There have to be rules; without them, the world would succumb to anarchy."

"And what's wrong with anarchy? It is the true nature of things, isn't it? Do lions have governments, religion... sin? Consider a moment. Wouldn't Homo sapiens be better without all these rules that suppress their creativity, their desires? Survival of the strong, the best, the wise. Do you honestly think for a moment that you are better off the way you are?" Reggie got up from his chair and put his hands behind his back, circling around the desk and then stopping to speak in Keenan's ear. "What if you could do whatever you wished, whenever you wished? What would you do?"

"Me?" The voice in his ear was starting to make too much sense.

"You. If you could do whatever you wanted without consequence?"

Keenan had to think about that one. Quit his job? Paint all day? Sleep for a week without ghostly intervention?

"Deeper." That voice was creeping into his cerebellum, wrapping around Keenan's pleasure receptors, and turning up the volume. "What are your desires? Where do your fantasies take you in the darkest part of the night?"

"Isabella," Keenan heard himself whisper.

"Yes," hissed in his ear. "Isabella, yes. But more…aren't there more desires buried inside you. Mind you, I have seen your dreams. What about two or even three women like Isabella to service you? Imagine it. Open your mind to the possibilities."

Keenan couldn't stop the pictures opening up as three women caressed and sucked every inch of his body, kissed and licked each other for his enjoyment, and then descended on his cock in pairs with their hot mouths and soaking pussies. He saw himself taking turns with each one in every orifice, sharing them with his friends as he watched them squirm, and making them lick each other's pussies.

"There is more." Reggie's voice was a salve against his resistance. "Money enough to buy every luxury, delicacies forbidden everywhere else, your enemies groveling at your feet, begging forgiveness. Think of it; you can live the way you wish without consequence. You can choose to skip bathing if you want to, punch out that guy that cuts you off on the freeway, take the neighbor's Ferrari, or his wife, if you wish, and use them any way you want. The world is yours and no one can take it away from you."

Keenan saw himself as a famous painter, rich beyond his dreams, in a mansion where the weather never turned cold. Servants waited on him, gave him everything he called for, did whatever you asked them to do. People worshipped his talent, his genius. He could do no wrong.

Reggie's words blended with the images in seamless perfection. "You see, my friend, there is no such thing as sin. There is only living the way you want without consequences, without fear of losing anything, without apologizing for wanting something you deserve. Take it, Keenan, live it the way you wish. I can make it all happen for you. All you have to do is trust me."

All you have to do is trust me...

There was something about those words that collapsed the images dancing through Keenan's head like old paint crushed in his hand. He had heard them before. That voice had whispered those same words—had convinced him to abandon something. Something important. Something special. The demon's voice smacked against an ancient memory inside him. It was so deeply buried, so old and far away, he couldn't dredge it up, but it was there.

The heat in his blood flushed cold through his veins like ice water on a spitting radiator.

Keenan jumped from the chair and stumbled across the room, crawling away from the black-eyed demon as fast as he hands and feet could carry him.

When he had gone as far as he could, he glared back at Reggie and his body quaked. Keenan was terrified down to the laces in his sneakers; he had come so close to succumbing that a few more seconds would have been all Reggie needed.

"Fuck you!"

Reggie shrugged, got an amused smirk to dance across his lips, and picked up his pipe. "Oh, well. I had to try. It's what I do."

The drink began to wear off, leaving a bad taste in Keenan's mouth. Reggie stood to one side of the room tilting his head at him as if summing up his expectations.

Keenan had enough. It was time for him to take a stand. So that's what he did, stood up. An old fatigue rippled through his muscles when he took stock of his position.

Reggie wanted his body. Amos told him he had to give it to him. Keenan hadn't been able to talk to Constance, which bothered him. And he prayed to God that he would find Isabella at his house after this was all done. That stopped him. So, what form would he be entering his house then? Ghost? Human? Angel? Demon? Hard to say, and the effort to sort it all out was making his left eye twitch. The only thing he could rely on right now was his instinct. That thought deepened his depression.

"I think I'm entitled to a few answers," he snarled at Reggie, running a hand through his hair and then rubbing a sore shoulder. "Explain why it is you're so hell bent on having a body. Trust me; they're not all they're cracked up to be."

"Granted," Reggie said, toying with a trinket on the table next to him. "But then, I have to have one to accomplish my goal."

"Which is?"

A little light flicked in his black eyes. "Patience, mon frère. Please, have a seat and I will alleviate all your curiosities."

"I doubt that." Keenan made his way back to the chair and sunk into the soft cushions. He closed his eyes and let his muscles settle into the leather.

"Do you remember when I told you in college that one day you would be great?"

"I remember you used to get me drunk, fill my ear with a lot of nonsense about running the world, and then get me to streak the football game."

The memory sent a bemused smiled across Reggie's face. "Ah, yes. I had forgotten that. But it doesn't change the fact that what I told you was true. You are about to become the father of the greatest creature ever born. And it's all thanks to me."

"Thanks." Keenan made it as dry as bone. "The way I see it, it won't be me at all, but you. Do I have that about right?"

"Well, yes, at this point you're just the sperm donor. But it doesn't have to be that way." The sly words followed him back to his chair as he sat down. Keenan was instantly alert.

"What doesn't have to be that way?"

"The sacrifice. I don't need you to die to inhabit your body. I just need you to—move over a bit. The human body is pretty large real estate. We could share the responsibilities and the perks."

Keenan nodded and sat up to put his elbows on his knees. "I get it. You move in with me—like roommates?"

"Precisely. Of course, you'll have to make a few concessions. But I think we could work out things quite nicely." He rubbed his hands above the desk and leveled those bleak eyes at Keenan. "I like you, Keenan, I always have. You have what we call in the vernacular a pure soul. A fellow who is untainted by lifetime after lifetime of degradation. Somewhere in your distant past, someone granted you a boon...a life without sin, if you will. Add your psychic abilities, your talent, your...physical gifts, and presto, chango, you've got one hell of a package. Because of that, I would prefer to do this with you intact. You bring so much to the table." He picked up his glass, sat back, and swirled the contents slowly. "It would be a pity to leave that behind. I'm giving you an incomparable gift here, son. If you agree, I promise your life will definitely take a turn for the better. Our son is brewing right now. All you have to do is help me raise him."

Keenan's brain was having some problems adjusting to the fact that he was a father. "Who's the girl—uh, the mother?"

Reggie shrugged, downed the last of the drink, and set the snifter down. "A witch, actually, although she doesn't know *that* yet. She'll find out soon enough. Right here in Portland, not far from here. Adorable little creature, though a bit dark for my tastes. She squealed like a chipmunk when I delivered... the bundle. A virgin, if you're interested."

Keenan gave him a look of disgust, folded his arms, and came to the only decision he could. "No thanks. I'm not interested in any of it, Reggie. You can take your proposition and shove it up your ass."

Reggie pulled a long sigh into his lungs and pushed himself away from the desk. "Very well."

In a swirl of color, the ceiling sucked the room away, taking the illusion and the light with it.

Chapter Nineteen

A Ghost of a Chance

When Keenan turned eighteen, his mother kicked him out with a hundred bucks and the clothes on his back. He had bought the clothes but assumed the hundred bucks was a lame effort to absolve eighteen years of guilt. Walking out the door, he didn't even turn back to look at her.

He had left lots of people in his life, simply walked away from them with promises he knew he'd never keep. Life got in the way, failed goals clogged up his ambition, and even those people he actually loved fell behind, his own guilt a roadblock to his re-acquaintance. His good friend Sally, a girl named Giana he left at the chapel steps in Florence, and a parade of caring people he had abandoned marched across his memory when the room changed.

Keenan suddenly found himself standing in the middle of the chapel again, the smell of reality musty in his nose.

Reggie appeared inside a yellow glow that settled down in front of Keenan. Behind him was Constance, who was wringing her hands and shaking her head so hard the curlers clicked. The worry lines were a roadmap on her face.

"Honey, are you all right?" She tried to take a step toward him, but Reggie threw up his arms and she stopped.

"What's she doing here?" Keenan demanded.

He was worried. Reggie knew how he felt about Constance. Just another way to get him to cooperate, he guessed, but he wished Reggie had chosen someone else. The only reason he was even considering this was largely because of Constance. The thought of this remarkable being writhing in hell would keep him up nights. He didn't want to walk away from her too.

"I need someone to help you...loose this mortal coil. Constance can do it without damaging the integrity of my new home."

Reggie moved toward Keenan and put a hand on either side of his head. "But first I need to do a bit of preparation. We don't want you dying of shock, now do we? That would be unacceptable."

In a sudden rush, Keenan's brain began to fill with a kind of energy. It was as if Reggie were giving him some super vitamin injection. Every ache or pain went away instantly; his mind cleared for the first time in days; there was a kind of vitality that seeped into his awareness. He had never felt so strong.

In that short exchange, however, something else shot into Keenan's conscience. It was strange, foreign, and when Keenan realized what it was, the violation left him cold. Reggie had planted some kind of seed inside him. It sat in him like a malignant cancer, beginning to unfurl at the edges. He wasn't alone in there anymore and the thought scared the bejesus out of him.

He pushed his eyes open and Reggie's satisfied grin greeted him.

"What a rush, huh?"

"Reggie, don't do this," Constance pleaded, frantically looking from one to the other. "You don't need to do this to him. Let him go. You can guide the baby just the way you are; you don't need to be human to do that."

"Shut up, Constance! She betrayed me, left me to rot in Italy. This is payment for her disloyalty. Dabria will suffer for every moment I was without her."

Reggie pulled an invisible string that propelled Constance forward. When she stood a few inches from Keenan, she tried to take a step back.

"I won't do it," she whispered.

When Reggie came up behind her, she crossed her arms and shivered.

"You will do it or the others go down right now."

With a click of his fingers, the ghosts appeared all around them, like a crowd in an arena. They were a frozen mass of ectoplasm.

Keenan searched the ranks and saw hundreds of familiar faces. It was odd. For the last twenty years he had wanted nothing more than to rid himself of these pesky poltergeists, had counted the days when he might have a moment's peace, had fantasized about being alone, if only for a minute. But now, as he considered each entity, his heart parked itself in a moment of pathos. These people had been his friends, his entertainment, his life for so long, he couldn't imagine his world without them. The thought of losing them was crushing.

The seed inside him shifted and a horrible thought came to him. He glared past Constance at Reggie and tightened his lips. Reggie's black soul was starting to come into focus.

"What happens to them when you've got what you want?"

There was the slightest flick of Reggie's chin and a ghost of a smile dusted his lips. "Nothing, of course."

The revelation hit Keenan between the eyes, but he had no idea where it was coming from. Reggie was lying, had been from the very beginning. Keenan took a step back and his mouth opened, but nothing came out. Reggie had no intention of letting any of them go. He wanted the world to himself—no witnesses. The thoughts bombarded Keenan's brain until he couldn't breathe.

In a rush of movement that amazed even Keenan, he jumped back, grabbed the gun out of his belt, and pointed it at Reggie.

"Let her go!" he demanded.

Those shark eyes glistened for only a moment. "What are you going to do, old bean? Shoot me?"

"No," he whispered.

Keenan did something then that would never have occurred to him in a million years. He pointed the gun at his own head.

Reggie stopped dead. The dark eyes sized up Keenan's courage in a glance. He allowed a relaxed grin to settle over his face and leaned against one leg. "You're bluffing," he stated as if he knew Keenan's every thought.

It was obvious he didn't. Keenan had never even contemplated suicide, let alone attempted it, and yet here he was. There was a certain kind of logic in what he was doing. Calm waves of ease took the shake out of his arms and stilled the hand holding the gun. He knew with absolute certainty that he could pull the trigger. The idea was freeing somehow.

"Don't bet on it," he answered quietly. "Let them go. All of them. Amos and Dabria, too. You do that, and I'll give you this body without a giant hole through the brain. Otherwise, you get it with air conditioning." A deep laugh came up from the bottom of Keenan's lungs when the irony became clear to him. "I'd love to see you start all over again, Reggie, so don't fuck with me."

Reggie searched Keenan's face a long time before answering. "Suicide is a one-way trip to hell, son. Do not pass go, do not collect two hundred dollars."

"Do you honestly think I care? No, Reg. You miscalculated. You called me a pure soul. Fact of the matter is I'm not *that* pure. I just don't like being fucked with. Let—them—go."

Reggie tossed his head back and finally threw up his hands.

"Fine!"

With a clap, the suspended ghosts became a whirling mass of energy again. The noise from their combined voices was deafening. But they did not move. Instead, they gathered around Keenan and hung suspended high above him, hiding behind arched beams and dark corners. Reggie eyed them suspiciously, but then shrugged and turned his attention to Keenan.

"Better?" Reggie asked.

Constance still stood between them, a huddled figure of clanking curlers and drab blue robe.

"Her, too," Keenan said.

"Come now. I think you understand that I need a way to dispatch you without harming the body. That will take a ghost. There is some kind of ironic justice in having it done by my fat little bundle of optimism here."

"It's all right, honey," Constance said sneering at Reggie and squaring her shoulders. "I'd rather do it so it won't hurt so much. I think I know what he's got in mind."

Keenan pushed the gun into his temple. "Where are they, Reggie?"

"I don't know who you are talking about?"

"Cut the crap! Dabria and Amos. Where are they?"

A slow grin spread over Reggie's face. "They're here," he said slowly. With a wave of his hand, Amos materialized as the entity behind him solid in his cloudy mass. "Dabria will be along soon. I'm not about to let go of my prizes until I know for sure you'll keep your end of the bargain. I don't know how I can assure you since I'm certain you won't take my word on it."

"Nope."

"Then how about this? You put down the gun and behave yourself and I won't mess up your pretty little girlfriend over there."

From out of a shadow at the end of the room, a golden light flared suddenly. There in the light, completely still, stood Isabella. Her face was soft, asleep, but in one hand she held the house key Keenan had just given to her.

"You son of a bitch!" Keenan rushed to her. When he reached her, she collapsed into him, warm and soft in his arms. He tried shaking her, but she was out cold.

"And just in case you doubt my sincerity…" Reggie wrinkled his nose and snorted a laugh. Isabella stopped breathing.

"No, no, no," Keenan whispered trying to shake her again and watching her lips turn blue. He laid her down and tried to get her mouth open for mouth to mouth, but she was as stiff as if rigor mortis had set in. Even when he pressed against her chest, it was like trying to revive a statue. He gritted his teeth and barked at Reggie, "Stop it!"

"Temper, temper. Do I have your attention now?"

"Yes," Keenan hissed wildly. "Let her go…"

Reggie put a finger to his ear. "And the magic word is…?"

Keenan clamped her against his pounding heart. "Please."

Isabella immediately softened in his arms. Her breath and heart went back to normal, and, with an effort, Keenan slowed his own. Gently setting her on the floor of the old chapel, he rose and crossed to the demon. There was nothing more he could do.

If he killed himself, he'd go to hell and Reggie would just start over again with another poor schmuck and destroy his friends in the process. If he allowed Reggie to take his body, then he would probably take up with Isabella, find the woman who was carrying Keenan's kid and take the child away from her, then raise it to be…what? Probably the anti-Christ's second cousin, for all Keenan knew. If he ran, there would be no place to go. They all knew where he lived. The piece of Reggie churning inside him settled in for the duration. He had to trust what Amos had told him, but it didn't come easily.

Keenan lifted his eyes to Constance, where he always went in a crisis. "What do I do?"

That profound dark face thawed into an expression that touched his heart. There was a moment when he saw not a ghost, but a human smiling back at him. "You trust in yourself and have faith in the future." The words were so quiet, he was sure only he had heard them. She put a hand next to his head and smiled. "I've always been with you. I'm not going anywhere now."

"Good boy." The satisfaction in Reggie's voice scraped against Keenan's anger, but he clamped his teeth down instead of speaking. "Now, drop the gun, turn around, and spread your arms and legs. We'll do the rest. You're sure you won't join me?" The words were now inside Keenan's head.

"Fuck off, Reggie."

"Too bad. It would have been fun."

Keenan spun around and threw the gun as hard as he could across the room where it hit one of the doors and clattered to the ground. He was half hoping the damned thing would go off and put a bullet into his brainpan. No such luck.

A voice filled the air at the back of Keenan's head and the next words took the breath out of his lungs.

"Before he dies, Reggie, you have to tell him the truth," Constance said.

"What?" Keenan asked.

Reggie folded his arms. "If he hasn't figured it out already, what's the point?"

"He has the right to know why you're doing this."

For some reason goose bumps rose on Keenan's arms. "Why *are* you doing this?" he asked Reggie.

The expression that came back to Keenan chilled him to the bone. "*She* knows."

When he nodded behind Keenan, he was almost too terrified to look, but he twisted his neck anyway.

Isabella stood in the middle of the chapel, her hair flying loosely around her, her arms outstretched. When she lifted her eyes to Keenan, her face was wet with tears.

A mirage of light danced around her, until he had to squint in the brilliance.

When the light faded, the succubus stood before him, her face now fully exposed. Keenan's heart caught in his chest.

"Isabella?"

He took a step away from her. Shock sent waves of numb up his legs, into his ass, and along his spine. He couldn't believe what he was seeing.

Those eyes. The opalescent eyes he had glimpsed in the darkness two nights before. Why hadn't he recognized them then? Now it seemed as clear as ice.

"He is doing this to punish me for disobeying him, but I don't mind now," she whispered, lowering her arms and floating toward him. "Azazel knew I would try to save you, just as I did centuries ago." She threw a loving look in the demon's direction and Keenan's insides turn to goo. "I can't remember now why I hid from him. It was foolish of me."

Keenan tried to get the words to make sense, but failed miserably. "I don't understand. You were human." He looked at his hands and brushed his lips with his fingers. "I touched you... I kissed you... You were real."

"She was human once," Reggie said leering at Dabria. "It is one of the perks of divine forgiveness, don't you see? Humanity is one of the fringe benefits. Unfortunately," he added pursing his lips, "something I have never experienced." A laugh echoed around Keenan.

Keenan bunched his fingers into fists and confronted Dabria. "Why?"

"Don't you see, old bean?" Reggie's voice filled Keenan's brain and he couldn't shut it out. "She has been protecting you from me since the day you died in Italy."

Keenan hardened his heart against the lust in Dabria's face as the monster spoke.

"When I found you here, I lured Amos from heaven and used him to capture my sweet Muse." Reggie cast a lascivious eye in Dabria's direction. She pulled her arms across her chest and lowered her chin. *Was she actually blushing?*

Reggie whispered close to Keenan's ear, "Helping me to get your seed was a test of her loyalty, and she pounced on the opportunity like the wanton whore she is. You must understand, old corker; who do you think gave me the idea of taking your body? A kind of delicious irony, don't you think? It is in her black nature to betray those whom she seduces; or did you think she loved you?" The throaty chuckle buzzed against Keenan's eardrum. "She could no more love you than she could love a slab of beef."

Keenan could no longer keep his heart in check; it broke against his ribs and sent rushes of pain into every part of his soul. It was like someone had kicked him hard in the nuts. He went to his knees, held his stomach to keep it from escaping, and put one hand on the dusty carpet to stay erect. His world shook when an involuntary shuttering breath finally allowed oxygen into his lungs. A plaintive *No* escaped his throat, but it did not stop the words.

Dabria lifted dark eyes to him and a slow smile crept upward. Keenan lost the last glimmer of hope. "You poured into me without a fight, my sweet." Her words tightened Keenan's chest forcing hot tears from his eyes. "Men are so pliable."

"I don't believe it," Keenan whispered. "How could you have set this all up? The office, the police station…?"

Dabria languidly crossed to Reggie and allowed him to run his fingers down her neck. Keenan watched her shiver under the caress.

"Your boss owed me a favor," Reggie said. "It was easy to disguise Dabria and put her in your path. I was going to let nature take its course, but you are the damndest idiot. Every time she tried to lure you, you turned the other way. Bad luck, really. I finally had to have her seduce you the old fashioned way."

Keenan balled his fists and struggled to his feet.

"You tricked me! You bitch!"

He reached out to grab her, but she vanished and his hands fell through a strange blue smoke. An invisible rope yanked him back and Reggie's voice insinuated itself into Keenan's neck.

"Can't have you damaging my property, chum. I've worked very hard to get us all to this point. All you have to do right now is stand perfectly still. Nothing easier."

Numb with betrayal, aching with agony, confusion turning his mind to slush, Keenan spread his arms, threw his head back, and screamed at the heavens. He stared at the skeletal chandelier and waited for it to be over.

Chapter Twenty

Past Tense

Keenan's mother was never one for nurturing when he was growing up. He spent most of his time with one neighbor or the other while she worked a job or two and put in her allotted three to four hours at the bar each night. There was an array of part-time father figures in his life, even one or two who actually threw a ball to him from time to time. But, for the most part, Keenan spent his hours alone.

He had never acquired much of a taste for television; not that he didn't spend hours in front of it, mind you, but there was always a scrap of paper on his lap and a rusty can of crayons, pencil stubs, and discarded pens next to his knee. Keenan's escape had always been his art. Dragons drawn on old mimeographed school assignments, coloring book backs covered in sketched soldiers with red crayon blasts coming out of gray guns, and gnarled pirates with black conical hats, marching across old newsprint, filled hundreds of tattered Pee Chees when he was growing up.

When he turned eight, the Carlsons (an engineer, his wife, and their four sprouting daughters) moved in next door and Keenan's life took its first major U-turn.

Having used up all her favors with the rest of the neighbors, Keenan's mom approached the new ones and asked if they'd be willing to watch her "little angel" (which was funny, because that's *not* what she usually called him when they were alone). Mrs. Carlson took one look at Keenan's face, smiled, and said she'd be glad to. Keenan's mom handed him off like a loaf of bread and ran for the bus.

Keenan was introduced to two things that day: girls (who he thought were gross at the time and then changed his mind a few years later) and Mr. Carlson's art studio.

Matt Carlson was an amateur sculptor and a damned good one at that. His specialty was wildlife: dolphins, eagles, lions, whales, and just about anything else you could think of. Every evening after supper, Mr. Carlson would rescue Keenan from the clutches of his adoring daughters. The girls, if not thwarted, loved to give Keenan a nightly "makeover" or some other diabolical plan to keep them entertained through the evening. Telling the females in no uncertain terms that this was 'man's stuff,' he'd take Keenan down to his sanctuary (which was actually a ratty unfinished basement) where he'd throw him a piece of clay and tell him to get to work. Just like that. It was the inspiration of those two years with Carlson that sent Keenan to the art museum, made him study hard for four years to get his degree (on his own), and took him eventually to Florence where he studied for another two years, until his money dried up.

Mr. Carlson used to say to him, "Keenan, if you want something bad enough, you've got to work hard, get it built in your head to the last whisper, and then promise yourself you won't forget it. Otherwise, your dreams won't survive beyond your everyday."

Keenan had contemplated that statement all his years through school, living abroad, and even the first two years of struggling to be a paid fine artist when he returned to the states. But hunger changed his priorities, a need to sleep out of the rain became an ambition, and life brushed that sentiment, along with many other ideals, under the ragged rug of necessity. The memory slipped away.

For the first time in many years, Carlson's deep voice echoed just inside Keenan's ears as he closed his eyes to wait for whatever it was Reggie was going to do to him.

...get it built in your head to the last whisper...promise yourself you won't forget it...

Keenan wasn't sure why the memory decided to slam into his skull just at that moment. Here he was about to take a one-way trip to the ethereal amusement park and his head was pondering broken ambitions. *Way to go, brain!*

Whatever Reggie had fed him was beginning to expand at Keenan's center like an inflating black balloon. Keenan knew he should be scared shitless, but he wasn't. There was a kind of fidgety calm growing from that same place and he didn't feel nervous at all. More like curious.

"Put your arms out, baby." Constance's voice meandered from one ear to the other, making it sound like she was on both sides of him. "No matter what happens, just do what I tell ya, ok?"

Keenan lifted his arms out to the side and attempted a feeble shrug. "Sure thing, Cee. What are you going to do?"

There was a long silence. A cold draft brushed the hairs on his neck, making them stand at attention.

"I'm sorry, sweetie." A deep sigh rolled over him like mist. "Brace yourself; this is goin' to hurt like hell."

Cold settled into his back, his outstretched arms, and into the base of his skull. It was like pressing his back into an iceberg. With a jolt that rocked Keenan from top to bottom, needles of pain stabbed into every pore.

Entangled in the arctic freeze, Keenan's screams grew louder and louder as winter moved through him. The intense pain caused endorphins to fire one after the other, but it was no good; they sputtered out as soon as they ignited, too weak to battle the overextended neurons in his brain. The only thing keeping him conscious was the black goo now growing exponentially through his body.

"Trust me." He heard the soothing words through his screams.

Scenes from Keenan's life flicked through his mind like an old nickelodeon. A fight with a boy named James when he was seven, cleaning up vomit after one of his mom's binges, holding a breast in his hand for the first time and the girl's sweet smile, tourists buying his first painting on the streets of Florence, breakfast with Isabella. The images picked up speed, churning out emotions like toothpaste from a tube; Keenan didn't have time to experience any of them.

Suddenly, just before the cold reached his heart, his endorphins threw in the towel. In one final thrust of agony, everything stopped and Keenan shut down for good.

Chapter Twenty-One

Living in a Non-Material World

Keenan couldn't open his eyes. There were no eyes to open. But he could see... sort of. It wasn't black, exactly, just a misty dark gray that swarmed around him. He could make out shapes, but they were fuzzy too. Behind him a presence nestled against the back of his awareness, warm, comforting, like the cocoon of the succubus. The silence was absolute; no background noise, no hiss of the world inside his head. No head. No heartbeat. No blood rushing through his veins. Nothing.

He was dead.

That realization was the first concrete actuality that penetrated the smoke of his existence. He was dead. He no longer existed. He was a...

Ghost.

If he had had a body, he would have screamed his lungs out. Keenan settled for the next best thing.

The single elongated word was as clear as a diamond in his psyche.

Fuuuuuuuuuuck!

It's okay, baby.

The thought fell through his understanding like icy water on hot feet.

Constance?

I'm here. Are you all right?

Where am I? I can't see anything.

You're with me, baby. The haze will pass quickly. Do you remember what happened?

Yeah...that son of a bitch made you kill me. What the fuck is going on?

You need to be calm, Kee, or the fog won't lift. I'm going to help you.

Keenan wanted to pull away from her but didn't know how. In fact, he didn't know how to do anything. Like being born, he imagined. He kept trying to get his legs to work, his arms to flail, his head to turn, his eyes to see, but none of those things existed. Thought was the only thing he had and it just didn't have the clout he wanted. His frustration was growing by the second.

Don't do me any favors. You want to help? Then get me the hell back into my body! The next thought was plaintive. *Why, Cee? Why did you do it?*

You have to trust me, Kee. You have to have faith that what we did we did for you and your kind.

Well, that was a big fat help. He didn't want to talk to her anymore and wished he could get away, but it was useless.

All at once, that soft soothing at his back intensified into something much less comfortable. The first sensation was like an increasing pressure building up around him. But it wasn't physical. It was as if someone was squeezing his thoughts. It was the oddest feeling. The gray eddies of smoke lightened.

The first things he saw were the other ghosts. They materialized one by one from a dreary blob to their more solid forms. Solid was a good word for it; not one of them was transparent any more. They were warm, complete, like living people. Even the scary parts were gone. A crowd of friends stood around him, some throwing him a tiny wave, others laughing at his condition, and still others ignoring him completely.

Keenan had just stepped through the looking glass.

"What you are seeing is a residual image of who they were, from their point of view," Constance whispered in his ear. "Look down at yourself."

Keenan patted down his *body* and everything seemed to be intact: jeans, faded T-shirt, feet, knees, stomach, arms.

He took his imaginary hands and ran them over his imaginary face to make sure it was still imaginarily there. Seemed the same, but you never knew.

When he turned around to glare at Constance, he had to take a step back. The change was drastic. Keenan hardly recognized her. She was still heavy and black, but the similarities stopped there. A glow like liquid fire radiated around her. Her black hair fell in beautiful waves to the back of her knees. She wore all white, making her coffee skin and black eyes as dark as midnight. But it was her face that got Keenan's attention. He had never seen her majestic before and it was a little alarming.

"Constance?"

"Yeah, baby. Sorry I couldn't tell you sooner, but I didn't want *him* to know."

"You're...you're an angel."

"Yes, Keenan. I'm Amos's friend Gazardiel. I have been with you for centuries."

Keenan blinked imaginary eyelids at her. "Now wait just one flipping second," he exclaimed. "What the hell do you mean centuries? Last time I looked, I'm thirty five next December."

Constance placed her hands into her sleeves and looked Keenan squarely in the eye. "You made this sacrifice of your own free will, is that right, son?"

Keenan prepared a scathing response, but his mouth clamped tight on a single sound.

Had he made this sacrifice of his own free will? He turned away from her and watched the meandering ghosts; had any of them made choices of their own free will? Reggie's word resonated soundly against his reason: *...humans were given the great gift of free will. In essence, the Father told them they could make their own decisions, good or bad, right or wrong; their fate was in their own hands. This royally pissed off our friends the angels... So, what are you going to do? I'll tell you; you're going to create a situation where the new guy looks bad every time he enjoys even one of those benefits. You're going to create* *sin.... who do you think whispered into the ears of those men in the beginning, started them on that long path?*

The Bounce, looking profoundly sad as always, had his hands behind his back and paced in small circles; Grumpy, still muttering profanities to anyone within hearing distance, was flailing his arms; Agnes, who now just looked very old and very tired, sat on the floor with her arms wrapped around her knees and rocked. *Did any of them become part of this other existence of their own free will?* He wondered. All of the ghosts looked miserable, tired, and lonely. For a microsecond Reggie's words punctured his assurance; doubt branded a kernel of hesitation into his soul. *Were they all just puppets to gods, angels, and demons?* It was then the human condition took over and he denied it all. Ego had come to his rescue again and he let it. Despite everything, he still had choice. It was the one thing that bound his soul and kept him from blowing apart. He sighed deeply at the liberating realization.

"Yeah, I guess I did," he said to Constance, searching the crowd. "But what difference does it make? Reggie's won."

"Not by a long shot, baby. We got a real chance here, but you got to do something for me."

"Yeah? What?"

"You got to remember, Kee. It's time for you to remember it all."

"Remember what?"

"The last few centuries."

"What?"

She put her hands on his shoulders and his head began to spin. "You got to remember and real quick. Sorry, baby, but this is necessary. It'll sting a might."

The spinning got worse until colors pin wheeled around his head. It was like being inside a taffy hurricane.

He was suddenly back in Renaissance Florence. It was very real, but Keenan couldn't get his wits wrapped around it. Someone was there, in the street, a very real someone. The man didn't look like Keenan, hell, not even close. But a realization was making him sick to his stomach; that man *was* him. Certainty clanged against his eardrums as he took in the scene. Keenan was under the wheels of a carriage…deader than yesterday's entree.

Chapter Twenty-Two

Eyes Flashing Before His Life

The images were fuzzy at first. Keenan was above the scene, staring down at Luciano's body cut in half under a wooden wheel. A pool of black blood coated the cobblestones on all sides of the wagon. Dabria stood stock still in terror. Reggie was behind her, a hand on her shoulder, pulling her away. A pang of intense jealously clouded Keenan's vision. He felt so useless. There was nothing he could do.

Truth hit him square between the eyes as the swirling picked up speed. Luciano… his name had been Luciano Moretti. The details of that long ago life flooded his memory like a wild tsunami. He had been married to Dabria, had loved her… did love her more than anything else in the world. Reggie filled his ears with sweet poison centuries before. And Keenan had let him.

Keenan remembered it all now; the demon had made it sound so good…and it was good. Reginald had tempted Keenan with irresistible pleasures one after the other until his resistance melted like fragile snow. Had it not been for Dabria and her bargain with the devil…

Keenan couldn't face the fact that it was his weakness that condemned Dabria to nearly four hundred years as a slave to this bastard. Because of him, she had been damned to exist as a night creature, forced to live off the sexual desires of men. But hadn't she just betrayed him? It was his fault. It was all his fault. The guilt churned up from his heart like black tar, suffocating his desire to go on.

Constance's voice in his mind soothed the pain and gave him courage.

No regrets, baby. You made up for it.

The swirl started to pick up speed and images pulsated through his memory. He wasn't remembering them exactly; it was as if an extreme 3D movie played all the way around him, fast-forwarding until it came to something interesting.

It was 1524 and Keenan had a new name, a new identity, a new body, and no recollection of the past. He was studying to be a chronicler, and his patron was introducing him to Giovanni de Verrazzano, a navigator commissioned by France to explore the west. Keenan was taken on as a scribe and sailed west with his captain.

Dabria had escaped him. Azazel knew the way to her was through you. Constance's voice sounded far away. *I had to get you out of Italy, off the continent. I hoped he would not find you in the new world... but I was wrong.*

The trip was a blur of blue ocean, shouted orders, smells of humanity, and persistent seasickness, but Keenan religiously kept the journals for his captain and even developed a friendship with the explorer.

Memories stumbled forward to the raw West Indies. It was hazy, but it seemed he was part of a small crew that accompanied the captain to explore the coast.

They didn't see the natives until it was too late. Hundreds of them scurried out of the deep brush and killed the entire landing party in less than a minute. Cannibals. Before the others on the ship could retaliate, the natives disappeared with their kill into the thick jungle.

Images snaked across his vision, a spinning top churning out colors and souls. It froze on a flame.

1562. Keenan was laughing with a group of natives, his friends, his family. They finished their meal, the bones in mounds next to their knees. A hunting party. There was a blast of gunfire. They scattered like leaves in the night, but it was too late. A net twirled out of the air above Keenan's head and caught him. The white men beat him down and forced manacles around his wrists and ankles. They took him along with hundreds of others into the bowels of a giant ship.

Nestled among dozens of dirty friends in the darkness, a white man appeared out of the shadows to speak to Keenan. He spoke their language like a native.

"You have given me quite the chase, old friend." The light in the man's eyes was so familiar, but Keenan had never known a white man. "It is good to see you again. When we land, I think I will buy you for myself. "

Keenan never made it to land. During a stormy night, he was visited by a spirit, a woman dressed all in white, shining like a lantern in the blackened hull. He heard her words in his head and it terrified him, but omens were sacred so he listened. The vision told him where to find a tin cup. She said to drink from it and it would free him. When he awoke from the dream, to his surprise, the tin cup was there. When he drank, he fell asleep and never woke again.

I could not let him take you. Not again. The regret in Constance's voice was clear.

A long period of black filled with only glimpses of eyes, then screaming as he entered into the cold bright world.

It was 1617. Jamestown. This was perhaps the strangest of all. Keenan was a woman. It was an odd feeling to be both familiar with the body and yet unfamiliar with it at the same time. He had adjusted.

While Azazel was in Virginia, I couldn't risk him finding you, so I disguised you as a woman, Kee. It was the only way to keep him from you. He searched and searched for decades. When you were 30, he discovered my diversion. I had no choice; there was only one way to hide you from him.

Keenan died on a winter evening in 1647 in an old Virginia house under mysterious circumstances.

But he did not move on.

The next hundred years were veiled, dreamlike. For some reason it wasn't his house anymore and yet he still lived there. Strangers came with all their things. He couldn't stop them. Their children grew older and replaced the parents; the children's children grew older and replaced them; generation after generation, each changing his house. Keenan could do nothing but howl in the night. His voice grew stronger with each new year. They brought priests and psychics to give him some ecclesiastical exercise, but he resisted their intrusion. The nightmare crawled into decades and then a century.

In 1750, Keenan found himself free.

I had to keep you from another body. As a mortal he is drawn to you like a moth to a flame. As a ghost, you are vague to him, hidden. It took me over a hundred years, but finally I convinced him through others that you had returned to Italy. Azazel was gone, and I thought I was finally rid of him.

I let you go after that, Kee, to live whatever life you wished without guidance or manipulation. You were a soldier, a painter, a musician, a poet. Each face he had possessed scrutinized him from ancient mirrors, like cards spread by a magician. *Every lifetime was richer than the last.*

I watched over you, protected you when I could, but let you go, hoping you would at last be free from Azazel's influence, and the maneuverings of angels. Over the many lifetimes, you became stronger, skilled, until your psychic abilities blossomed into something that stunned me. I had no idea where they would lead you.

In 1988, I couldn't stay away from you any longer. Your gift had doubled over the years. It would soon manifest itself in ways that would make it impossible for you to cope or for society to accept. I knew when you reached adolescence you would start seeing them... all of them. That was when I appeared to you, Keenan, to teach you how to live with your gifts.

Unfortunately, just as I had sensed your abilities, so had Azazel. He found you through your art and came back to use you.

When you told me of this new ghost friend in college, I thought nothing of it. Reggie was very clever; he made sure I never saw him. I would have recognized him at once, if I had. You spoke of him so fondly, I was happy you found at least one other ghost you could relate to. After all, you needed a friend, someone who could guide you as a man, who seemed to have your best interest at heart. Reggie was the perfect companion to help you deal with your special gift. As he took over, I felt confident you were in good hands. It was only when Amos descended from heaven that I learned the truth and so did Dabria. She came here to look for you. What she found instead was her old master and her mentor. Azazel used you both to capture Dabria. There was only one way to stop him.

You had to die.

Chapter Twenty-Three

Death Becomes Him

You had to die.

The words twisted his ethereal middle into knots.

Keenan was back with his friends, staring out into a real world that was distinctly surreal.

He could see a very human Dabria/Isabella backing away from the body lying on the floor, the chapel musty and small in front of them. In one corner was the storm cloud of Amos suspended there like gray cotton candy. The body wasn't moving and a twinge of hope surfaced; maybe it didn't take.

"Is he dead?"

Constance said nothing.

Every ghost held his or her breath for what seemed like an eternity, but the body did not move. Isabella pressed against a wall, biting her thumb. Was it hope or grief he saw in her eyes as she watched the still body? She wasn't breathing either. It was the most held breaths Keenan had ever witnessed.

After several minutes, murmurs of joy leaked out of the ghostly mass, tentative at first and then picking up volume. Constance squeezed Keenan's arm until it hurt, something he found very curious since he didn't have nerves to speak of, but he didn't mind. Maybe just the act of giving up his body had been enough. He let out a *whoohoo* and touched her hand. Azazel still didn't move.

Just at the height of their joy, a strange shout came from the back of the room and Keenan's relief turned to mush.

"Swanson!"

Sergeant Thompson made a beeline directly for the body, got it laid out flat with a quick tug, and started CPR and mouth-to-mouth, shouting at Isabella between breaths to get down on the floor and put her hands on top of her head. Confused, Isabella followed his orders.

Thompson flicked a switch in a blur and continued compressions, shouting into his radio, "I have a man down at the Old Church on Broadway. Get me a unit right now."

Two more compressions and a fateful miracle exploded under his hands. Reggie's chest heaved and he rolled over on his side with a coughing fit. Thompson fell back apparently startled the cadaver had come to life. He helped Reggie to sit up and suddenly looked very cross.

"What the fuck now, Swanson? You are one lucky son of a bitch! I've called an ambulance."

"That won't be necessary, officer." Apparently, whatever Reggie had put into Keenan's body was working for him. His recovery was nothing less than miraculous and Thompson scowled at him. "I'm fine, really."

"You were dead a second ago, buddy. You're going to the hospital."

Reggie bounced up from the floor with the grace of an acrobat and performed a full spin for Thompson. "As you can see, I am quite all right, officer."

Thompson laid one ear near his shoulder and brought those brutish brows close to the center of this forehead.

"What's with the accent? You ok? Did you knock your head on something? Name's Thompson, remember? Sergeant Thompson. How many fingers am I holding up?"

"Right." Reggie smoothed his face into an expression Keenan was sure *he* never had in his life, but it looked like Thompson was buying it. "Sorry, Sergeant." The accent was perfect. "Guess I must have hit it when I fell. Three fingers."

Thompson didn't look too convinced, but he headed over to the door where his service revolver was lying.

Picking it up, he inspected it briefly then pointed it at the girl on the floor. "Up, sweetheart."

Isabella got off the floor and looked like she was going to make a break for it, but Reggie was quick. He darted to her side and wrapped an arm around her waist.

"Who's this?" Thompson asked.

"My girlfriend." It was an expertly executed lie. He tightened his grip on Isabella and she gasped under the pressure. Keenan was sure the smile she gave Reggie was forced. It confused him.

"The one you were talking about earlier?"

"Yep." Keenan could tell Reggie was struggling with the accent, but it was coming easier with each word.

"I oughta take you in and throw the book at you, asshole! Just for taking my gun... not to mention my cruiser." Thompson scratched his head and surveyed the room. "Not sure what happened back there, but looks like maybe you saved my life."

"Well, I wasn't going to say anything..."

"Shut up, smart mouth! You sure you're ok?"

"Never been better, offi...I mean, Sergeant. Unless you want to force me, I don't need to go to the hospital. Maybe the clout to the head knocked some sense into me."

Thompson snorted and holstered his gun. "I wish." He pressed the button on his radio. "Dispatch, this is 7-2-2. Cancel last request. We're all dandy here."

"So are you arresting us?" Reggie adjusted his grip around Isabella's waist and whispered something quick into her ear. She touched his cheek and gave him a quick kiss. Keenan bunched his fingers together.

Thompson folded his arms and bent one knee. He glared at the two for a count of ten then said, "I should, but not today. Waste of time."

"Thank you."

"You got a lot of explaining to do about that stunt last night. You come down to the station tomorrow and we'll get it all sorted out. Right now I'm beat." He rubbed his eyes and adjusted his belt. "You want a ride home?"

Reggie glanced at Isabella and sent a shining smile back to Thompson. From the look on the cop's face, Keenan figured this whole thing was creeping Thompson out.

"Actually..." Reggie drawled. "...any chance you could take me to a house in the southeast? It's very close to the station."

"Sure. Let's go."

Reggie scanned the room as if searching for something. "Tell you what; I'll meet you out there in a jiff. I need to find my coat."

Thompson headed for the door. "Don't take too long. I'm leaving in five minutes." He lumbered out the door.

As soon as he was gone, Reggie grabbed both Isabella's arms and shook her. Keenan had never wanted to hit someone more than at that moment.

"Where are they?" Reggie snarled.

"Who?"

"The fucking ghosts and Amos... Where are they?"

Isabella looked straight at Keenan and it startled him. Were those tears in her eyes?

"Look at me, you bitch!" Reggie shook her hard with each syllable. "Where the fuck did they go?"

"He can't see us," Constance whispered in Keenan's ear.

"Why?" Keenan whispered back, struck for the moment by Isabella's beauty. It was very distracting.

"Because he doesn't have your abilities as a human, Kee. He's blind because he's seeing through mortal eyes. It's the best piece of news I've had all day."

"Tell me!" Reggie shouted at Isabella.

"I... I don't know. They left." Her lips quivered under his hard stare and her eyes were wild.

"Fuck!" Reggie screamed up at the rafters. He grabbed Isabella by one arm and pulled her toward the door.

Just before they went through, Isabella managed to turn her head. The expression she shot at Keenan before they vanished burned into his heart. Sadness, hope, adoration, all rolled into that face in an instant. Before he could return it, they were gone.

Chapter Twenty-Four

The Devil in the Details

For some reason, Keenan had always suspected that ghosts were just kind of "born" into the condition, instantly knowing everything they needed to function in an un-living world. Had he realized how difficult it was to adjust to his new surroundings, he would have been much more understanding.

When Constance grabbed his hand and "pulled" him forward with a shouted, "Come on!" everything twisted around him into dark multi-colored blurs. The *physical* universe melted into the ghostly universe, creating a watercolor world that he flitted through like an oak leaf twirling in the wind. He was flying, or at least that's what he preferred to call it. It was actually more like creative flapping.

They rushed out of the church so fast Keenan was having a hard time getting his bearings. That coupled with the fact that the world had turned into melting ice cream around him and Constance a bright beam of light, it was no wonder he resisted her pull. She was apparently unaware of Keenan's plight since it didn't even slow her down.

"What are you doing?" He didn't need to shout; there wasn't any particular sound going on around him. It should have been noisy as all hell so it was a natural inclination.

"I'm sorry I didn't tell ya, Kee. When Amos went after Dabria at *The Hotcake House*, I panicked. I was so afraid Reggie might have him grab you, too, and we weren't ready." She stopped talking only long enough to swerve around a sharp corner. "This is why we needed you to give up your body, Kee. So Reggie would go to the girl."

Keenan's legs were pulling colors off the tops of frosting cars as they flew past. If he still had his head, he was sure he'd have a splitting headache. "What girl?"

Constance's face materialized out of the bright light to smile at him. "You really need to keep up."

"Granted." His feet went through a shining yellow parking meter and got tangled in an old woman's hair, but bounced back at him instantly, sending out waves like ripples in a cup of coffee. They picked up speed. "I've never died before, so my wits are a little scrambled this morning. What girl?"

The light took Constance's face back and they sped after the cruiser sailing through a ginger bread world. "The vessel… the woman who has been impregnated with your seed. We need to reach her before he does."

It was as if he had missed every other chapter in a mystery novel. "Ok," was all he could manage. "And then what?"

"You'll see."

The silence that followed was stern, if that was possible. Keenan knew Constance would not answer any more questions.

To entertain himself, he focused on getting things to settle down around him. Cars, buses, houses, buildings, everything manmade had a cake-like texture. A thirty-year-old birthday wish flashed through his skull; he had always wanted to live in a candy world. *What a stupid wish!* Natural objects, people, animals, trees, grass, and the like all had a golden or red hue around them.

The cruiser stopped abruptly at a street light, and the gang of ghosts collided against itself in a roiling cloud of entities. When it got itself sorted out, Keenan's universe solidified and everything around him turned normal again. It was disconcerting as all hell. When the cop car fired across the intersection, the mass de-constituted itself and followed like a cartoon swarm of bees. Keenan decided to hitch his ass to the inevitable, as if he had a choice.

When they reached Maywood Park, Thompson took a sharp right onto 102nd and floored it. Six blocks down, he screeched around another right and the group of ghosts almost missed the turn. They caught themselves en-mass and had to bank hard left to make the turn. The cruiser was just pulling up to the house on the right when they got behind it.

Maywood Park, a tiny city within the larger city of Portland, was a triangular neighborhood built between 1920 and 1940. The neighbors had filed for independence when the state threatened to park an interstate highway in their backyards. The highway stayed despite their efforts, but the neighborhood was now an isolated oasis in the middle of concrete, asphalt, and expansion, fighting them all with manicured lawns, clockwork dog walking, and stern refusals to budge. It was a mighty midget amongst municipal giants.

The house they stopped at was typical for the area; small, with a conical tower and a large yard surrounded by a white slatted fence. The grass and hedges were neat and trim, the large front porch clear of debris, and, except for the color, it was a perfect example of Maywood Park's best. The house was black, all black, from the perfectly placed plywood covering the crawlspace, to the ten-foot high brick chimney spewing smoke against fluffy white clouds. It looked like Dorothy had caught the wrong tornado and missed Oz by at least eighteen hundred miles.

Constance didn't let Keenan examine it for long. Before he knew it, they had hauled him into the yard and set him in front of the five stairs leading to the railed porch. The black swing bench hanging from black chains rattled once in an ethereal breeze then remained still.

Constance expanded herself to her full size and puffed out massive white wings, a brilliant snowstorm against the black house. Without hesitation, the rest of the ghosts fell into place, linked shoulder to shoulder, facing out, like soldiers standing in a line. When Keenan craned his neck, he watched them click into place like colorful piano keys. They must have extended all the way around the house.

"What's happening, Cee?" The words came out of Keenan's mouth a bit tattered, as if they were afraid of something.

Constance's wings folded around his shoulders and took the fear away. "This is where we finish the fight, honey."

"Fight?" Keenan watched as Reggie opened his door and pulled Isabella out with him.

Constance pulled on a wayward feather and straightened it. "For thousands of years we have waited for this. It is here we take our stand."

"Against Reggie?"

Those soulful eyes fired with passion when she turned her head to him. "No, Keenan." She turned it back, squared her shoulders, and twisted her neck from side to side. "Against hell."

Keenan swallowed hard, knowing down to the sinews of his soul that whatever happened next he was absolutely unprepared for.

Chapter Twenty-Five

The Spirit of the Dead

When Keenan was very small, he had a babysitter (or maybe one of his mom's boyfriends) who loved to juggle: fruit, balls, toys, dishes, shoes, anything he could get his hands on. One hot summer afternoon, apparently bored and not too bright, this young man decided it might be a hoot to juggle the baby. Young Keenan, barely walking at the time, scooted out of the danger zone as quick as his chubby little legs could carry him. Unfortunately, due to the nature of an eighteen month old body, the exercise was one of futility; a hand the size of a basketball (or so it seemed to the infant Keenan) scooped him up by the bottom and balanced him in midair, while the other hand filled with some kind of fishbowl squished together with a very angry kitten.

Keenan had to admit the initial attempt was an astonishing accomplishment; he flew over the tall man's head and plopped down onto the opposite hand at the same time the bowl plopped down into the other and the cat remained, for the moment, suspended in the air above the man's face. Regrettably, inertia and the jumbled contortions of the unfortunate feline were apparently something the skilled acrobat had not contemplated before attempting the feat. With a loud meow and a resounding un-kitten like hiss, the cat lodged itself squarely on the young man's face, wherein he attempted to dislodge it. The bowl flew up out of his hands to shatter an expensive looking chandelier, and Keenan, for the first time in his life, knew what it was to fly... if only for a moment.

It was that gravity defying emptiness that filled him as he watched Reggie and Isabella enter the gate.

His ghostly existence clarified for him in that moment; the world shot into a reality that was almost painful. Everything looked so... alive. It was the only word he could think of. The trees, the grass, even the houses around them shimmered with a kind of vibrancy that made his ears hurt. The ghosts filed away from him on either side and disappeared around the corner of the house. The glow of each was bright yellow as if some kid had stolen a highlighter and, during the glee of insanity, outlined them all. Behind him, the black house was a midnight sky, full of holes.

It was hard to look at Isabella. So many emotions coursed through Keenan's blood when he did. He was royally pissed that she had lied and betrayed him, even more so at the fact that she didn't even try to fight Reggie in the end. That emotion, despite his best efforts, was quickly melting under those angelic brown eyes. Every time he saw her, his blood coagulated into glop and his heart grew twice its normal size. He couldn't help it.

"You need to focus!" The words screeched against his chalkboard brain. When he glared at Constance a rush of guilt flushed through him. Strain was red in her face. She was working to hold the group together and Keenan had let his mind wander through casual thoughts without a care.

"Sorry." He forced his head around and concentrated on the couple.

"Are you ready, Isabella?" The words came out of Constance silently and Isabella gave the lightest tilt of her chin. Keenan's confusion deepened.

Still holding Isabella's arm, Reggie slammed the gate and gloated at the house. "Come on, lover. It's time to meet the third sixty degrees in our triangle. Haven't I always told you what fun a threesome can be?"

Isabella pulled her arm out of Reggie's grasp and spread her feet on the cement path.

"I don't think so, asshole."

Shock parted Reggie's lips. "What?"

"You heard me. I'm done taking your crap."

Reggie lifted his hand and pointed a finger at her. "I made you, bitch. I can destroy you!"

"You're right. You did make me, Azazel, along with a lot of other Muses, but you were as much an asshole then as you are now."

He balled his fists and shook them. "I loved you," he hissed through his teeth. "You should have followed me. I was your father."

"There is only one Father, Azazel, and you betrayed Him. You got what you deserved!"

Apparently, Reggie was trying to blast her or something with his hands, but he frowned at them when nothing came out.

"Missing something?" Isabella sneered. "You're human now. Impotent! As limp as you've always been."

Reggie shrugged and the side of his mouth curled. "Yes, well." In a quick movement, he brought the back of his hand across Isabella's cheek and sent her flying. She crumbled in the middle of the lawn. "You're human too, in case you haven't noticed, my little bit of muslin. I do have my resources. I'll deal with you when I'm done. Count on it."

Turning around, Reggie walked toward the stairs leading to the front door of the house but stopped abruptly. His faced tightened and he raised one brow. He was nose to nose with Keenan.

A charge of anger clouded Keenan's responses. He wanted to punch this guy but hard. It took self-control and Constance's whispered, "Don't move," to keep him still. When Reggie shrugged and moved forward, he pushed into Keenan's chest. Keenan's body softened under the pressure, caving in just enough to create a little resistance.

Reggie took a step back, frowned, and tried it again with more force. This time Keenan pushed back harder. Reggie bounced off Keenan's chest as if it were a rubber mat. He flew back and almost fell. Catching himself, he glared at Keenan without seeing him.

"What the hell?"

Taking a running start, Reggie plowed toward them at full speed. He hit hard this time, making the line of ghosts buckle and Keenan take in a gasp. It wasn't physical, Keenan had to remind himself, but it still felt that way. The line held, and Reggie went flying this time, propelled upward and back. When he landed on his ass, Keenan cringed a little. That had to hurt, and, still somewhat attached to his body, Keenan knew it was going to leave one hell of a bruise. Pins and needles glanced through his shoulders in empathy.

Reggie got up stiffly. He put his hands on his hips and locked his jaw. "Who's there?" he screamed. "Gazardiel, I know it's you. You and your ghost friends. I will send you all to Hell!"

"Not without your powers, you won't. Human, indeed. You have been such a fool." Isabella rose from the ground, her succubus form flowing like tunneling water now. Where her arms should have been, graceful sleeves of black night poured into massive random shapes. From her feet and sides more starry blackness emptied into the air around her. A sound, a melody, vibrated from those masses, drowning out every other noise. Keenan knew that sound and couldn't help smiling in response. He held his breath, wishing he could hear it forever.

Reggie's scream broke through the resonance and he doubled over covering his ears. In an instant, the mass enveloped him, wrapping around his arms, his legs, and his torso until he disappeared into the darkness. It muffled his voice.

At almost the same time, Isabella flew out of the mass in a blur and snapped into Keenan as if he were lime gelatin. In an instinctive move, he caught her in his arms.

She wrapped her hands around his neck and pulled him close. "Do you love me?" Her voice and her eyes were desperate.

Keenan couldn't answer. The pain of her betrayal still lingered like acid in his mouth. Everything from the last few days buried him under mountains of doubt. Anger mixed with hope, joy with pain, and confusion jumbled his brain.

In the boiling turmoil, one thing remained steady, strong at its center, despite his better judgment or common sense; Dabria/Isabella had given him the only real joy in his life. The other experiences, good and bad, anchored themselves around that and came to an abrupt halt.

"I do love you," he said to her upturned face. When her eyes softened in relief, he knew it was absolutely true.

"Then kiss me, Keenan."

Without hesitation, he pressed his lips to hers and the world went away.

Chapter Twenty-Six

Back to the Netherland

There were only three times in Keenan's life that were truly, exquisitely, absolutely perfect. The day he got his first bike, the day he sold his first painting, and that first kiss in the restaurant from Isabella. This outshone all of them.

Watery static ignited when their lips touched firing every nerve in Keenan's ethereal body. Isabella's soft moist lips seemed to merge with his mouth; it was hot, sensual, and yet pure at the same time. A white light seemed to go off in Keenan's head, blinding out every other thought until there was nothing in his existence except that kiss. His bliss was complete. Keenan's body melted into Isabella's until there was only one.

What happened next Keenan was aware of on a plane of existence he could later only describe as bizarre. He was not himself any more. Keenan as a person disappeared. Some kind of floating spirit replaced him, one that melted everything around them. Keenly aware of his surroundings, he absorbed the universe, as if both physical and spiritual had merged. Isabella was part of him now, wrapped around his psyche until he had difficulty knowing where he began and she ended. At the heart of this awareness was an emotion Keenan had always struggled with, had always kept at arm's distance, had always turned his back on. The dam burst and love flowed like lava through his phantom heart.

A white roiling circle exploded out of him into the physical universe. It lingered for a moment, delicate, alluring, a ring cloud full of light. Then it shot out on all sides.

A tendril of cloud caught Keenan by the chest and ripped him from Isabella's arms. Overwhelming energy propelled him toward Reggie. The surprise on Reggie's face was satisfying as Keenan got nearer.

In a last blast, the ring of fire engulfed Keenan's physical body and pulled something from it like a fly from pancake batter. A black hole opened. It was deep, spherical, like a cookie cutter had removed a piece of reality, a horizontal tornado turned inside out.

The ghostly form of Reggie popped out of Keenan's body in an instant. He was a spirit again. The look of surprise irised from his face like a camera shutter. It stayed that way for only a moment. Terror replaced it. Reggie's scream shattered against the ghosts, the house, and Keenan. It was a high-pitched banshee cry that filled the air. Reggie struggled against the vortex, clawing at the air, those shark eyes now pale and pleading. Keenan watched as darkness enfolded Reggie's form, twisted around his chest until it imploded upon itself. In a blink, he was sucked inside.

Keenan had no time to respond. He plunged into his own body with such force it flew back toward the vortex.

The wind howled inside his now corporeal ears and sucked the breath out of his lungs. He couldn't open his eyes. Fire took over his brain. Debris smacked against his exposed hands, throat, and face. Keenan couldn't even lift his arms to protect them. His body dangled against the torrents and flapped in the winds like a car lot banner. The pain was excruciating. Keenan was helpless.

With a last push of strength, he managed to get his eyes open. His first sight was Reggie disappearing into the black hole at the tornado's center, his hands outstretched, those black soulless eyes wide with terror. Then he blipped out. *Blink.*

Keenan knew this was the end. It should have scared the living piss out of him, but for some reason it didn't. A kind of calm settled over him. He knew he had saved the world and Isabella. That was enough.

A gray cloud appeared suddenly in front of him that materialized into Amos. The angel unfurled his wings and smiled at Keenan. The forceful winds didn't seem to bother him.

"Nicely done, boy," was all he said and Keenan frowned. A rope or a hand would have been much more helpful. The hole was closing around Keenan and he bowed to the inevitable.

A hard jerk caught at his legs and he stopped. Twisting around, he saw a hand on his ankle and then another. They clawed at his jeans together and pulled.

Keenan flipped over and landed in a heap on top of someone. The vortex shut down in a loud ear-splitting bang that shook the ground and everything went quiet.

When Keenan looked down into the face of a sputtering Sergeant Thompson, joy got the better of him. Without hesitation, he grabbed Thompson's stern face in his hands and kissed him soundly. He had never been happier to be alive.

Chapter Twenty-Seven

Aftermath

Thompson gave Keenan a good shove and he landed on his back, staring up at a glorious blue sky and billowing clouds. He was so weak he could barely turn onto his side, but strength was creeping into his legs and arms, and the pain was receding. When he searched the yard, the ghosts and the angels were dancing in pairs or groups, kicking up their ethereal heels, and laughing so hard ectoplasm came out of their collective noses. Amos and Gazardiel locked elbows and did a jig. The air filled with jubilation.

Getting to his feet, Thompson crossed to the prostrate Keenan and helped him to sit. "You okay?" he asked gruffly.

"Yeah." Keenan rubbed his forehead. "Got a splitting headache and I'm as weak as last night's sitcom, but I'll live. You?"

"Fine," he said. He motioned to the group of dancing specters. "Where the hell did these guys come from?"

"You can see them?" Keenan was flabbergasted. No other human being he had ever known could see the ghosts.

"Of course I can see them! I'm not blind."

He left Keenan abruptly and crossed to a heap of figure on the ground. A shot of fear sent pinpricks up Keenan's arms. Reggie?

But when Thompson bent down to help the figure up, Keenan fought to get to his feet to cross to them. As graceful as a newborn giraffe, Keenan took Isabella into his arms and swore he would never let her go again.

Kissing her softly, he touched her face not believing she was real... and human again.

From behind them Keenan heard the squeak of a rusty screen door and turned around. There on the porch was a young woman no more than five feet tall and as pixie like as Keenan had ever seen. Maybe twenty or twenty-five, everything about her said gothic, from the black nail polish on her delicate little hands, to the tattered black skirt hugging a very trim waist. Two large brown eyes rested at the center of a pale face framed by spiky jet-black hair. On her right cheek a tattoo of two delicate angel wings laced down along her jaw. Her black lips accentuated an adorable porcelain face. She frowned at them and looked around her yard.

"What the hell are all you people doing on my lawn?"

You could have heard a feather fall. Even the angels seemed surprised.

"Hi." The voice came from behind Keenan. When he looked back, his mouth fell open.

Thompson's eyes had gone dewy. It was scary as all hell. The insipid grin on his face looked like a pod person had taken over.

"Hi," the girl said back. Her face softened and Keenan had no trouble figuring out why.

"Uh," said Thompson, looking down at his hands. "Name's Thomp... Cecil."

Cecil?

"Hi," she repeated then looked down. A blush brightened her cheeks. "I'm Dyna... Dyna Campbell."

"Hi." The response from Thompson was so uncharacteristic, Keenan wanted to slap him. But having been in love himself, he let it go.

Keenan kissed Isabella soundly, letting the waves of relief and joy wash through him without caring about anything else.

When he broke the kiss, he saw Thompson on the porch talking to the girl and winked down at Isabella. "So, she can see the ghosts."

"Yes," she replied softly.

"And so can he."

"The ring affected everyone it touched. The girl, Thompson…" She stopped and touched his cheek. "And you, Keenan."

"How did it affect me?"

"It freed ya, Kee," Constance said from behind him. When Keenan turned around, she was back to her old self again. Amos stood next to her holding her hand.

"You and Isabella can move on with your lives now, without interference."

"Wait." Something caught in Keenan's throat when he saw the brilliant smile Isabella was giving him. "You mean Isabella's…"

"Yes, Kee," said Constance. "She's human. As human as you are. It was the least we could do for all we've put her through. It's the only way she can get back into heaven; like any other human soul, she'll have to earn it."

Amos touched Isabella's cheek. "If that is what you wish."

In response, tears filled Isabella's eyes and she kissed the angel's hand. "Thank you," she whispered. She fell into Keenan's arms.

"As for you," Constance said to Keenan and her eyes misted. "It has been an honor knowing you."

"Come on, Cee. You're not going anywhere."

Constance glanced at Amos and back to Keenan. "I'm sorry, Kee. In a few hours you won't be able to see us."

Keenan let Isabella go. "What?"

"You don't need us anymore, Kee. You are stronger than you know and in the days to come, you'll discover that. We might return from time to time, when you need us most, but for the moment we have to move on."

Grief pulled at his cheeks. He surveyed the milling crowd of ghosts, the ancient whisper of smiles fading as he watched. "No."

"I'm so sorry, Kee. It is out of our hands. Dyna and Thompson need us now. The child she carries is important to the future… your son, Kee. He will need our guidance, our love, and our strength to see him through what he must face."

"If he's my child then I should take responsibility for..."

"No, Kee. You have your own road to follow, you and Isabella. Perhaps one day your paths will cross. Who knows? But for now, the child needs Thompson's strength and skill, and his mother's magic to guide him. You can do nothing to help him."

Keenan didn't like the fact that he could do nothing for his own son, but then realized the kid was probably as much everyone else's as his. He searched Isabella's face and touched her brow.

"Tell me what to do."

She took his hand, kissed it, and rubbed it against her cheek. "The choice is yours. All I know is the child could not be in better hands."

He kissed her again and turned to Constance. "Can I at least be part of his life?"

Constance pulled a long sigh into her lungs and looked at the ground. "I'm so sorry. You must not have any contact while the child grows. This is the real sacrifice we need from you. And who knows?" She ran her hand around his face and smiled. "Perhaps one day you will meet again. I see interesting times ahead." She glanced at the couple on the porch. "For all of you."

Chapter Twenty-Eight

Eight Months Later…

"Hand me the cleaver, will you?"

Keenan grabbed the large knife from the cutting board, turned it and put the handle into his wife's dainty hand.

"Thank you."

From this angle, the protruding belly made her legs and arms look small. He grinned to himself. Even with seven months of baby in there, Isabella was still as breathtaking as she had ever been. Maybe even more so.

He turned back to the turnips and continued cutting. "So, explain it to me again, will you?"

"I told you, I'm not sure how I got pregnant, or why I didn't get pregnant before. Maybe they changed something in me this time. Who knows? I'm not going to jinx it by wondering. Honestly, you worry too much."

"I'm just curious, that's all. You don't think the baby will turn out to be…" When Isabella leveled stern eyes at him, he stopped. Keenan shrugged. "What? It could happen."

"This baby," she said evenly, "will be as human as you are. I told you before, the ultrasound showed a perfectly healthy, *normal* baby girl." She folded her arms. "Nothing more."

Keenan put his hands up defensively. "All right, all right. Just want to make sure there isn't some kind of angel in our future. I've had my fill." A pang of loss fell into the turnips when he went back to them.

Isabella's face softened and she put down her knife. Taking his chin in her fingers, she reached up to kiss him lightly. "You miss them, don't you?"

Keenan turned his head back to the vegetables and let a sigh out for some air. "Yeah. Maybe."

"They'll be back, Keenan. You'll see them again, I promise. In the meantime, you'll have to settle for me."

That did it. He put down his knife, swept her up into this arms, avoiding the big bumpy part in the middle, and smothered her with kisses. In the middle of a nice juicy one, a foot (or maybe it was an elbow) caught him right in the solar plexus. He let out a puff of air into Isabella's mouth and she pushed away from him. Her belly twitched when she touched it.

"Oh," she huffed when another kick distended the skin at her middle. "That was a good one. Man, she's strong."

"Yeah." Keenan held his stomach trying to get air back into his body.

Out of the corner of his eye, he saw Isabella's eyes get big at something behind him. When he turned around he instinctively put a hand in front of her.

Suspended in the air were the two knives they had been using, twirling on their tips. Keenan pushed Isabella back against the refrigerator and watched as the knives did a little dance over the cobalt blue tiled counter. Then, in a quick swoop, they charged at the cutting board and chopped through the vegetables in record time, then laid themselves in the sink for washing.

Keenan waited a good count of sixty before moving to investigate. Isabella held his arm and tucked herself behind him (pushing just a bit, he thought). Keenan approached the vegetables now diced on the counter in neat little piles of green and white. Fear was making Keenan's eyes and nose hurt.

"Tell me you did this," he whispered to his wife. He could feel her shaking her head against his arm.

"Not me."

"Hello?" he called to the air in general. It didn't answer back. "Is someone here? Constance? Amos? Anyone?" The only reply was the rain against the kitchen window.

Keenan swallowed hard when a new idea crept up his neck.

"You don't think…"

"No." The word came out long and uncertain from Isabella's mouth. "It couldn't be."

"Are you sure? She could have inherited your abilities…"

"It can't be, Kee. She's mortal, human…"

"Hear me out. I had psychic abilities… you had angelic ones. What if some of that transferred to her. What if she inherited them from us?"

"That's just too scary to think about. Can you imagine the trouble we'd have?"

Keenan turned around and touched Isabella's belly with his palms. "I want to try something."

Isabella took a step back and put a protective hand against the bulge. "I don't think we better…"

"Trust me," he said, covering her hand with his. "I just have to know."

She twisted her lips to the side and looked down at his hand. "All right, but be careful."

"I won't hurt her, I promise."

Keenan got down on his knees so his face was level with the baby and pulled up Isabella's shirt. The glistening stretched skin looked almost golden in the gray afternoon light spilling in from the garden.

He pressed his ear against it and spoke very softly. "Hey, sweetie. It's Daddy. Can you hear me?"

A small tremor brushed his ear and Keenan smiled. A rush of satisfaction relaxed his earlier doubt. He was talking to his little girl.

"Hey, baby. Mama and I want to know if you can hear us, if you can understand us."

"You look ridiculous," Isabella said laughing. "What if a neighbor came in right now?"

He glanced up at her. "Hey, I'm experimenting here. Lock the door if you're worried." He kissed her belly and readjusted his ear to a different spot. "It's Daddy, baby. Can you hear me?"

A gurgle echoed against his eardrum and he got very excited. "I hear her!"

"I think you're hearing lunch, sweetie."

He ignored the jibe and tapped the skin. "Can you touch Daddy, sweetie? Just a tap?"

Nothing happened for several heartbeats and Keenan gave up. It was probably just one of the ghosts coming in for a quick visit. In a way, he was kind of glad. Maybe Constance was right. Maybe he would see them again.

He moved quickly to stand and all at once, he found himself flying through the air. The counter caught him square in the back and the entire house shook. Air came out of his lungs in one great whoop. The cabinets behind him teetered for a moment and he could hear the wood crack. A knife fell from the counter behind his head, point down. It wedged itself a good half inch into the floor right between his legs, two inches from his jewels.

Gasping to get air back into his lungs he saw Isabella with her mouth open, looking down at her pregnant belly, caressing it softly with her hands.

"It's okay, baby." She lifted her chin to him. "Daddy didn't mean to frighten you."

Struggling to his feet, Keenan moved, very slowly, toward his wife.

"She's… uh, got quite a kick."

"Yes."

"Don't suppose you know where this is going, do you?"

Isabella gave him a nervous little laugh. "No."

Keenan nodded. "I guess we'll find out eventually."

"Yep."

He nodded again. "All right then."

Taking her gently into his arms, watching to make sure there wasn't another blast coming, he kissed her on the forehead.

Keenan turned to look at the vegetables on the counter and frowned.

"Maybe we'll go out to eat. *Hotcakes?*"

Isabella patted his arm and examined the counter with him. "Sure, I'll get my coat."

They never talked about it again.

The End

About the Author

Somewhere between thirty and dust...red hair, blue eyes...six kids, one slightly used husband, and any number of pets from time to time... wanttabe hippy... wanttheirmoney yuppie... pro musician and actress for 20 years... native Oregonian... lover of music, beauty, and all things green. Willing slave to the venerable muse. Minnette currently resides in Portland, Oregon with her husband, having replaced the children with one dog. The dog, Pierre, pretty much runs the show.

Additional titles available from Minnette Meador: *Starsight Vols. I & II* (Stonegarden Publishing) *The Centurion & The Queen* (Resplendence Publishing) *The Edge of Honor* (Resplendence Publishing) *A Boy & His Wizard* (writing as M. A. Smith)

(All titles available from Amazon, Borders, Barnes & Noble, and other fine book locations)

COMING SOON:

The Gladiator Prince (Resplendence Publishing) — August 2011
The Bell Stalker (Resplendence Publishing) — October 2011

www.minnettemeador.com
minnettemeador.blogspot.com
Also visit her on Facebook or Twitter

We Kill Dead Things by Sommer Marsden
Book One in the *Zombie Exterminators* Series

Poppy thinks her life is weird working the food court at Parktowne mall, until in one brief moment of creeper killing, things change forever. Now she's a freelance zombie exterminator along with her long lusted after co-worker Garrity (her not-so-secret crush), a somewhat lusted after bad boy Cahill and pretty gay boy Noah. When the four are hired to do a ballsy zombie clean up at St. Peter's Hospital, Poppy finds out just what's more scary than creepers. The Evoluminaries, a zealot cult who think zombies are part of God's chosen, who happen to end up thinking Poppy might make a mighty good zombie incubator. She finds herself finally sleeping with Garrity, being hunted by a crazy preacher man and stumbling over the fact that Cahill and Noah have become lovers somewhere in the chaos. And that's all on the job. Just another day in the life when you kill dead things...

Reawakening by Charlotte Stein
Forever Dead Series, Book One

June has spent the last two years of her life trying to avoid death at the hands of murderous psychopaths and ravening zombies. So when Jamie turns up on the scene, careless, still whole and promising her safety on a little paradise island, she isn't quite sure she can trust him. Especially when he tells her that it's just him, and his equally big, burly, handsome friend Blake.

But Jamie and Blake are even better than her wildest dreams—sweet and funny and charming. And worst of all: sexy as hell. Though they're trying to be gentlemanly with her, all she can think about is how much she wants to get tangled up in them, and forget the nightmare the world has become. She's waiting for her reawakening—back to life and happiness and love.

And they seem like just the right sort of men to wake her—body and soul.

Dark Paradise by Temple Hogan

Molly Prescott, small town librarian, was leading a normal, if boring, life until one stormy night, sexy forensic psychologist and vampire hunter extraordinaire, Matthew Stanislaus, walked into her library. When Vasilek, one of the ancient ones, bites Molly, Matthew is able to save her life for the moment, but he knows Molly may turn and he may have to kill her despite his sizzling attraction for her.

Molly has never known such a hunger for a man, but the gorgeous Hungarian with the sexy accent turns her temperature gauge sky-high, even while she's trying to outrun vampires who want to kill her and Matthew's brother, Lucas and his Holy Order of the Brotherhood, set on destroying her. She refuses to accept the fact that she's become one of the undead by seducing Matthew and showing him what an imaginative, half-turned vampiress is capable of.

Overlord's Chosen by Bronwyn Green
Dark Destinies Book One

Elizabeth Louden has been chosen to provide Micah Bleddyn, the Overlord of Maelgwn, with an heir. However, she's not interested in the honor. In a land where only men are allowed to use magic, women found to possess supernatural abilities are punished—often by death. She knows it's only a matter of time before her secret is revealed.

Micah has no desire to rule his father's empire, but after his older brother vanishes, he has no choice. Faced with invading forces, treachery among his own people, and now, a mate hell-bent on escape, he's had enough. Realizing they have no allies but each other, Micah and Elizabeth reach a reluctant truce in their bid to stay alive and keep Maelgwn safe.

Three Ways to Wicked by Melinda Barron

Bestselling Author Krisily Carmichael needs a break from her life. Her horrid ex-boyfriend sold naked photos of her, and now she's plastered all over the nation's largest skin magazine. So when an advertisement for a rental cottage near Bath appears in her mailbox, she snatches up the offer.

When she arrives at the remote English cottage, she finds a charming country home with a huge botanical garden...complete with four magical beings trapped inside.

Victim of a wayward spell, the Sorcerer Uriel and his alchemist cousins, Bythos and Acolius, have spent centuries trapped inside their garden with an evil witch who wants their secrets. Krisily's arrival sets off a string of events foretold to bring about the witch's end. Unfortunately, they have to contend with the witch's curse, which took one sense from each of the men.

But the four of them find a way to communicate, and they come together in a blaze of passion that helps them to destroy the witch and meet their destiny.

Coyote Savage by Kris Norris
Phases: Book Two

February's full moon is rising, only this year, it's bringing a new brand of hunger...

For coyote shifters Caden and Talon Brady, the upcoming hunger moon has ignited a different kind of appetite. They've been waiting several years for a chance to court their intended mate, and now that she's finally in their sights, they'll stop at nothing to win her over. But when local livestock start disappearing, their coyote refuge is put in the hot seat, and more than just their way of life is suddenly in jeopardy.

Sheriff Rebecca Savage never planned on returning to Beckit Falls, or for falling for two handsome men. But fate seems to have different plans for her. Unfortunately not all of them are sexy and look fantastic in jeans. The local mayor is trying to run the Brady boys and their coyote refuge out of town. Nothing seems to make sense, but when she starts digging deeper, a new danger rises with the full moon—one that just might get them all killed.

Alpheli Solution by Anny Cook

Bootcamp class seems to be the answer to her prayers. In her wildest dreams, she doesn't consider meeting not just one, but two hunky vampires who take her—in the car, in the shower, in the living room, in the hot tub, in hand—as they teach her everything she'll need to know about her new vampire life.

For centuries, Pierre has loved and pursued Julian with no success. After a hostile takeover of Julian's financial assets, Pierre is positive Julian will have nowhere else to turn. Julian, though, chooses to teach the Vampire Bootcamp class rather than surrender to Pierre on unequal terms. When one of Julian's students approaches him for help identifying her sire, Julian is stunned that she is his alpheli—an extremely rare mate whose blood will allow him to subsist on real food. What will that mean to his love-hate relationship with Pierre?

There are just one or two problems. Danamara is descended from Pierre's bloodline. And she's on someone's hit list. Julian and Pierre find unexpected erotic rewards and eternal love when they join together in a brutal war to protect their alpheli's life.

Oriana and the Three Werebears by Tia Fanning

Oriana Ricci has taken over the family business—flying cargo and rich tourists around Alaska's barely inhabited Kodiak Archipelago. When her plane malfunctions and she's forced to make an emergency landing, she finds herself stranded in the middle of a National Wildlife Refuge. With no civilization for miles and no hope of rescue, she thinks all is lost... Until she stumbles upon the entrance to an underground bunker.

Jack, Jordan, and Jonathan McMathan own and operate a secret intelligence firm contracted by the US Government. Hidden away in an old Cold War spy station located the middle of the Kodiak National Wildlife Refuge, the brothers are not only able to do their top secret jobs safely without fear of discovery, but are better to protect their other, more personal secret: They have the ability to shift into Kodiak bears.

Like a fairy tale gone bad, the brothers return home to find their lunch tasted—or eaten, their computer chairs adjusted—or broken, and a beautiful blonde sleeping in one of their beds. This situation poses a big problem for the brothers… Their location is now compromised. But more importantly, what are they to do with the lady?

Bewitching Bite by Destiny Blaine

A descendant of The Blood Countess, Matilda is transformed during the blending of bloodlines and becomes a supernatural creature empowered by a damning legacy. Intrigued by the future she reluctantly embraces, the spunky young witch completes the bonding and blending of bloodlines with a vampire who isn't quite ready to reveal his precise place in her future.

Armand is a Russian vampire in search of a blender, a mate destined for him because of peculiar mutual ties to the past. The knowledge Armand has about Erzsebet Bathory, a distant relative of the one chosen for him, is frightening. Armand discovers the only way the dead will stay buried is if he can bond with a witch and empower her with the blood of the one vampire Erzsebet Bathory wanted, but couldn't have.

Dragon's Blood by Brynn Paulin

For centuries, there have been legends of Vampires—the fault of one careless dragon. But humans only know part of the story. Walking amongst us are Dragons—shape-shifters who feed on blood.

Reluctant Dragon Elder Janos Aventech's vacation in New York is about to come to an abrupt end. Riding on the subway, he stumbles across a Dragon mate—one of the few human women with whom his people can unite and be truly happy. And his people's enemies are out to get her. As his attraction to this woman grows, he knows he must find her mate and see her safely into that man's arms. It's destined. But as every minute passes in her company, Janos begins to see he'll never willingly let her go, mate or not. If only she were *his* mate…

On the subway, Scarlett couldn't stop staring at him—then he turned crazy. When he essentially kidnaps her off the train, she knows she should be irate and terrified. Instead, she finds her initial attraction growing. But what's all this stuff he's spouting about mates and enemies? She only wants to return to her life, not get caught in the middle of a war. But it's too late for that. She's destined for a Dragon's bed, and in Janos' arms, she can only hope it's his.

Find Resplendence titles at these retailers

Resplendence Publishing
www.ResplendencePublishing.com

Amazon
www.Amazon.com

Barnes and Noble
www.BarnesandNoble.com

Target
www.Target.com

Fictionwise
www.Fictionwise.com

All Romance E-Books
www.AllRomanceEBooks.com

Mobipocket
www.Mobipocket.com

1 Place for Romance
www.1placeforromance.com

Made in the USA
Charleston, SC
04 August 2012